T.B. KRAMER

The Fourth Branch

2076

To my three reasons for being:
Steph, Johnny, and Lucy

Contents

1

Homeward Bound

"Welcome to the city of brotherly love, killers," crackled the conductor's voice over the intercom. Victor unbuttoned his uniform collar and wiped his brow as he listened, grumbling quietly about the lack of air conditioning in the military train car. He regretted not taking civilian transportation, but being a lowly corporal, he was left little choice in the matter. Above, the conductor's droning voice blared through the circular speaker.

"It's a tropical ninety-four degrees outside today, folks. Almost makes you wanna be back in sunny Haiti. Am I right?"

The conductor's lame stab at humor added no relief to the shabby ambiance. Sweat continued to trickle into Victor's eyes, making him rub them with both bawled-up fists. He blinked rapidly in hopes of relieving the stinging sensation.

Despite the obnoxious announcement, it provided Victor with a jolt of elation. *I'm finally going home.* Yet, notions of seeing his mother and friends gave way to an unsettling anxiety about where he had been and where he had to go now. Before he could go home, he had one more official act to do as a corporal in the US Army. A trip to the mysterious

E.C.H.O. Chamber, courtesy of Uncle Sam. He caught a glimpse of his reflection in the train car window. Unkempt short black curls of hair were starting to grow long, with two cowlicks causing an unintended but stylish tuft of hair to creep onto his forehead. A chiseled face with handsome features, yet with large puffy eye bags, stared back at him. His stomach groaned loudly. *Damn, I need a haircut, and when was the last time I ate?*

After he stretched his tired limbs a bit, he heard a faint whistling from inside the train car. An older-looking man dressed in an all-white officer's uniform was whistling a strange tune to himself. *Had he been there this whole time? Maybe I dosed off at the last stop.*

He sat five rows in front of Victor but faced his direction. As Victor focused on him for a fleeting moment, he thought the stranger rolled a small black flame between his white leather-gloved fingers. An oddity, he trumped up to his mind playing tricks from the heat. He had seen more than his fair share of weird things in his short twenty-one years, but seeing someone casually playing with fire was an absurdity he could dismiss.

He looked away but felt the stranger's stare pressing on him. It grew uncomfortable. *Should I move to another seat? Take another glance.* His eyes lifted for a moment only to find the man's intense gaze still focused. *What is this guy's problem?* Victor cursed softly.

In the twinkling of an eye, the man pushed himself upright and whistled his bizarre song down the aisle, his cane thudding solidly as he moved.

"ETA to 30th Street Station is ten minutes," blasted the conductor's voice.

The old officer's whistling grew louder with each thud of his cane. *Did it just get hotter in here?*

As the officer drew closer to Victor, the silver eagles on his shoulder boards shimmered in the lights. *He's a colonel.* Instinctively, Victor leaped from his seat to a crisp position of attention.

Up close, he appeared younger than Victor thought. He was dark-complected like Victor, though with a scar that crossed his lips and up to his left cheek. Both eyes were a pale, piercing gray with a hint of blue in their centers. His cane topper was the shape of a grotesque spider. And when his trench coat parted, it revealed a holstered silver pistol with an ivory grip. The colonel ceased his whistling once his eyes locked onto Victor.

He leaned heavily on his cane as he spoke with a southern drawl as thick as molasses. "Corporal, why didn't you ask my permission?"

Victor stammered stupidly. "Permission, sir?"

"Yes, permission," he repeated slowly. "For eye fucking me for the past five minutes."

Victor was well-versed in coarse military humor. After all, he was a soldier. His response to the colonel would be risky since it was one thing to joke with someone in your squad or platoon but another thing entirely to smart-ass a superior officer.

"I was unaware I needed permission, sir," he said, feigning ignorance. "You were wearing protection, after all." He inclined his chin toward the man's sidearm.

The colonel moved closer, his eyes narrowing into round, focused orbs. "Well, now, seems as though I've discovered a regular joker," he said, tapping his pistol. With a smooth, practiced move, he unholstered it and pointed the muzzle lazily in Victor's direction.

"Selena's seen more men bleed than you have years. She doesn't take kindly to people who lay eyes on her. Least of all, the likes of some snot-nose kid. She's liable to get…ornery. You wouldn't like to see my baby girl get ornery."

Victor knew he stirred a hornet's nest. *I just had to be a smart-ass.*

The colonel cracked a grin and re-holstered his weapon. "It's not every day you meet someone with a pair of nuts." He nodded approvingly. "Take a seat, corporal…?"

"Gates, sir."

The genteel southerner removed his glove and shook Victor's hand firmly. "That's a strong grip you've got there, Corporal Gates. I am tickled pink to make your acquaintance. My name is Colonel DeThroe." He slowly took a seat, clasping his injured leg gingerly with one hand while lowering himself into the seat with the other. Out of courtesy, Victor waited until he was seated before lowering himself into his own seat.

"Gates, Gates, Gates." He snapped his fingers with each word, then rubbed his smooth chin in thought. "Where have I heard that name before?" DeThroe's gaze wandered around the car as though searching for an answer on the walls. "No matter," he said, waving a flippant hand. "I'm sure it will come to me at some point. How many years have you been deployed, corporal?"

"Three, sir," responded Victor, thinking it felt more like an eternity.

"All in Haiti, I presume?"

"Yes, sir," said Victor, wishing the train would go a little faster. He vainly attempted to change the conversation. "Where are you heading, sir?"

"I loved Haiti," said the colonel dismissively. "Now, mind you, it was nothing like my little sugar cane plantation near New Orleans, but the stories the Haitians tell…well, they are just marvelous. Goodness knows I love a good story." He chuckled.

He paused to pull a silver cigarette case from his coat pocket. Taking one, he lit it and blew a puff of smoke. "Those locals sure do tell a good story, don't you think, corporal? Perhaps that's how I grew so fond of storytelling. I'm Haitian on my mother's side. My personal favorite is about a fierce voodoo priestess by the name of Cecile Fatiman. Her bone-headed father, no pun intended, this is voodoo after all—" DeThroe gave another hearty chuckle. "I do apologize." He wiped a phantom tear from his cheek.

"You see, Cecile's father didn't want her to complete her initiations as a priestess. You have to understand her father's position. He had a rather colonial mentality and had been convinced by the colonizers that voodoo was an aberration against all that was holy. His daughter thought otherwise. She'd worked too hard to get where she was. She nearly completed her training to become initiated. There was absolutely no way she would roll over and relinquish the prestige and status that she would obtain by becoming a full-fledged priestess."

DeThroe propped his cane between his crossed legs and faced the spider's head in Victor's direction. "Cecile's last rite of initiation into the voodoo tradition was to sacrifice a pig with a ceremonial dagger. Her father said if she sacrificed the pig, he would excommunicate her. Well, do you think that stopped our fierce heroin? No, sir. She cut that pig's throat from ear to ear. That righteous display pleased the Gods of war. They were so pleased, in fact, that they sent a bolt of lightning to blow that pig to kingdom come. Cecile's people viewed this as a sign to begin to fight."

He took a long drag from his cigarette. "And that, young corporal, is how the Haitian Revolution in 1804 was started." He exhaled the gray cloud in Victor's direction. "Now, what do you think the moral of our story is?"

The train car's heat, along with the thick plumes of smoke, made Victor nauseous. He tried to crack the window, but it wouldn't budge. "Buy your meat at the grocery store?" he said, giving up on the window and slumping back into his seat.

"Fathers will always disappoint you, of course," said DeThroe coldly.

Fathers. The lesson of DeThroe's parable struck a personal chord with Victor. He imagined the story leading to some great lesson about war or some other obscure notion, but it didn't. *God, I just want to get out of here.* Instinctively, he searched the train car for an exit. But there was no escaping his past, least of all his own identity.

The colonel looked decidedly pleased as if he had solicited the reaction he wanted. His face contorted into a look of surprise. "Hold on! I just recalled your name. You are *the* Corporal Gates from the battle of Les Rouge." Victor straightened and met DeThroe's eyes with a nod.

DeThroe puffed a few rings of smoke into a small cloud forming overhead. "How embarrassing of me. I've been in the presence of a genuine legend this whole time. What you did down there was nothing short of miraculous, son. The lives you saved and the rebels you killed…Truly marvelous."

Victor could feel his upper lip begin to curl but masked it with a smile. *No one knew what really happened over there.*

"What now, corporal? Getting some R&R before getting back into the fight?"

"No, sir. I'm starting to out-process from the Army this week." Victor craned his neck to catch a glimpse of the neon clock on the front of the car.

DeThroe puffed on the last bit of his cigarette. "That's a shame. The Army will hate to see you go, especially after everything you've done," he sighed. "What you did down there may have nearly resurrected your family's reputation."

Victor took another deep breath, guessing what would come next.

"Especially after your traitorous father dragged it through the mud. He is the worst kind of human being. The very worst. But you're not like him, are you? You, sir, are a *friend* of our great nation. I reckon if your father was standing before us right now, I could hand you Selena, and you would blow him and his band of Omega hooligans straight to hell where they belong."

Victor hated being tested and that is exactly what this felt like. Regardless, he answered honestly. "He deserves a traitor's death, sir."

"I'm happy to hear that," said DeThroe as a smile turned up the corners of his mouth. "Don't go changing your mind now, ya hear? By the way, I've had the good fortune of just being appointed as General VanHeller's Chief of Security. So if you hear so much as a mouse fart from those Omega bastards, I'm the man to tell. Understand?"

Victor gave a quick nod. "Yes, sir."

DeThroe opened his window to toss his cigarette butt out. "Ladies and ladies, we have now arrived at 30th Street Station, Philadelphia, Pennsylvania," the conductor announced. "Time to collect your belongings, trash, and war trophies. The doors will open momentarily."

Victor rose, grabbed his heavy duffel bag, and made his way to the doors.

"Will you be doing your out-processing brief at the E.C.H.O. Chamber?" asked DeThroe.

"My friends are picking me up from the station and taking me to the chamber. I'm a little confused about what to expect. I've only heard rumors."

"Ahh yes, the chamber," exclaimed the colonel without veiling a giddy unease. "Your out-processing includes a shiny new neurograft, courtesy of The Fourth Branch. And you won't forget your experience. The neurograft calibration process is quite…memorable." He laughed uncomfortably. "I should warn you not to be late for your appointment, though," he said, freeing an intricately cast silver pocket watch from his breast pocket. "General VanHeller occasionally attends E.C.H.O. Chamber appointments for VIPs, and I reckon that you make the cut. Good luck, corporal, and hail The Fourth Branch!"

Victor snapped to attention at the door threshold and saluted with the customary greeting, "Hail The Fourth Branch!" And with that, he stepped onto the platform.

He looked down expectantly at a small black tattoo that resembled the number four on his unfurled left hand. *Why's this damn thing not showing the time?* He turned to the train conductor, a scraggly-looking draftee standing in the doorway of the train car. "Hey, Private, looks like my sociograft is busted. What's the time?"

The private looked down at his own sociograft device. With a flicker of his fingers, a holographic image of "9:30" levitated above his hand. "You have yourself a *glorious* Army day, corporal," said the man with an unmistakable dose of sarcasm.

9:30. I have a whole two hours till my appointment at the E.C.H.O. Chamber. As the train pulled away, a lump formed in Victor's throat. The mere thought of going to the chamber produced a powerful wave of anxiety. Save for seeing his family and friends, Victor had thought of little else during the train ride. DeThroe's parting words only deepened the feeling of existential dread and tension that were already building inside of him.

Taking a slow look around to gain his bearings he saw the 30th Street Station had changed little after his three-year absence. Its historic, once beautiful, towering limestone walls were still a grimy shade of white, and there was chewed gum on nearly every surface. Likely the same discarded gum that had been there since he left for Haiti three years ago. Perhaps it was out of necessity to cover the grease and grime of the walls, or maybe it was the need for advertising space, but most of the walls were covered floor to ceiling with posters. A whole section of which was devoted to "*Wanted – Mobius Gates, Dead or Alive,*" posters picturing a mugshot of his father staring grimly back at him. Victor quickly moved past these to another section of wall and took a closer look at some of the flashier-looking tri-centennial posters. They reflected a holographic image to the viewers. The messages were mostly patriotic. "*Happy 300th Birthday America!*" "*Freedom Through Strength,*" "*Liberty Not Moderation!*" "*Disunity IS Unity!*" and "*Cyberocracy Dies in the Dark.*"

They were all pretty self-explanatory, but one caught his eye. It said,

Cyberocracy Can't Survive Without the Mandate! The poster depicted a family all smiling widely with their neurografts displayed prominently on their temples. As he studied it, he realized the message must be referring to the upcoming chant vote, where the people will decide if a neurograft mandate is enacted.

He stared for another minute, pondering its meaning as an altercation between two men broke out. A crowd was already gathering. Victor watched and listened as they traded obscenities.

"Suck it, you four-head fuck!" one shouted.

The man with a four-shaped neurograft on his forehead cracked his knuckles. "That's pretty rich coming from a filthy moderate. You're all the same; just a bunch of drones!" yelled the other. Cheers and jeers alike came from the onlookers.

"Oh, *I'm* the moderate? Why I oughta'..." This display went on for several minutes with no side staking a decisive victory. Soon enough, the two men simply parted ways, adjusting their respective collars while giving an added spectacle of spitting in each other's directions. Victor had seen these 'cyberduels' before his deployment but was shocked to encounter one immediately after stepping off the train.

"That was the most pathetic cyberduel that I've ever seen," said a few onlookers as they began to disperse.

The weight of his duffel bag was digging into his shoulders. He had already done several laps around the main atrium only to realize he was alone. It felt as if he had been stood up by a date. With a long sigh, he tossed his bag on the floor and sat on a bench to catch his breath and scan the crowd for his friends, Eli and Rocky.

The first thing he noticed was that most people in the station already wore neurografts. The devices were red in color with a purplish-blue tint around the outer edges and resembled a tattoo in the shape of a number four. Victor had heard rumors in Haiti that there was going to be an upcoming chant vote that sought to mandate the neurograft for the entire country. The grafts were relatively new, so he was not quite sure what they did, but he knew they were controversial and could only be installed by technicians at the E.C.H.O. Chamber.

He heard several horror stories about the chamber but discounted most since they were second or third-hand accounts. One guy in another battalion swore his cousin had nearly drowned in one of the chamber's many preparation pods. Others said their best friend barfed harder riding the pods in the chamber than on any roller coaster they'd ever been on. It all sounded like barracks gossip and speculation to him. Still, it didn't sound like something you'd ever want to try twice. He looked at the clock on the station wall. Over an hour had passed since he arrived, and there was still no sight of his friends.

They promised to meet him at the main atrium of the train station. "What a couple of duds," he mumbled. Thinking they might have forgotten, he called them. He made a few motions with his left hand, moved the number four looking tattoo closer to his mouth, and spoke, "Call Eli and Rocky."

"Error. Cannot connect. Hail The Fourth Branch." responded a terse voice emanating from his hand's device along with a hologram of the same message. He began poking the device in the center of its number four slowly in a vain attempt to make it work.

"This stupid sociograft is broken again!" he grumbled, jabbing it even harder with his middle finger. *Totally worthless.* Hoping he could borrow one, he tried to flag down several passersby's attention. He received nothing more than blank stares and a few obscene gestures. Finally, an old, and pleasant-looking man sat near him on the bench.

"Excuse me, sir," asked Victor, "can I borrow your sociograft? Mine appears to be broken, and I need to get in touch with my friends."

The man's face lit up with a wide grin that wrinkled all the way up to his neurograft. "Of course you can. Anything for one of America's heroes." He stretched his hand towards Victor and pointed the sociograft's number four tattoo directly into his face. The digitized tattoo appeared to glow for a moment as though it was trying to scan Victor's face.

"Unable to synch. Hail The Fourth Branch," blurted the device loudly from the man's hand, and directly into Victor's face.

"Sorry about that, young man." The old man eyed Victor and his Army duffel. "Are you heading home or going back to the fight?" His short gray beard hardly hid his affable grin.

"Going home. I live in the Fair Heights neighborhood of Philly," replied Victor.

"Good. I'm sure you're looking forward to seeing your family again."

"Yes. I know my mother has missed me terribly."

"I can imagine. And what about your father?" asked the old man.

Victor crossed one leg over the other. "He's not in the picture anymore."

"Well, I'm sure wherever he is, he misses you."

"I seriously doubt it. Wherever he is, he wanted to be there a lot more than with my mom or me." Perhaps it was the man's disarming nature, but Victor was surprised to lower his guard in front of a total stranger.

"Look, son, no one is perfect. Take that young family there, for example." The old man tilted his head toward a soldier with his wife and small son, who was just learning how to walk. The mom had just let the little boy walk toward his father, who was bent down on one knee and gave him a giant hug. The kind of hug where you forget everything around you. "Would you say that that man is a bad father?"

"No," said Victor, without hesitation.

"Now, how can that be? He is willingly leaving his family," said the old man with a narrowed brow. He rose to his feet and pulled a pocket watch out of his purple blazer to check the time.

"It's his duty. He's doing it for his family and his nation," said Victor.

The old man looked back with curious amusement. "He's doing it because he must. He doesn't *want* to leave. He *needs* to leave."

Victor took a harder look at the family of three. The mother and father had knelt down and embraced each other with their young son in the middle of them. The little boy took his father's military hat off and put it on his own head. Even from a distance, Victor could see tears rolling down the father's cheek.

"We all have choices. For some, family cannot come first." Victor turned his head to respond, but the stranger had vanished. *Wherever he went, he must have been in a hurry.* With a shrug, Victor's attention went to a nearby tellvision broadcasting the morning news by Philadelphia's action news reporter Cliff Mifflin.

"These recent sightings of Omega terror suspects within city limits are very concerning indeed. However, the mayor has reiterated that there is no reason to be worried, going on to say the city has adequate defense measures at its disposal. We're live now with Mayor Goldie." A man wearing a flamboyant golden-colored blazer with a popped gold collar appeared on the screen. He seemed to be in the throes of an argument with someone offscreen. "Mr. Mayor, good morning."

"Is it on? Did you turn it on? I didn't see a red light!"

"You are *on*," whispered a disembodied voice.

"I'm live? Okay. Good morning, my fellow Philadelphians," he said with a toothy smile. "This is your mayor speaking. We have so many wonderful upcoming events. First, July third is nearly here. That means the annual chant is nearly upon us. Of course, we will do the usual voting for our next president, congress, grand architect, and *mayor*." He interrupted his own speech with a theatrical wink.

"But this year is most important since we are deciding whether to mandate neurografts or not. Also, we have exciting activities planned for the Independence Day celebration. We are blessed

to be living in the birthplace of our country. Philadelphia is like the hospital where little baby America was birthed into the world. And we all love babies. But do you know who doesn't? Those soulless scumbags from Omega. They are evil and have no place in our cyberocracy. My goal is to smoke those drones out with all the means at my disposal and slap 'em around!"

He began making aggressive and offensive hand gestures, encouraging his producer to cut the footage back to Cliff.

Victor looked at the clock on the wall of the station. *It's 11:00.* Colonel DeThroe's final words sprang into his mind. 'Don't be late,' he had warned on the train. With another forty-five minutes to spare, Victor stood up and grabbed his bag. *I guess I'll have to walk there.* Throngs of people poured out of the platforms. Each passerby either eyed the military-clad Victor approvingly or with a side-ways glare that stung with malevolent intent. They swarmed menacingly like a hive of hornets as they made their way to the exits. Victor wanted out. He elbowed his way through the crowd.

A familiar, raspy voice with a British accent echoed throughout the cavernous station halls. Victor's jaw dropped. His friend Eli was in the center of the raucous cyberduel crowd with fists raised and teeth clenched. Eli stood about eight inches taller than his opponent and was far more muscular to boot. Despite being shorter and less stocky, his spunky adversary, wearing glasses, taunted Eli with a 'come get some' hand gesture. Eli shook his head and cracked his knuckles.

Except for today, Victor could not remember the last cyberduel he witnessed. This was the second one today, and it involved one of his best friends. He muscled his way to the front to get a better look. Those in the front row had a particularly hateful glint in their eyes. They stood in stark contrast to those in the back of this angry mob. Some folks looked on with mild boredom at the brawling pair, apparently unimpressed with the ferociousness of the fight. One disengaged onlooker mumbled, "What a couple of lightweights," before walking off to catch his train. Others held up their sociografts to their faces to livestream their commentary of the spectacle.

The bespeckled man unbuttoned his wrist buttons and rolled up his sleeves. "Well…we going to do this or not?"

"Your funeral," said Eli.

The two men held up their sociografts to each other and shook with their left hands. A faint glow of red emanated from the palms of their hands, and the crowd went wild.

"It's starting." A woman clapped gleefully.

"Here we go," said a little boy, craning his neck around the rather large man in front of him to get a better view.

The instant their hands detached, the man in glasses threw a cheap right hook, landing squarely on Eli's jaw.

Eli spat at his opponent's feet. He was never one to yell, but he channeled a guttural growl to say, "Listen, you fucking four-head twit, that was a lucky shot. You only get one of those."

The insult must have done the trick because the man lunged at Eli with a hearty war cry. This was, admittedly, the only real move he could make against a physique any outside linebacker would be jealous of. Eli grabbed his attacker, spun him around, and got him in a chokehold.

"Squeeze that little VanHeller loving squirt," cried a woman.

"Throw his stupid four-head-loving ass on the train tracks!" shouted a short, round man with a mustache.

Eli's forearm and bicep formed a vice-like grip around the man's skinny neck. At first, the man flailed and smacked at Eli's face in vain to be released. But seconds later, he began to lose consciousness, sending his eyes rolling back in his head. The fight ended with the man's pitiful gurgle before he slumped to the ground. Eli began to pummel him with his fists.

Victor felt like an unwitting accomplice in this collective crime of inaction. A black hole descended on the crowd, sucking out any shred of humanity they possessed. Time itself seemed to stop. Waves of anger and hate swept over the shouting bystanders as they watched with blood lust in their eyes. The blood splattering from the man's lip, the contorted faces of rage from the onlookers, and the utter neglect of passersby were overwhelming. Someone had to do something.

Victor dove toward Eli's arm, grabbing his elbow to prevent the next punch from landing. Eli was unrecognizable and looked much older than before. To be fair, he was ten years older than Victor, but there were already gray hairs peppering his previously jet-black sideburns. His eyes were sunken in with heavy bags underneath. Covered in blood and sweat and face red with rage, he was a man possessed. It took Eli a moment to recognize his friend.

"Hey, man…this guy's had enough!" Victor stumbled on his words but summoned the strength to address the crowd. "This…whatever this is, it's over. Move along. F' off already!"

"What? Where you all going?" Eli chided as they traipsed away. "Had enough fun for one day? I bet none of you sissies even has the balls to ask for a refund. If you do, you can get it at the corner of First and Go-Fuck-Yourselves. That's right, just walk away, you bunch of miserable twats." No one paid him any attention.

"Looking fine, hero," said Eli, his raspy voice raising a few octaves as Victor gave him a tight handshake hug.

"Are you out of your mind? You were about to kill that guy! What's your problem, man? Did you even know who he was? Why did you get in a fight with him?"

"He saw my sociograft tag and challenged me."

Victor paused. "What the hell is a sociograft tag?"

Eli cracked a grin. "I've forgotten how big of a rock you live under when they send you down to play in the Jungle."

Victor was okay living under that rock for a few more minutes. He had bigger fish to fry now. "Whatever man, you can explain on the way. We need to leave right now. My appointment at the chamber is in twenty minutes!"

2

Hellish Proposals

The two rushed from the station straight into the humid July morning. The sparrow's last morning songs echoed between the concrete buildings along Market Street, where Eli's car was parked. 'Car' was a generous word for this hunk of junk. It was a nearly forty-year-old Ford Bronco with a constellation of poorly done, rusty bodywork on nearly every square foot. The bumper, apart from being held up with bungee cords, was riddled with every manner of politically charged stickers.

"How is this beater even still street-legal?" asked Victor.

"It's not. Hasn't been in twenty years. Hop in."

"Surprised they haven't impounded it on you," said Victor, opening the creaky passenger door to clamber inside.

"Well, it's not for their lack of trying. Give the glove compartment a look. There's about a hundred citations inside." With a turn of the key, they sped toward downtown.

"So let me get this straight. You beat the shit out of some stranger, you have an ass load of speeding tickets, and you drive like a madman! Jesus, Eli, slow down!" Victor was already getting whiplash from the erratic driving.

"I'm not a madman. You only think that 'cause you're such a freaking boy scout." Eli chortled. "I suppose you'll go bonkers when I tell you I became a cop?"

"You're joking! You should be in jail right now, man. How in the hell are you a cop? I can barely even look at you right now. That shit back there was awful. What do you think Jacky would think of that if she saw it? How is she, by the way?"

"She wouldn't see it. I barely get to see her anymore as it is. I have her every other weekend from that cunt mother of hers. But you're right. She'd hate it. Probably see me as a wild animal or something."

"So you're a cop, and you get to see Jacky again. That's good shit, man. That must mean you've been laying off the neuroenhancements?"

The pair's last visit was rough. Eli was in bad shape before Victor deployed. His buddy had addiction issues, none of which helped his parental rights custody case.

"Been sober for nearly three years now, soon after you left. I got my badge nearly two years ago," said Eli, speeding through a three-way intersection. "And so you know, that bloke back there challenged *me* to the fight. And *both* people have to accept the fight. It's not like you can just walk up to anybody and clock 'em."

"What are you talking about? What do you mean 'accept' the fight?"

"Right. Allow me to unearth that big ass rock you've been living under. There's been some major upgrades to the sociograft since you've been gone. They made it so that you can flag people down or tag them using any kind of search criteria. Tags is what we call 'em."

"What kind of 'tags?'"

"Well, it depends on what you adjust your settings to. Most people just use it to find sex. That miserable sod back there must have had his settings searching for people who hate VanHeller and the neurograft mandate. Mine is set to every anti-VanHeller, anti-neurograft mandate setting you possibly can. And his must have been set to 'bend me over and let me have it Fourth Branch.' So naturally, when we crossed paths, our sociografts started going off like a five-alarm fire."

"I don't get why you hate VanHeller. If it wasn't for him, we'd be in another War of the Moderates."

"What a crock of shite, Victor. He's a power-hungry maniac. Anything else you need to know?" Eli swerved hard to the left, narrowly avoiding hitting a woman strolling her baby.

"I've been gone three years, man. Cut me some slack. I'll be asking you basic questions for at least the next month. So what's new with the 'neuromandate?' There were a ton of posters all over the station running on about 'democracy can't survive without the neuromandate.'"

Historic downtown Philly, with its tidy stoops and decorative wooden front doors, grew smaller in the rear-view mirror as Eli drifted the Bronco around a long bend in the road, sending thick plumes of smoke from the rear tires onto nearby pedestrians. "Neurograft mandate. You'd vote against it during the chant vote if you knew what was good for you. Its mind-control. It's not enough that VanHeller and his Fourth Branch goons want to go to war with every group of military-aged men doing jumping jacks in the jungle. Now they're going to wage war with your mind, mate!" said Eli, looking thoroughly deranged. After letting Victor digest that for a moment, he added, "You have to vote 'no' during the chant, and don't you let Rocky talk you out of it on your first vote. God knows he'll try."

"Looks like we're almost there," said Victor, trying to switch topics away from the neurograft. He didn't know anything about it, but he was pretty sure the grafts had nothing to do with mind control. Eli always got overly excited about controversial issues. This one was no different.

"What did you mean back at the station when you told all those people that they can't get their money back?" asked Victor. "From watching the cyberduel. Did you guys charge or something?"

Eli shot him a sideways glare. "Victor…I was being sarcastic. No one charges for these things. But you know, maybe that might not be such a terrible idea," he added. "You might be a war hero, but you're still dense as hell."

Victor shifted uncomfortably in his seat and told Eli a little louder than he intended, "Would you please stop calling me a hero."

Hero. Victor could barely string those two syllables together without cringing. In their short-lived discussion, Colonel DeThroe pierced the veil shrouding Victor's insecurities, making him feel exposed. The colonel, like everyone else, knew the young corporal was desperately trying to get out from under his father's shadow. Though no one really knew what had taken place in Haiti. Some call it heroism, and maybe some of it was, at least on the surface. But Victor knew that the deeper you dig, the dirtier you get.

After a minute, Eli broke the awkward silence. "Listen, mate, I'm not trying to get your knickers in a knot. I know what you've been through, and I know what you're going through now." Eli slowed down, trying to make random eye contact while driving.

"I was down in the Jungle Gym for three years myself. But I didn't want to be there. I was drafted. You volunteered, you crazy bastard. Every day, I counted the seconds till I could come home. Every single day, it felt like I was in survival mode, keeping my head down and doing the bare minimum to not get myself shot. You're different, mate."

The Jungle Gym. It wasn't where kids go down slides and swing from the monkey bars. It's a tongue-in-cheek way of calling the battlegrounds now raging in Haiti, where the battle of Les Rouge was fought only a few short weeks ago. Victor cast his gaze out the window and lowered his voice. "None of that matters. I'll still just be my father's son in everyone's eyes."

"That's bullshit, and you know it. Firstly, what you did in Haiti had nothing to do with your dad. Secondly, there'd be a lot of young grunts who'd be lying dead in some jungle somewhere if it wasn't for you. You did what no one else would or could. That's the Victor Gates I know."

Eli's Bronco weaved and bobbed through traffic. Apart from Eli screaming road rage-induced expletives at other drivers and the occasional pedestrian, the car ride was otherwise quiet. With each passing block, Victor's palms grew slick with sweat. Anxiousness was settling in, making his stomach churn. He had one place to be today, and somehow he screwed it up. He hoped Colonel DeThroe was wrong and General VanHeller would not be present. *What were the chances of the head of the military for the entire United States of America showing up?* His heart raced.

"I'm going to be court-martialed," he muttered.

"No, you won't. They'll kick the piss out of you…maybe make you peel potatoes, but they won't court-martial you." Eli didn't inspire a lot of confidence. Even he sounded unsure of his own message. Both of his outcomes sounded decidedly unappealing. Victor wasn't one to sit on his ass and peel potatoes. He somehow was always in the thick of it. "Besides, getting court-martialed isn't *that* bad…" Eli cleared his throat. "After all, I can speak from experience." He let out a morbid laugh while narrowly avoiding an old woman in a wheelchair crossing the street.

Eli was outdoing himself. If Victor was hanging on to the 'oh shit handle' during their drive from the train station, then what he needed now was a parachute cord to rip. Ice cream trucks and hot dog stands all barely survived as Eli dodged them by inches.

They screeched into a makeshift parking spot by violently drifting its rear end onto the curb. Victor turned green as Eli kissed the steering wheel. "Old girl never lets me down," he said lovingly. "We're here."

Victor clambered out of the car and started in a sprint. Eli called after him, "Oi, I'll see you at your house tomorrow morning. We'll go to Rocky's together.

* * *

Victor stepped onto a grassy expanse at the epicenter of Philadelphia. It was rectangular and flanked on all sides by towering glitzy office complexes. In years past, this place had been called Independence Mall. Some still called it that, but it was more commonly referred to as 'the drop.' So named because of the E.C.H.O. Chamber, an enormous purplish-red colored teardrop-shaped building that now dominated the whole northern end of the mall. Victor focused. He checked his watch. It was now 11:35. *I'm already late.* He sprinted toward the entry point of a large wrought iron fence that surrounded the chamber complex. He showed his ID to the guard, who checked a manifest on his computer.

The guard looked back and forth between the ID and Victor. "Damn, this doesn't look like you. You look like a little kid in this picture."

"It's me," Victor said impatiently. The picture on the ID he handed the guard *was* of a kid. It was taken right after he graduated from high school. It's shocking what four years of lifting heavy things and living on an Army diet will do to a physique.

"Well, of course, I know it's you, Corporal Gates. Your face is plastered on everyone's sociograft feeds." The guard pressed a button on a console to open the entry gate for Victor.

Officially, this place was not called the "E.C.H.O. Chamber." Instead, it was known as the 'Emotive Calibration Helix Optimizer,' but the name didn't matter. The complex was ground zero for all things mysterious and intriguing. It was common knowledge this was where people received their neurografts, but beyond that bit of half-truth, the whole place was shrouded in mystery.

Victor took two steps at a time as he raced up the marble stairs. He came to a sizeable landing and looked around. Near the teardrop, he saw the outside was a reflective dark purple, though it did not remain a constant color. Its metallic exterior pulsed and swirled into an ominous, almost angry, red. The bottom of the drop pointed upright on the landing which served as its pedestal. Perhaps if a giant had stomped into center city Philadelphia, he simply could have rolled the drop right off its stand and into Independence Hall.

Given the menacing exterior, Victor assumed there would be an equally grand entrance. To his surprise, the only visible way inside this behemoth was through a small circular cutout, one just large enough for one or two people. The hatch opened automatically as he approached. He stepped inside a cavernous, sterile white room, thinking he had just entered a ceramic bowl like the ones in his mother's fine dinnerware cabinet. The interior held only two pieces of furniture. A teardrop-shaped white chair was placed in front of but at an awkwardly far distance away from, a sweeping white marble desk. He walked over to the desk and peered over it, half expecting to see someone behind it. *No one.* Just an empty chair and a lot of strange-looking buttons. *Where the hell is everybody?*

"Ahem…" Another hatch opened and a man dressed all in white with slicked-back hair and the thinnest mustache Victor had ever seen came strolling towards Victor and sat behind the desk.

Victor adjusted his shirt collar and swallowed hard. "I'm sorry I'm late for my appointment. My name is—"

"Hail The Fourth Branch, Victor Gates. Yes, we are expecting you. I am the Sentient Caretaker." He spoke in terse, broken snippets, barely even lifting his eyes to acknowledge Victor. "Please take a seat." He motioned to the large teardrop chair placed far from his desk. "The

Chairman of The Fourth Branch is expecting you. He will be here soon."

Victor's ears turned hot. He wondered if they were as red as they felt. My blood pressure must be through the roof, he thought. *Great. Any moment VanHeller will walk in and chew me a new asshole.*

He attempted to take his mind off of that unsavory thought by taking stock of his surroundings. There wasn't much to this place. Just white, white, and more white—with a splash of white. The man at the front desk was staring him down like he was about to catch fire. Once they locked eyes, the man averted his gaze and looked down at his desk, the front of which had a Latin inscription emblazoned on the front of it:

E UNUM PLURIBUS

Victor had a gut feeling that he should try to get on the good side of the caretaker and at least take a stab at conversation. He cleared his throat and asked, "Sir, what does 'E Unum Pluribus' mean?"

"It means 'out of one, many,' It is the motto of The Fourth Branch. How on Earth do you not know that?"

Victor nodded politely, rolled his eyes, and continued scanning the room. Opposite the entrance hatch across the vast elliptical expanse was the cutout of another small hatch where the caretaker entered from. The hatch was barely perceptible and would have been nearly invisible had it not been for a large symbol that looked like a misshapen yin-yang etched into the wall above it.

Behind the caretaker's desk were several portraits of high-ranking members of The Fourth Branch. He recognized the two big bosses: General Kurt VanHeller and Grand Architect Valter Lucier. Even someone living under a rock would know who Valter Lucier was. He was the head of The Fourth Branch and someone Victor admired. Lucier pulled the country out of its darkest period twenty years ago—

when Victor's father was trying to topple civilization.

Suddenly, the entry hatch opened. It made Victor jump. *This is it. He's here.* He listened intently for VanHeller's footsteps and was nearly ready to rise from his chair to greet his superior.

It quickly dawned on him there were no footsteps. Only the sound of a rickety pair of wheels squeaked across the mirror-finish floor. Curiosity got the best of him, and he peeked around his tear-shaped chair. A boy in a wheelchair was approaching the desk.

"Hello, my name is Innocius Rios. I'm sorry I'm late." The boy was thoroughly out of breath. His left arm was being nursed by his right, and his clothes were more tattered than the ones even Victor had grown up in. He looked exhausted and uncomfortable.

The man rose and squared his shoulders. "You will need to reschedule when you learn how to read a watch," he said before lowering back down in his chair.

The boy looked distraught. "Sir…I couldn't take the bus today. I…"

"I'm afraid that isn't my problem or the problem of this office. Now, kindly remove yourself from the premises." The caretaker never glanced up as he replied.

"He can have my seat." Victor stood. "I can make another appointment."

Before the caretaker could reply, a voice came over Victor's shoulder, "No, Corporal Gates, I'm afraid we can't have that. We've been expecting you for much too long to delay our rendezvous any further."

Victor and the boy turned to face an entourage of military officers staring at them. The one with the most medals, who seemed in charge, had spoken first.

"*The* Victor Gates. I've been looking forward to this moment for a very long time." He outstretched his hand. "I am General Kurt VanHeller." He smiled broadly as they shook hands.

Victor noticed he had an impeccably straight, easy smile, one that would make a dentist blush. It belied his more common characteristics of a high-ranking military officer; a pointed chin and curved cheekbones.

"Now, Mr. Raucks, what is all the commotion going on in front of our special guest?" VanHeller asked the caretaker, half-mockingly, all while commanding a serious response.

"General, this…*boy*…is two hours late. Only Corporal Gates is scheduled for this time."

VanHeller eyed the youth seemingly for the first time and leaped backward with dramatic astonishment. His neck oscillated back and forth between Victor and Innocius. "Have you two ever been told that you look remarkably alike?"

There is a bit of a resemblance. The boy had a little more childhood pudge on his face, but his bone structure, compared with Victor's, was uncannily similar, with a high forehead and a straight nose. They both had the same bright brown eyes and complexion. Even their curly black hair was cowlicked in all the same places. Victor shrugged off the comment as nothing more than a coincidence. "We've only just met, sir."

"Huh, well, if I didn't know any better, I would say you could have been brothers," said VanHeller. His eyes still darting back and forth between the two boys. He shook his head dismissively to come back to his senses. "Well, there you have it, young man. As Mr. Raucks said, we are going to have to see you another time."

Tears welled in Innocius' eyes. *It must have been a harrowing journey traveling here in a wheelchair.* "Sir, there is plenty of room in here. Can you make an exception for him?"

Raucks sprang from his chair, looking upset. "Corporal—you have no idea how this process works or what you are—"

"What the caretaker means," the general interrupted, "is that your military de-brief process coupled with your neurograft upload is fairly complex. There could be unforeseen consequences if you both enter the E.C.H.O. Chamber together." Raucks leaned back with a smug look of vindication.

The general went on, "But that risk is quite low, isn't it, Raucks? Besides, how could I convince America's most famous hero to join the grand architect and I during the Fourth of July Celebration if I rub him the wrong way on our first day of meeting one another?" The general seemed to make it a habit to ask questions in a half-joking and patronizing sort of way. "Let's reschedule this young man's appointment for, oh, how about ten minutes from now?"

Raucks' reddened face signaled an imminent internal gasket being blown, but he kept it together enough to say, "As you wish, sir." Innocius breathed an audible sigh of relief.

"Corporal Gates, you represent everything good about our great nation," said VanHeller, looking pleased with himself. "You're a fighter, and God knows we need more fighters in this country. Ones willing to struggle for what they believe in, even if it means getting a little… dirty. This is your shot to get into the big leagues, corporal. Together, imagine the good we can do for this country."

At face value, this all seemed like a pretty fantastic offer. But Victor started to warm up to the idea of hanging his uniform up for good. His new life would involve going to backyard parties and day drinking on his porch with his friends. All he wanted was to blend into a life of relative obscurity. As VanHeller eyed him, he shifted his stance and folded his arms across his chest, hoping the general would catch his drift that this was not a hill worth dying on.

VanHeller's lip curled up, and he teetered back and forth on his heels. Instead of retreating, he was repositioning for a new tact. "You're a genuine hero, son. We can't let that go to waste. What I'm offering you is a chance to chart your destiny. How many people can say they are offered that gift-wrapped opportunity? Grand Architect Lucier and I are trying to rally this country together. Lucier saved this country two decades ago by developing The Fourth Branch and now we need your help in keeping Liberty alive and well. With you by my side, we'll have the American people just smitten by my good looks and your heroics. So what'll it be, Victor, destiny or destitute?" VanHeller moved closer to Victor and whispered. "Like your father..."

Victor had not thought about his father his entire time in Haiti. And now, on his first day home, he had already endured multiple painful reminders. He barely even remembered the man, but everyone seemed to do that for him. His father was a traitor and the most wanted man in the world. That was a good enough reason for everyone else to hate him. In truth, Victor could hardly remember why he hated Mobius Gates.

Even Mr. Raucks' grumpy frown evened out a bit in the presence of Victor's glow. Before he could stop himself, he said confidently, "I think this is just what I'm looking for, sir. I'd be happy to join you on the fourth."

"Splendid." VanHeller's smile grew. "I'll send a car to pick you up. I think I've kept you boys long enough from your appointment with Mr. Raucks. Plus, I'm late for an appointment with my new head of security, Colonel DeThroe. Mr. Raucks, they are all yours. Be gentle," he said with a parting wink.

Victor, Innocius, and Mr. Raucks were now the only three occupants in the teardrop's spacious foyer. Valter Lucier and Kurt VanHeller starred down lifelessly from their nearby portraits. Mr. Raucks feverishly pressed buttons on a console. A second teardrop-shaped chair rose from the floor next to the first.

"You both need to take a seat, please," said Mr. Raucks.

Realizing the shape of the chairs would make this simple task difficult for Innocius, Victor offered to help the young man into the chair. Innocius smiled appreciatively as the corporal settled him into the teardrop while avoiding putting pressure on the arm he had been nursing. "What happened to your arm?" asked Victor.

"Sometimes the boys at school…they like to pick on me 'cause I'm paralyzed, and…sometimes things just get out of hand." Innocius looked away, embarrassed.

Victor searched for words to comfort this boy who didn't deserve the hand he was dealt in life. "I got bullied all the time when I was in school. You heard VanHeller talk about my dad. Well, no one likes him. The entire world hates the man with an undying passion. So when I was in school, the boys would beat me up a lot."

"I can't imagine anyone picking on you. I've heard stories about how brave you were," said the boy with admiration in his eyes.

"I just got lucky. I doubt if half the stories you heard are real." Victor knew Innocius would shudder at the thoughts of what happened in that jungle in Haiti. The truth would only terrify the boy. "But do you know what's brave?" Innocius shook his head. "Facing down bullies and recognizing them for what they are. Nothing more than pathetic, miserable bastards. Next time they mess with you, just tell them they can sit on a fat one and spin." Innocius snorted with laughter. Victor realized he should probably keep things G-rated in front of the kid. Running his hand through his hair, he apologized, "Yikes! Sorry kid. I shouldn't have said—"

Mr. Raucks' voice interrupted, "You are about to enter into the Emotive Calibration Helix Optimizer. But before you do, I need to give a short legal brief." He droned on as if reading from a script since he had given this speech thousands of times. "The neurograft procedure is irrevocable. By entering into these chairs you have consented to have a neurograft device, patent pending, permanently affixed to your body. The device will be calibrated by harvesting a small amount of your DNA. This device can transmit certain neurograft theta activity waves at a frequency of 7.3hz for an undisclosed range. The neurograft is capable of receiving certain artificial forms of theta waves in limited capacities. The programming used to generate the theta waves is strictly proprietary information of The Fourth Branch. By undergoing this procedure, you are eligible to waive any compulsory mandate the government institutes on its citizens to receive a neurograft device." Mr. Raucks looked up from his panel. "Are you prepared to receive your devices?"

Victor and Innocius nodded in unison. Raucks clicked more buttons, engulfing their bodies within the chairs, save their heads, which protruded like a couple of hatching chicks. The chairs then tilted to lay flat back.

"Is this a roller coaster or something?" said Innocius, trying to turn his head to face Victor with a smile.

"It is nothing of the sort," replied Mr. Raucks, again pressing more buttons. "Your vessels," he cleared his throat, "that is to say, your chairs will guide you to several points within the E.C.H.O. Chamber. At all stages during the process, you must keep your legs and arms in your vessel at all times. Do you understand?"

The two nodded again before stifling small giggles as their eyes met. Raucks' safety speech confirmed this was just a fancy roller coaster.

Unable to suffer these indignities any longer, Raucks pressed one final button like a maestro finishing the last note of his orchestra. At that, the chairs began to rise, higher and higher still. As they rushed toward the ceiling, Victor squeezed his eyes close. He never saw the two holes in the ceiling open to allow them passage.

3

The E.C.H.O. Chamber

The two boys were now on a level that looked very similar to the first one; sterile and void of any color. He couldn't tell for certain, but Victor was sure that they were on one of the top floors of the teardrop-shaped building because the room they were in was tiny.

Their chairs began behaving in a very peculiar manner with a series of quick motions. First, they reclined flat so the boys could only see the top of the ceiling shaped like a narrow dome, confirming Victor's suspicions they were at the top of the teardrop building. Then, the chairs passed through the floor as though being absorbed by it.

An icy cold liquid formed a pool that surrounded their heads, covering their ears. Innocius let out a cry as Victor tried to calm him.

"Don't worry, I'm right here with you. We're going to be okay. Alright, little brother?" Victor could see some of the fear melt from the boy's face. He was pleased he helped take some of the boy's anxiety away. Now, if only someone could do the same for him.

Victor's head was now nearly submerged in this liquid, but even so, he remained buoyant so that his face remained on the surface. He could breathe normally, but if Innocius, or anyone else, were talking he wouldn't be able to hear it because his ears were submerged too. Once submerged, a transparent casing began to envelop itself around their heads. Now Victor was completely cut off from Innocius.

The eerie silence was like nothing Victor had experienced before. He felt wholly separated from the world outside, utterly alone. Once that feeling washed over him, he felt his lower limbs jolt involuntarily. It felt like he was falling asleep, and the hypnic jerks were beginning to kick in to try to wake him up. All at once, he felt so tired, so at peace. Awake, but only just.

***

His ears rang loudly as a weightless sensation gripped him. It felt like he was hovering. No, floating. Floating into a place that seemed so foreign but horribly familiar. Below him, a wide ocean with large waves crashed against a rocky shore. Near the coastline, a half dozen men were gathered amongst the shrubs, crouching low to the ground as if hiding. Farther ahead, tall, emerald-green mountains speckled the horizon. There was a small village at the base of the towering hills.

Victor fought to wake up from this dream but had no control. As he was whisked closer to the crouched men, he saw their faces. They remained blurry, but he recognized them. They were his squad of soldiers he led in Haiti at the battle of Les Rouge. Their lips were moving as if they were speaking to him. He concentrated on their words.

"Corporal Vic! Yo, Corporal Vic? Can you hear me, man? Did you go deaf or something?" said one.

Victor quickly understood he had become one of them. He was *inside* one of them. Specifically inside this dream game as an avatar. *God damn, this is too weird.*

"Ain't that the truth? Company is on the radio, man. They want a

SITREP."

Victor took the handset from his radio operator, Lewis, and spoke into the mic, "Alpha6, this is Tengo7, SITREP to follow, break. We are at the operational rally point and have a UAV visual on the target break. Awaiting orders to conduct assault, over."

Victor heard a familiar voice reply, "Tengo7, this is Alpha6, wait one." He knew that meant 'hang on a minute while we unfuck something on our end.'

"Good copy, Alpha6, holding position." Victor handed the mic back to Lewis and looked at his men. They looked tired and weather-beaten. "Hey Chan, give Sullivan a nudge to wake him the fuck up. No sleeping, and head on a swivel alright? Pull security till we move out, got it?"

Chan nodded and poked Sullivan, whose cheek was propped against the stock of his rifle as he slept. "Time to wake up sleeping beauty. What'd you dream about?"

Sullivan's cheek rolled off the rifle stock, lurching him awake. "What'd I dream about? Taking a nice long walk on the beach with your sister."

"Well, you're only gonna get half your dream asshole." Chan laughed and flicked some sand in Sullivan's face.

"Corporal said to knock off the grab-ass you two," said Lewis sternly.

The squad looked ahead at the thick vegetation separating them from their target. With their backs to the sea, they were now sitting ducks for an enemy attack.

"What's taking so long? We need to get moving," Victor murmured to Lewis.

"I don't know, man, those company fucks better pull their heads out their asses. This shit's about to get wack. I can feel it."

Just then, the radio chirped to life. "Tengo7, this is Alpha6 proceed to your objective. Rules of engagement are as follows: weapons-free. I say again, weapons free, break. Intel reports heavy enemy activity in your AO, proceed with caution, out."

"Good copy, Tengo6. We're moving out," answered Victor. "Hey, knuckleheads, we move out in two minutes. Rojas what do you see on the UAV feed, anything?"

"No, corporal. Just some villagers in the town and some farmers in the fields. Also, does anybody's cock get harder than concrete whenever we get the green light for weapons-free?" 'Weapons-free' is military talk for 'shoot anything that looks remotely threatening.'

"What about in the jungle?" said Victor, ignoring the concrete cock comment. "Use the thermal filter. Do you see any warm bodies out there?"

"Let me look again," responded Rojas. "Holy shit, corporal—"

He never finished his words as a hail of bullets began pummeling the rocks they hid behind.

"Sullivan, Chan lay down suppressive fire. Rojas, Lewis, I need targets. I'm going up on the Scyther board and taking the wingman UAV with me."

Next to Victor lay two large metallic surfboard-like pieces of equipment. Two propellers were embedded in the front and back. He ran to one of them and put his sociograft hand on the board's control interface, initiating a start sequence and causing it to hover above the ground. He ran to the other and quickly did the same thing, but also donned the board's targeting mechanism, the Heads Up Display (HUD). He jumped on the Scyther board, planting his feet in the auto-bindings just as bullets whizzed past his ear. Victor used intricate motions with his sociograft hand to propel the board into the air and navigate it above the Jungle canopy while the wingman UAV followed, mirroring his board's every move.

The boards flew high and fast away from the coast, heading toward the village. Victor glanced back at his team, who were still pinned down by a concealed enemy. "My guys are good. They have good cover and plenty of ammo. They'll be alright for a little while," he muttered, trying to convince himself leaving was the right choice.

He didn't have much time. He had to get to the objective. His commander and the whole company were relying on him.

As he rose higher, he saw other squads in the same predicament. They, too, were pinned down along the coast. Small pockets of intense firefights happening simultaneously could only mean one thing; the enemy had been expecting them.

His company had all been lured into a complex ambush with no support to exit the island. Thankfully, the other squads also had board pilots who were going to attack the objective. Currently, though, they were all fighting for their lives, and Victor was flying solo.

"Damn, I need to hurry." His plan was to get in, bomb the target to hell, and then make his way back to the coast to help the squads. The mission always came first.

As he neared the village, he saw his objective—a small compound surrounded by fortified concrete barriers. Targeting cross hairs appeared in his helmet HUD with the compound directly in the middle of them. He silently thanked the inventor of the heads-up display. *This was going to be easy. That must be the enemy command post.*

He radioed Lewis. "Tengo1, I have the target in my sites. Request confirmation, over."

No response.

He tried again. "Tengo1, need confirmation of my visual, over."

Nothing.

He tried once more, "Tengo, two, three, four, come in over. Anybody, come in, over. Damn!"

Either their radios malfunctioned or something bad happened to his squad. The decision now fell to him. *Destroy the target without confirmation or abort.* He chose the former. He navigated his board with subtle motions of his sociograft hand to close in on the target and trained the HUD's cross hairs on the target. With a flick of his wrist, the ports to the direct energy weapons on the noses of both boards opened. And with a closed fist of his sociograft hand, both his board and the wingman UAV companion unloaded a barrage of hellish fire on the building.

It never had a chance. Alright, that shit's done. Time to go help my guys.

Victor headed back for the coast to help the squads closest to him that were under fierce attack by the enemy. He closed in with his board and wingman UAV, obliterating the enemy's jungle positions. Though he could not see exactly where he was firing, he was certain whoever was down there was unhappy. After Victor laid waste to the enemy with his board's direct energy weapons, he would dismount his board to load up casualties onto the boards. If the enemy was still pummeling the rocky positions where the casualties were taking cover, he would orient his board and the wingman to strike enemy positions while dismounted to perform lifesaving aid to his comrades. A spunky medic named Private Foster at Romeo Squad's position was fighting off the enemy while bandaging up his fallen comrades behind the rocks. Despite Victor's protests, Private Foster insisted on staying with Victor while he made his rounds to the other squads to assist him in the company's recovery operation. Victor and Private Foster flew to the next squad, and the next, and then the next. Each one was in a worse shape than the last. Sometimes, there were a few survivors, though most had only a few with many injured. Two squads had no survivors at all, and Victor and Foster loaded all the bodies onto his boards and took them to the evacuation (EVAC) site on a small hill near the coast. One by one, they assisted all sixteen of the company's other squads. There were many casualties, and only a few of them would ever see home again.

At last, he was returning to his men at the Tengo squad. As he approached, the silence was deafening. He expected to hear the chaos of active combat, but only the waves crashing against the rocks filled his ears.

He landed, horrified at the sight before him. He was too late. His squad's mangled bodies lay lifelessly on the rocks. There was no enemy now and nothing he could do. Lewis's radio and his body were lying on the beach, riddled with bullet wounds. With trembling hands, Victor took the mic to give his report.

"Alpha…Alpha6, this is Tengo7," he said with a shaking voice.

"Send it, Tengo7."

"Alpha6, enemy compound destroyed. They knew we were comin'." Victor took a deep breath and then keyed the mic again. "There's… casualties."

"Tengo7, what's the status of your squad?"

My squad…they're dead…they're all dead!" Victor shouted.

"Tengo7, calm down. We're sending an extraction team to get you out. Be advised, you destroyed the wrong target."

"Alpha6, say again. Wrong target?"

"Be prepared for debriefing after evacuation."

As soon as Victor thought it was over, he was sucked back into a memory of immediately after he and the other survivors were air evacuated from the battle. He was now pacing outside of his commander's tent, still dressed in his bloodied fatigues, waiting for the debrief. The same thoughts relentlessly swirled like a hurricane in his mind.

Tengo Squad. My guys. How are their families going to find out what happened? Who will tell them? It needs to be me. Wrong target? What did the CO mean the wrong target? The HUD showed me the target, and it's never wrong.

The flap to the tent opened, and Private Foster emerged from within. Foster grabbed Victor by the shoulder. "You did what you could, Vic."

"Corporal Gates. Enter," shouted a voice from inside the tent. Victor walked in to find his commander sitting at a table smoking a cigarette. There was another officer there typing on a computer station in the back. Victor approached the commander, stood at attention, and saluted.

The commander returned the salute. "Please sit, Corporal Gates." He took a long drag of his cigarette, put it down, and ran his hand across his bald head. "How you holdin' up, Gates?"

Victor didn't need pleasantries. He wanted to cut right to the point. "What did you mean I destroyed the wrong target, Captain? My HUD showed a positive identification of the target. It's never been wrong."

"Corporal, you've been through a great deal today. There'd be dozens of young men who wouldn't see home were it not for you. That's what we need to focus on now. You're a hero, son."

"Captain, I want to know what you meant. If I didn't destroy the target, then what did I destroy?"

The commander picked up his cigarette, took another long drag, and then put out the butt on his table, squeezing the last bits of tobacco onto the grassy floor. "Scribe. Stop recording," he called out to the other officer sitting at the computer. She lowered her hands from the keyboard and sat back.

"It was a school, Gates. You destroyed a school."

How could this happen? How many innocent people did I kill? How many were kids? How could I look at myself again?

His ears rang loudly, and he was back lying in the pod of E.C.H.O. Chamber goo. He couldn't tell if it was the goo on his face or tears falling from his eyes. He still felt tired, so very tired, as he floated away, and his ears again rang loudly. Far away to another familiar place. He was at home in the foyer, sitting on the floor like a little boy again, sitting crisscross applesauce, playing with a toy. A man and a woman walked past, talking loudly. They were arguing and kept glancing in his direction. Victor barely recognized the woman, but she had to be his mother, Carmenta. She wore stylish clothes, with her hair done up in tight interlocking braids. She looked beautiful and more youthful than Victor had ever seen her. The man was his father, Mobius. He was easy to recognize from the wanted posters.

Mobius raised his voice with Carmenta. She cried as he continued. Victor couldn't understand what they were saying. He was just a little boy playing with a toy truck. He knew something was wrong, but he was powerless to act.

His parents moved toward the door where Victor was playing. They were yelling so loud that Victor stopped to cover his ears. Mobius opened the door, stepped into the dimly lit street, and kept walking. Victor looked at his mom, who clung to the threshold for a moment. His eyes went to the door toward his dad as he crawled closer to get a better view from the porch.

Events blurred again, like a chalk painting being washed away by rainfall. He was floating again, maybe back to the E.C.H.O. Chamber. *Please let this be over. No more, please, no more.*

A small boy cowered in the corner from a fearsome man who looked just like a younger Victor. *Innocius.* He was frozen in fear and couldn't run even if he wasn't wearing leg braces. There was a woman on the bedroom floor who looked remarkably like his mother, Carmenta. The man was beating her. Beating her so hard that she didn't get up again.

Victor jolted awake with a gasp. He was lying in a bed in the sterile room. He was puzzled how he came to be on a firm, scratchy bed. How long had he been in that horrible chair? Hours? Days? "Hey, is anyone here?" he called.

"Ah, Corporal Gates. You're awake. Good." A young woman in medical scrubs peeked around the hospital curtain that surrounded his bed. "Can I get you anything? Are you thirsty?"

"Yeah, I'm parched, actually."

She brought a large glass of water, which he emptied in seconds.

"Where's my friend I came with? His name was Innocius."

"Yes. He was a sweet boy. He was discharged about an hour ago."

Victor leaped from the bed only to realize he was naked. The nurse dropped the water jug to place both hands over her eyes.

"Oh God, jeez—sorry about that. Can I have my clothes, please?"

The nurse pointed to a cabinet in the corner. "They're in there. Though, Corporal Gates, you can't leave just yet." She ventured a look as he dressed. "You have a significantly large…amount of paperwork to fill out."

"Mail it to me," he told her while slipping on his pants and shoes. He walked toward the door. Finding Innocius became his only mission. *That last memory wasn't mine. Was it Innocius?' That couldn't have been part of the normal procedure.*

He left the room, found an elevator, then headed to the lobby. As the door opened, he was shocked to find it deserted. Even Raucks was gone. Victor walked into the sultry night air where he exited the grounds of the E.C.H.O. Chamber.

4

Mother Earth

Victor's mind raced. How was he going to find the boy? He *had* to find him. He searched up and down the street and across the grassy field toward Independence Hall. There was neither a soul in sight nor a star in the night sky. He folded his hands on top of his head in frustration, *Dammit.*

"How bad was that for you?" a small voice asked from behind him.

Victor turned around to see Innocius slumped down low in his wheelchair. "It was bad little man. Really bad. At least we got a couple cool mementos out of it." Both Innocius and Victor now had a neurograft affixed to the left side of their foreheads. Like the sociograft, the neurograft was embedded into the skin like a tattoo and resembled the number four. Though unlike the sociograft, which was normally black in color, the neurograft burned a fiery purplish red. If Victor looked at Innocius' graft a certain way, it glowed in the dark.

"Can you help me get home? I don't want to go by myself," said Innocius wearily.

"Sure, I'll go with you. There's a bus stop on the next corner up."

Innocius tilted his head down and exhaled in frustration. "SEPTA stopped doing service to Fair Heights after dark."

Victor couldn't believe it. "You live in Fair Heights?"

"Yip."

"That's crazy, little man, so do I. Screw SEPTA, we'll use your wheels. They're probably more reliable anyway."

Victor pushed Innocius' wheelchair on the sidewalks next to Independence Hall. The hands on the clock tower read one-thirty. *How is it this late?* It didn't feel like he was in the E.C.H.O. Chamber for more than a few minutes, and yet nearly half a day had passed. Victor pushed Innocius' wheelchair through the windy roads of Philly's historic district. Soon, the neat rows of stately brick homes gave way to iron bars on windows and broken shutters. The two boys made most of their journey in silence, exhausted by their shared ordeal in the E.C.H.O. Chamber. *What the hell was that thing?*

Victor knew these thoughts were weighing heavily on Innocius, too.

"It made me relive my *worst* memories," said Innocius in exasperation.

"Yeah, me too. The craziest part about it was that I felt like I was there, you know? Like I had somehow possessed my own body and relived those moments all over again. I can't even explain it. It's like an out-of-body experience or something like that."

"I saw where you were," said Innocius. "In a big forest with your friends, and they...they were..."

"I'm sorry you had to see that. I wish you hadn't..." Victor's memory flashed back to the woman being beaten. She looked so much like his mother, Carmenta, and yet he knew the woman on the floor was not his mother. "Was that your mother? I...I think I saw your memory of her being beaten by that man. I couldn't see his face clearly, but the woman looked so much like my mom."

"Yes. That was my mom. I didn't even know I had that memory." said Innocius. His voice drifting off.

Victor tried to change the subject. "Why didn't your mom drop you off at the E.C.H.O. Chamber?"

"She doesn't have a car, and she had to work tonight. She's the one who wanted me to get the neurograft. Which is super strange because up until last week, she *hated* the neurografts. Then a couple days she heard from someone that it could cure my paralysis. I guess that wasn't true, or else you wouldn't have to push me home."

Victor thought back to the cyberduel at the train station where the two men were fighting over the mandate. "So your mom is an anti-neuro?"

"Oh yeah. She would always go to all the protests to stop the neurograft mandate from going through. She would call people who got them 'pathetic mind-controlled four-head drones.' My mom's not normally an angry person, but the idea of the mandate really brought something out of her."

"My friend Eli and your mom would get along great. He said that when you get the neurograft, you become mind-controlled. I don't believe him, though. He's always had all these crazy conspiracy theories. He means well, but I know to take what he says with a grain of salt. I mean, the guy's a cop, and he has about a hundred speeding tickets in his glove compartment."

The two didn't speak again for a while. Victor couldn't stop thinking about the last vision he had in the E.C.H.O. Chamber. The image of Innocius' mother being beaten on the floor was now branded in his mind. If Innocius had seen him and his squad in the jungle, and Victor had seen Innocius' mother, then the thought was too ridiculous to entertain. *How is that even possible?* If that's the case, then maybe Eli and Innocius' mom were right. How else could he have seen what Innocius was imagining in the E.C.H.O. Chamber? Judging by the confuddled look on Innocius' face, Victor was sure he was thinking the same thing.

Victor yawned deeply. Right now, the only question that mattered was how long he was going to sleep for once he curled up into the bed he hadn't slept in in three years. They were now firmly outside of the touristy district of historic downtown Philly. They found themselves in a seedier part of the city as they neared Fair Heights. Most of the streetlights were blacked out, and a whole kennel's worth of dogs were barking against the backdrop of near-constant police sirens.

Innocius finally broke the silence. "Hey, I'm not supposed to go this way home."

"Yeah, I know what you mean. This place is even more of a dump than I remember it was."

"No, what I'm saying is I was told not to take this way home…by some of the boys in my school."

"Don't worry, kid, you're with me. Nothing bad is going to happen," said Victor reassuringly.

"Well, they told me not to go this way, or else they would…they'd beat me up."

"Kids are such assholes. Don't worry about it, it's so late right now, I bet they're all sleeping. Plus like I said, I'm not going to let anything bad happen to you, okay?"

Innocius nodded but began twisting his hands together into a nervous knot.

Victor kept pushing Innocius, though his pace quickened faster than before, and his eyes scanned the houses as they rushed past. "Hey, are we getting close? What street do you live on?"

"It's just about five blocks ahead, on Jacobs Street."

"Okay, almost there," said Victor. Up ahead on the corner, Victor could see some people lurking in the shadows. He didn't know what they were doing there at this hour, but he knew they weren't selling cookies.

The pair crossed the group of five burly ruffians along the sidewalk when one of them called out. "Hamster boy! I said I was gonna stomp your ass if you came anywhere near my corner again."

"We didn't mean to Big T, but it was late, and we got turned around coming back. We had to walk all the way from downtown."

"Does it look like I care about literally anything you just said, hamster?"

Victor folded his arms. "Why do you keep calling him hamster?"

Big T and his cronies exchanged smiles. "Cause he's on wheels. Get it? Like a hamster wheel." They howled with laughter.

Victor was stone-faced. "You really are as stupid as you look, aren't ya?"

Big T was clearly trying to think that through for a minute. "So, not only did you come here, but you brought your soldier bitch with you too." The boy called Big T wasn't much older than Innocius, but he was built like a linebacker for the Philadelphia Eagles. Big T's friends were smaller, but not by much. "Wait a minute, I recognize you, soldier bitch. You're that guy they keep showing on our sociograft feed, right boys?" They all nodded and looked very pleased with themselves. "You got money, right? You're famous. I'll tell you what, you pay the toll, and we'll let you go. But you gotta leave the kid, alright?" The gang cackled with laughter.

Innocius looked petrified. These boys were twice his size and clearly made his life a living hell. God only knows what they would do with the boy if Victor left him with them. And he definitely wasn't planning on letting that happen.

Victor was tired, but he'd been more tired before. He wanted to get home, but he could wait a little longer. The odds were five on one, and he'd definitely seen worse. These punks needed to be taught a lesson. *This is going to be a wipeout.*

Victor stepped between Innocius and these bunch of assholes. "There's another option here. You all get your punk stench off *my* street for good, and I never want to see you here again. How's that for a deal?"

Big T rushed toward Victor, who grabbed a trash can lid next to him and smashed the boy's face with it. Big T stood in a stupor for a few seconds and then fell onto Innocius' wheelchair arm, causing both of them to fall to the ground. Big T's friends exchanged nervous looks and hightailed out of sight.

Innocius lay helpless in the street but had the wherewithal to yell after the fleeing hoodlums. "Sit on a fat one and spin!"

Victor walked over to him, laughing hysterically. "Hey, little brother, you handled yourself pretty well, you know that? I've seen people take shorter falls than that and end up way more jacked up."

"I didn't do anything. I was about as fierce as my pet rabbit, Snuffles."

Victor chuckled. "Well, looks like Snuffles knows how to handle himself. You hurt?"

"Just a bit scratched up, I'm alright though."

"Good. Let's get you back in your chair," said Victor, reaching down to help him back into his chair. When he lifted Innocius off the street, their hands interclasped, and both of their sociografts began to go haywire. They transmitted holograms that were a jumbled mess of unintelligible symbols. Victor wasn't an archaeologist, but it looked more like hieroglyphics than anything else he had seen outside of a museum.

What's more, when the two boys joined hands, Victor felt an overwhelming sense of peace. The likes of which he had never felt. After having experienced those horrible memories in the E.C.H.O. Chamber, it felt like a warm embrace from both his parents that he never remembered getting. The immediacy of the sensation was such that Victor felt like he had been hooked on an IV and had a direct injection of pure joy. Whatever it was, Victor could see that Innocius felt the same connectedness between them.

They continued to stare at the sociograft malfunction like it was some kind of miracle. In the pitch black of the dimly lit street, it seemed like one. Flashes of spectacular colors and holographic symmetrical symbols that resembled yin-yangs made it seem as though this malfunction was by design. And just as quickly as it started, the transmission disappeared.

"Wow," said Innocius.

"Yeah…what the hell? I mean, I couldn't even make a local phone call with this stupid thing this morning, and now it looks like it's talking to aliens or some shit," said Victor as he hoisted Innocius back into his chair. "We need to get you home, let's go."

Victor returned Innocius to his home's stoop, which was only two blocks from where he lived, and carried him up the small flight of stairs to his door. "Do you want me to wait till you make sure your mom is home?"

"No, I'll be okay. You've done so much for me tonight, Victor. I can never repay you," said Innocius earnestly.

"Anybody would've helped you, kid."

"No, they wouldn't. I'm young, but I'm not naive. This place, sometimes…it can be…"

"Miserable?"

"Yeah."

Victor didn't want to leave the boy feeling down in the dumps, and what's more, he felt somehow connected with him now. He had an idea. "Hey, I have to go get my sociograft repaired at my buddy's shop tomorrow. How about I swing by your place afterward?"

"Hey, yeah, that sounds great!"

"That gives us probably five solid hours of sleep. See you tomorrow, champ."

Victor walked the several blocks to his mom's row home. It was a shabby little brick thing with worn shutters and metal bars on the windows. A single bulb next to the door provided a bit of light on the otherwise dark street. It wasn't much, but his mom took care of what she could. Flowers were still pouring out of the window boxes, and a handmade wooden sign on the door read "Home is where the heart is" welcomed her guests.

He knocked on the door as quietly as he could. No one answered. He knew his mother must have fallen asleep. Victor instinctively turned the doorknob, and it creaked open. "Mom, what the hell?" he said in a hushed tone. *She must have forgotten to lock her door.*

Victor opened the creaky door slowly, not wanting to wake his mother. The home opened into a small living room. A lamp in the corner was turned on and he could see his mom fell asleep on the couch. He walked over to her, kissed her on the cheek, and turned out the light.

He walked up the stairs to his old childhood bedroom which looked completely unchanged from when he left. *Christ, what a long day.* He started out on a plane from Haiti, then rode the train with a very odd colonel. He stopped his friend from killing a guy and smashed a punk's face with a trash can, but not before reliving his most horrific memories and that of someone he had just met. *And* to top it all off had probably communicated with God, aliens or something else entirely.

* * *

Victor woke the next morning to the smell of bacon wafting through his room. He looked out his open bedroom window to the sights and sounds of a warm northeast Philly morning. Not exactly the French countryside, but it was what he knew, and it was home. The T-shirt he pulled out of his dresser didn't fit at all anymore. A glance in the mirror confirmed it; he left this house a punk teenager with the body of a boy and returned to it with that of a full-grown man.

Starved out of his mind, he tossed on a pair of jeans and went down the stairs. His mom heard his footsteps and came to the foot of the stairwell. Victor skipped the last five stairs and leaped into his mother's arms.

"Oh, my baby. I can't believe it's you. Is it you? I'm not sure if it is. Just look at you, son! My handsome boy has returned the most handsome man," said Carmenta, holding Victor's cheeks in both her hands.

"I knew you were going to say that, Ma."

"Well, it's the truth," she said as she wiped a face full of joyful tears away. "Now come on to the kitchen, and let's get you some breakfast."

They didn't have to walk far to go from the bottom of the stairs to the kitchen. On the first floor of the row home was a small living room, kitchen, bathroom, and a closet under the stairs. It may have looked like a dump from the outside, but on the inside Carmenta made sure it was kept immaculately clean. The house wasn't decorated in the 'typical sense.' In a previous life, Victor thought she must have been a farmer or herbologist or something like that. She cleaned rooms at a hotel downtown to pay the bills, but everyone who knew her well knew that she was born with a green thumb. "Mom, do your co-workers still call you—"

"Mother Earth? Yes, sometimes. Every Christmas, I don't give out cards. I give little terrariums!" She howled with laughter.

Every wall was stacked from floor to ceiling with plants, terrariums, and some very exotic-looking flowers on floating shelves. The bay window, despite having bars over it, provided ample light for all her "greeny babies," is what she called them. She doted on them like she was their mother, hummed delightful tunes, and watered them with glass beakers. For some of the bigger indoor plants, she rigged up an irrigation system from the water picket outside, where she kept a lovely little garden. Victor grew up in this green menagerie, and he wouldn't have had it any other way.

Victor took a seat at the kitchen peninsula while Carmenta lovingly filled a plate with grits, bacon, chicken, and waffles and a separate one with biscuits and gravy. "Mom, there's no way I can eat all of this."

"What? You don't like it?"

"No, I love it, I just—"

"So, you want more?"

"No, Ma, this is fine," relented Victor. No matter how poor they were, Carmenta always made sure the kitchen was fully stocked. It was a blessing and a curse; Victor could never walk away from the kitchen without eating two people's worth of food. And God forbid he didn't eat all of it, or she would get the idea something was undercooked.

Carmenta put her hand on her hips. "You are skin and bones, Victor Gates. Now eat up." She grabbed a broom and started sweeping the white linoleum floor. "You know Eli called yesterday? He said that he was going to stop by and pick you up before you two went to Rocky's. I figured maybe he might want a bite, too, so I did make a bit extra. You know he's been so nice to me since you were away. He'd stop in every couple of weeks to check up on me. He's a good boy, that Eli."

Victor laughed on the inside at the thought of Eli being a "good boy." He wasn't, but he was a hell of a friend, and he took care of those he loved.

Victor scarfed down one plate like a starved wild beast. He had been eating 'Meals Ready to Eat' (MREs) for as long as he could remember. Sometimes, on holidays, he and his squad would kill a deer or wild hog to cook over an open flame. For some reason, Lewis, who was from coastal Maryland, would carry around a shaker of Old Bay flavoring to spice up the meat a bit. And how could he forget the time Sullivan and Chan stole a pig from a farmer? They made a pen for it until it was time to butcher it. When they tried to get it out, it slipped and ran into the woods. Those two went tripping over every branch in the forest to chase that fast little bastard down. They never did get it. *Tengo squad.*

"You okay, baby?" Carmenta noticed Victor appeared distant suddenly.

"Yeah, I'm okay, Ma. Just glad to be home, that's all."

Carmenta ran her hand through his hair. "I know. You've been away for so long," she said lovingly. "You need to take the time you need to get alright, you hear? God only knows what you've been through, and now I'm gonna be with you, too. Every step of the way."

Victor gave her a half smile between chews. He was nearly done with both plates of breakfast when the glass from the bay window shattered, and a large rock skipped across the floor. The loud crackle of glass was enough to make Victor leap across the peninsula to cover his mom from any shards that broke free.

"Are you okay?" Victor asked Carmenta and then bolted outside to see if he could catch a glimpse of the punk that did this. They must have been in a car because by the time Victor looked up and down the street, nothing was moving except for the birds on the power lines.

On the living room floor lay the softball-sized rock. Victor was furious.

"It's alright. Don't let this get you down. It's just a little hole in the window. We can patch it up just fine," said Carmenta.

"Ma, we have to get you out of this dump," Victor said a little more loudly than he meant to.

"Please don't call this place a dump. It's my home. It's our home."

"You know what I mean. I just never should have left you by yourself."

"Victor, you know damn well that I can take care of myself. That was probably just some neuro-junky getting down off his high."

Just then, there was a knock on the door. "I'll get it," said Victor as he opened the door for Eli.

Eli walked into the living room and sneered at the mess of glass on the floor. "Fuckin' neuro-junkies," growled Eli. "Good to see you, Mama Gates," he said with a quick peck on Carmenta's cheek.

"Do you want some breakfast, Eli? I made some extra for you."

"Thanks, but I'm alright. How's your garbage disposal working for you?"

"It's doing just fine, thanks to you, Eli," said Carmenta while walking to the closet to grab a broom and dustpan. "I told you, Victor, I've been just fine. And whenever I needed an extra hand, this stud muffin was always here to help."

Eli didn't blush. At least, Victor could never see him do it through his thick bushy beard. "You're a peach, Mama Gates," he said in an octave higher than his normal tone. One of Eli's very few tells that he was pleased with something. He even smiled a bit before his eyes landed on Victor's forehead, and did a dramatic double take. "Sweet merciful fuck, Victor. What in all that is holy is on your forehead?" He moved in closer to inspect the red neurograft tattoo now affixed to Victor's forehead.

Victor rolled his eyes. "We should get rolling, Eli. I met some kid at the E.C.H.O. Chamber yesterday. He lives down the street, and I invited him over to Rocky's shop. And something…something really weird happened last night when we were walking back home. We got jumped by these punks at that three-way corner near Jacobs Street. And…I don't know. I can't explain it. Our sociografts just started spewing all these weird symbols and lights, and—"

"Ouch!" Carmenta cut her hand on a shard of glass.

"Oh, Ma. Are you okay?"

She started to shoo them toward the door. "Yes, I'm fine, baby. Why don't you and Eli get going to Rocky's? Eli, will you be coming over for dinner?"

"I'm sorry, Mama Gates, but I can't. Those twits put me on the night shift for the whole week. Rain check?"

"Of course, Sugar," she said, giving Eli a big hug. "You're family here."

Victor hugged his mom, and he and Eli made their way out onto the street.

5

Mr. Rizal's Cyber Parlor

Outside, Victor took a deep breath and filled his lungs with the familiar daytime smells native to this side of Philly. It was neither sweet, fruity, nor fragrant in the classical sense. It was mainly comprised of car exhaust, mingled with hot asphalt and the occasional heavenly whiff of barbeque or halal. It wasn't for most, but it was all he knew, besides a three-year stint in Haiti and a handful of Army bases.

The Fair Heights neighborhood in northeast Philadelphia would even be recognizable to a time traveler from the late twentieth century. It wasn't a neighborhood built for tourists like the quaint streets lining Independence Hall and City Hall. Rather, it was made for hard-working people who couldn't seem to ever catch a break.

He and Eli began the short walk down the narrow sidewalks to Rocky's dad's store. Victor took in all his surroundings that he never knew he would miss so dearly over the past three years. It wasn't a paradise. Far from it, in fact, but these streets had raised him. And even if they were lined with buildings that had bars on their windows or trash strewn as far as the eye could see, you never forget who raised you.

Eli carried on about how The Fourth Branch was secretly construct-ing bunkers for an Apocalypse that they themselves were planning. It had to do with something about how the neurografts created a gateway to the sentient artificial intelligence that was the 'man behind the curtain' for the cyberocracy. Victor was too busy taking in the sights to pay too much attention. Some kids right next to where they were walking had opened the valve on a fire hydrant, and on the next street up, a small crowd gathered to spectate a cyberduel. Eli got so carried away and animated with his storytelling that he never saw the toolbox lying on the edge of the sidewalk. He tripped over it and fell chest-first onto someone's car side mirror. "Bloody hell!"

Two gorgeous women emerged from behind the car's hood that was popped open. "Nice job, asshole, you broke the freaking mirror," said one of them.

"Oh my God, Victor? Victor Gates? Is that you!" said the other, with her hands on her hips. "Victor Gates. How long have you been back? Stacy and I have been seeing you all over our sociograft feeds." The girls swooned in Victor's direction.

"Eli…" said the girl, shooting Eli the nastiest resting-bitch face she could scrounge up.

Eli got up and dusted himself off. "A-bitchy-ana…it's been much too soon. Sorry about your mirror. Good thing you brought *tools* with you. Even if you do leave them in the worst spot imaginable."

"Eli, go off yourself," said Stacy coldly. Her and Eli started a shouting match while Victor stepped closer to Abiana.

"Abiana, how long has it been?" asked Victor, trying desperately not to let his voice crack or let his eyes wander.

This was particularly challenging, even if Abiana was dressed in jean overalls covered in grease and oil stains. She was even prettier than he remembered. A tall, curly-haired blonde with a smile that went for miles. She probably turned at least a dozen heads on her way to this part of town.

Thinking about that last part, he asked, "What the hell are you doing down here? I mean, it's incredible to see you again. But God, this neighborhood has gotten so shitty. Aren't you still living on the other side of town?" Victor thought Abiana may still be staying with her rather wealthy parents.

"Stacy and I had to go to one of the mills down here to pick up some parts for our power circuit board. There's a race tomorrow night! Victor, you should come. She saved one more nasty look to flash at Eli as a clear sign that there was only one invitation on the table.

"Jeez, I haven't been on a circuit board in forever. I think I'd need some practice first."

Abiana winked. "Just like riding a bike."

Eli and Stacy had stopped bickering, and he clearly couldn't take it anymore. "Alright, that's enough sexual tension for one morning! Now we all need to be getting to Rocky's, right? Abiana, it's a shame they don't sell grease to lubricate bitchy personalities."

"You are such a tool bag you know that?"

"Jeez, knock it off, you two," said Victor, trying to be the adult in the room. "Yes, we will definitely see you there, Abiana."

"Good. See you there, hero," said Abiana as she and Stacy waved goodbye.

Eli looked disapprovingly at Victor. "So she can call you hero, and it's alright? Good to see you're not still thinking with your dick," he said sarcastically.

"What's with you two?"

"Nothing's wrong with me. She's the one who's a neuromandate-loving flaming bitch. I just happened to break up the last power circuit race that she was in."

"There it is. I knew there was something."

The two-story brick building that they were now walking toward looked completely and purposely ordinary, except perhaps for the chicly designed sign above the door that read "E. Rizal Cyber Parlor" in bright red, white, and blue lettering. Underneath it a smaller sign read "Custom Sociografts and NOW offering Neurograft Repairs." Flanking the door were two large windows, with many colorful pictures plastered on them of people's exotic sociograft designs. Victor hadn't been here in several years but remembered that Mr. Rizal only used a portion of the front of the building for his business. He'd never been into the back before.

Victor had never been in a 2040s-style tattoo parlor, but this is exactly what he imagined it may have been like as the bell above the doorway welcomed them inside. The floor was a black and white tile in a checkered pattern, and the walls were decorated floor to ceiling with WWIII-era paraphernalia. Tattooed pin-up girl posters were the most common décor, but there were also many portraits of colorfully painted elongated Army Jeep chassis called Jeepneys that served as public transportation in Manila after the post-war years. There were eight retro-style reclining leather chairs that hugged the walls, and each had a small ornate wooden table next to it with all kinds of intricate silver instruments. A woman was seated in one of the chairs with her hand resting very still on the armrest while a sociograft tattoo artist dressed in a white apron held one of the silver smart ink pens carefully above his customer's hand. Victor and Eli approached the pair, careful not to disturb the technician's concentration. The artist used the pen to carefully graft the smart ink onto the woman's hand in the shape of a snake. When he was finished with his work, she tested it with a flick of her wrist to reveal a blue holograph image of a snake floating above her hand.

"Oi, where's your boss?" Eli snapped from behind the young artist.

The technician jerked his arm in surprise and shot Eli a nasty look before pointing his pen toward a large metal door in the back that looked decidedly out of place.

"I don't remember that door being so big or…metal," said Victor, scratching his head.

"It's new," said Eli. "It's a good thing this guy makes one hell of a custom sociograft tattoo. Otherwise, I don't know what he'd be good for." He held his hand up to show Victor his sociograft tattoo, made in the shape of a bird taking flight. "Here we go." He rolled his eyes.

Eli knocked on the door in a rhythmic pattern that sounded suspiciously like the beginning of the theme song to the Rocky movies starring Sylvester Stallone.

Deh…deh, deh, deh…deh, deh, deh…deh, deh, dehhhhhh.

Within seconds, a narrow panel on the door, at about head height, slid to the left, and a thick set of eyeballs appeared on the other side, wearing what could have been spyglasses for spectacles. The big eyeballs must have been attached to someone with a very big mouth because a loud voice yelled, "It's you!" Rather than sliding or swinging, the large metal door dropped beneath ground level.

"It *is* you!" exclaimed the spectacled individual wearing a tank top and brown leather apron. Underneath the apron was a densely muscled physique with black tattoos covering every inch of his body below the neck.

"Of course, it's us, who else would know the secret knock to your fortress of solitude is that stupid song."

Rocky lunged toward Victor to hug him and then took off those enormous glasses to reveal a normal-sized pair of brown eyes. "Look at you bes', how are you not surrounded by dozens of gorgeous women right now, hero? You caramel-skinned stud! And rocking a brand-spanking new neurograft to boot! If you need it fixed you know where to come!" Rocky had a habit of frequently mixing English words with his native Filipino tongue of Tagalog, with the occasional sprinkling of Spanish here and there.

Rocky turned to Eli and gave him a decidedly less affectionate, one-handed hug. "I guess it's good to see you too, you kupal."

Eli patted Rocky on the back. "Yeah, I suppose it's not bad to see you either. You ever get rid of the cockroaches?" said Eli with a mischievous smirk.

"Look at this British cabron," said Rocky, throwing his hands half-jokingly in the air. "I haven't seen him in months, and he's already talking shit. There has, nor will there ever be, cockroaches in this place."

"Oh, come off it," replied Eli. "If we're talking about who has the biggest bone to pick, I'm pretty sure Victor wins that one."

"What's he talking about?" said Rocky, casting a confused look at Victor.

"Maybe if you'd take off those stupid glasses once in a blue moon, you'd look at your sociograft and be able to tell when you're supposed to pick up your best mate from the train station," Eli growled judgmentally.

A look of sheer terrorized embarrassment came over Rocky. He brought both hands to his face and started hitting himself repeatedly while pacing back and forth on the sidewalk. "Ay dios mio, I sent you a message, buddy. Shit was going haywire in the back of my dad's shop for a while, so I couldn't make it. You didn't get the message?" Rocky just kept hitting himself while rapidly sputtering unintelligible Tagalog profanities.

"Don't sweat it, man. No harm done. I wanted to stop in and say hi to you and your dad, but I didn't get your message cause my sociograft is busted. Can you look at it for me?"

Rocky put his telescope-sized glasses back on and grabbed Victor's left wrist, holding his sociograft up toward the ceiling lights. "Damn, bro," said Rocky. "What'd you do to this thing, drag it through the mud for three years? I'll need the Insta-Scan for this one. There's one in the back." He motioned for Victor and Eli to follow him through the metal door and into the building. "My dad can't wait to see you, Victor. And I have to show you guys something awesome he's been working on. Like I said, it was acting up this morning, but now, it's all good, baby."

Rocky led them through the threshold and into a small, narrow room chock full of white lab coats and protective gear. Victor and Eli put on whichever garments that fit them the best. Rocky entered a code on a keypad at the other side of the room, causing a door as thick as the outside one to retract downward. They all walked into an even smaller room that was pitch black. The floor began to rotate while a bright green light showed down and scanned their bodies. After the scan, Rocky moved to the other side of the room, where a small device scanned his retina. This caused yet another large metal door to disappear through the floor.

"Paranoid much?" said Eli, turning to Rocky.

"It's my dad. He had to put in all kinds of new security stuff in here because of the government contract he just got. Oh, uh, don't tell him I told you that!" said Rocky, smacking his head repeatedly. "It looks normal from the outside, right? The only thing that looks like it shouldn't be there is that big ass satellite dish on the roof, but you can't even see it from the street."

The boys passed through the final door and into a cavernous space that was big enough to fit a small cathedral inside. Victor was immediately greeted by the chilly air pumping through the massive overhead ducts. He crossed his arms and wedged his hands underneath his armpits. A deluge of light now flooded Victor's retinas. He blinked and squinted to adjust to the darkness of the last room. This bright

LED lighting illuminated rows upon rows of computer server stacks that stretched to the ceilings. The second and third floors had been removed, and in their place were large steel beams that crisscrossed up to the ceiling to support the structure. Thousands of ethernet connections seemed to converge into one large pipe suspended above.

"This isn't even the best part!" said Rocky, clapping with excitement and leading them to the belly of this inner-city enigma.

Victor cleared his throat to reduce the chance of sounding judgmental. "Rocky, wow…Um, this is really something." He didn't succeed. At best, he sounded curiously dumbfounded. Victor figured he must have bought out the next three tenants in the building to make room for all…this.

Eli was a little less delicate. "This place is weird."

"*You* would say that cabron," said Rocky. "Like I said, he got this big government contract and had to renovate the shop. That's all I know. I just work here, you know? But check. This. Out." He motioned to the center of the building to a large, round, open enclave carved out at an intersection between the server stacks. At this point, Rocky thrust his arms into the air like an orchestra conductor, taking in the reactions of his guests. "Ta-da!"

Eli and Victor craned their necks back to take it all in. The big pipe overhead, with the cables inside, ran down from the ceiling and emptied into a large purplish-red teardrop-shaped object, probably about fifteen feet high. The teardrop was so reflective. For all Victor knew, it could have been made from stainless steel. And Victor couldn't be sure, but it looked as though it was subtly pulsating an ominous glow.

Eli clenched his fists. "What in the unholy fuck are you doing with a mini E.C.H.O. Chamber?"

"What? No, dude, this isn't an E.C.H.O. Chamber. There's only a handful of those around the whole world. Plus, that thing is way bigger than this," said Rocky, spreading his muscular arms up and down to demonstrate the difference. "This is called an E.C.H.O. Booster. The E.C.H.O. Chamber implants the neurograft. The E.C.H.O. Booster provides a low-frequency theta wave to power the neurografts. See, big difference."

In typical Eli fashion, he didn't mince his words. "This right here is some devious, fourth-branch shit you got here. You said it yourself. Your dad just nabbed some 'big government contract,' right?"

"Wow, *now* who's the one being paranoid, Eli, my big angry siopao."

"Don't call me a…what did you just call me?"

"It's like a dumpling, but better. My point is you're being ridiculous. But you know, even if it was E.C.H.O. Chamber-ish, what's the big deal? If we didn't have it, we'd probably be back in another War of the Moderates again."

The two of them began bickering loudly. Victor put his hands together in the shape of the letter T. "Guys time out. You're speaking gibberish. I just want to know why the E.C.H.O. Chamber was so horrible."

"How about before we give you guys the 411, you let me take a look at your sociograft Victor," said Rocky.

Victor nodded in agreement while Rocky turned around toward a large utility cabinet behind him and fumbled inside its deep drawers. He partially disappeared momentarily while leaning into the cabinet, haphazardly throwing its contents on the floor with metallic thuds. The thing he was looking for was at the bottom because he shimmied himself out and proudly proclaimed, "Eureka!" He blew the dust off of what he called an 'Insta-Scan.'

Rocky set the Insta-Scan on a fold-out table he produced from the utility cabinet, along with a small stool. He motioned for Victor to take a seat. Then he asked him to place his hand on a few indentations inside of the Insta-Scan and hold it very still. Rocky turned the machine on, and once it started making a loud humming sound, he started running his fingers up and down its circular exterior. He could see something that Victor couldn't because his eyes were darting back and forth quickly from Victor's hands to his controls and back again. He ran his fingers through a rhythmic pattern on the machine for several more minutes. Victor sat still as a board, only moving his eyeballs to catch Eli staring menacingly at that big red teardrop.

The machine made a few buzzing noises, and Rocky looked satisfied. "Just like riding a bike," he said, basking in his achievement. "Now, Victor, you need to stay perfectly still. Like, I'm talking statue still. You're sociograft needs to be in the Insta-Scan for at least five minutes to perform its diagnostics and remapping, got it?" Victor nodded obediently, and Eli snapped out of his teardrop trance.

"So, now can we talk about neurografts and E.C.H.O. Chambers?" asked Victor out of the corner of his mouth—trying not to move an inch.

"Okay. I'll start," said Rocky, casting a mischievous smile at Eli.

"Right, and I'll finish it," growled Eli.

"E.C.H.O. Chambers are where they give you the neurograft graft. It's not a surgical procedure or anything like that, but before they can place it, they need the mind to be...calibrated."

"Calibrated?" asked Victor.

Rocky checked the settings on the Insta-Scan. "Yes, calibrated. They need to make sure that they establish a baseline for your emotional state so the neurograft can determine what emotions you are feeling at the time."

"But it felt like I was forced to relive all the *bad* memories I had," said Victor.

"All my customers tell me the same thing when I fix their neurografts. Eliciting memories is how the E.C.H.O. Chamber does its calibration. And the strongest memories most of us have seem to be bad ones."

Still trying hard not to move, Victor just moved the corners of his mouth to talk. "Okay, now what about the neurograft?"

Rocky was clearly excited to get to the good stuff. "So, if you thought the sociograft was cool, the neurograft is the biggest thing since indoor plumbing..."

"Cause there's shit everywhere," interrupted Eli.

Rocky barely skipped a beat. "...If you have one, you can control all the functions on your sociograft. Just by thinking it! The technology is similar to sociograft. It's a tattoo that's put on the temple of your forehead. What makes this tech so unique is that it can read the emotional state of its wearer. It can transmit this information to the sociograft which acts as a relay to the information contained in the cloud. So if you feel sad, the sociograft will prompt you to go buy a puppy or something. If you feel lucky, it will tell you to go to the casino and put it all on black. Don't ask me how I know this one."

"You're completely touched in the head, you know that Rocky? It's evil incarnate. It is, quite literally, some Book of Revelations Mark of the Beast shit. Mind reading Victor, plain and simple," said Eli with a nod to Victor.

"I don't think so. I mean, it's basically a highly sophisticated mood ring."

"So what's stopping The Fourth Branch from turning everybody into a bunch of pissed-off four-head having fucks who just fuck each other up?"

"The E.C.H.O. Booster puts out super low-frequency theta waves. Even the E.C.H.O. Chamber itself doesn't put out that much. I'd have to do the calculations..." Rocky began whispering some quick calculations he was trying to noodle through. "You'd probably need a couple of thousand E.C.H.O. Chambers, concentrated at one fixed point to control someone's thought patterns. Plus, why would The Fourth Branch want to make us 'pissed off four-head having fucks who just fuck each other up?' Pretty sure you're doing a good enough job of that already, amigo."

Rocky moved over to a console next to the E.C.H.O. Booster and typed in some commands on the interface. "This is the coolest part. Check it out." They all moved closer to Rocky, except for Victor, who just craned his neck back to see what was going on. "You can see a map of where the E.C.H.O. Booster has a theta wave connection with the neurografts. See, all these little dots on here are people. Here, let me show you something really cool." He typed in a few more commands and the map zoomed to a large dot downtown that signified the location of the E.C.H.O. Chamber. "See how big the E.C.H.O. Chamber blob looks on the map? Think that's big? Well, check this out." He moved the map over to where Victor's old high school was. "Look at across the street from the high school." Rocky pointed to it, but he didn't need to.

Victor could see a large blob many times bigger than the E.C.H.O. Chamber's theta wave signature emanating from where an old convenience store used to be.

"I've never seen an anomaly this big before, ever. It only just showed up this morning. I plan on taking my Theta Wave Detector there in a bit to check it out." He rewound the video feed. "See, last night at about midnight, there was a huge energy surge at the E.C.H.O. Chamber." The data feed showed a huge energy sphere that appeared over the entire city for a few fleeting seconds and then collapsed back onto the E.C.H.O. Chamber. "And then, a few hours later there was *another* surge down on Jacobs Street."

Victor pulled back from the screen, his hand on the back of his head. *I was at the E.C.H.O. Chamber and on Jacobs Street last night.*

"Enrique Rizal!" shouted a booming voice across the shop floor. Victor knew Mr. Rizal meant some serious business when he used Rocky's full name. That, and Rocky instantaneously turned a queasy shade of white. When Mr. Rizal appeared from between the server stacks, he made a beeline directly for Rocky with an outstretched finger wagging furiously in his direction. "Can you even *comprehend* how much trouble you could have gotten us all into Enrique? If your mother (may she rest in peace) could see how reckless her only son has become!"

Mr. Rizal, red in the face and shaking, finally seemed to notice who he was standing next to. "Victor? It is you, my boy!" Mr. Rizal's shaking fists unclenched and he grabbed Victor into a tight embrace. "You look so thin, but you're alive! Salamat sa Dios. And Eli, it's been too long. Seeing you boys all together again really brings back the memories."

Eli nodded and shook Mr. Rizal's hand firmly. "Thank you, sir. If your son wasn't such a git all the time, maybe I would stop by more," he said with a smirk.

"It's good to see you too, Mr. Rizal. We were just stopping by to fix my sociograft. It needs to be updated...or, er, something like that." Victor knew he sounded as technologically savvy as a goat using a touchscreen.

Rocky lifted the Insta-Scan off of Victor's hand and put his giant spectacles on again. "Looks good, buddy. You should be good to hook. No charge," he said with a smile.

Talk of business seemed to reignite Mr. Rizal's fury at Rocky. "I'm glad we can help you, Victor, but *someone* should have let me know we would have guests so I could move certain things out of sight!"

Victor noticed a green icon light up on the Insta-scan contraption. "I think this thing is done," he said timidly. Rocky walked over to him and pressed a few buttons on a nearby monitor.

"Yep. You should be all good, mi amigo. Once you take it outside, out of the building, it should get its updates, and you should be good to hook," said Rocky, forcing a smile. Victor knew the moment that he and Eli walked off the shop floor, Rocky was in for it. Sure enough, one look at Mr. Rizal's folded arms and tapping foot was a dead giveaway that all the goodwill drummed up from seeing Victor again had quickly evaporated.

"This shop is too dirty for guests. How about you boys leave and come back soon for some lumpia," said Mr. Rizal kindly but forcefully.

"Sure thing, Mr. Rizal," said Victor. "Bye, Rock, thanks for getting me fixed up. See you in a few?" Victor wasn't quite sure about that last part as he walked past Rocky toward the exit.

"See you soon, sir." Eli nodded respectively to Mr. Rizal. He took a more sarcastic tone when bidding goodbye to Rocky. "I reckon I can't say the same for you. You're deader than a doornail."

As Victor and Eli approached the only door in and out of the shop, they heard a thunderous eruption of what could only be presumed to be a tirade of expletives in Tagalog from Mr. Rizal directed at his son. Victor quickly walked through the doorway, having to tug a snickering Eli by the collar and off the shop floor.

6

Omega

"You really like getting Rocky all riled up, don't you?" asked Victor as they stepped out into a warm late-morning breeze.

Eli smirked sinisterly. "I make a sport of it now, if I'm being honest."

"Wow. My sociograft is blowing up right now. Look at all these messages," said Victor as a stream of blue notifications started swirling in and out of view on his news feed.

"I'm going to get walking home for a nap before my shift. You all set now?" asked Eli.

Victor wasn't paying attention. Too many messages were rolling in. "Yeah, I'm good. Oh wait, on second thought, do you still have the MDD practice circuit board in your garage? I think I want to go a few practice rounds on it before tomorrow."

"Right. Don't want to look like a bag of smacked ass in front of your chick. I get it. Swing on by tomorrow afternoon before my shift, and we'll get some reps in."

"Later, man, thanks," said Victor, still distracted from watching his sociograft feed updates roll in. *God, this is going to take forever to update.*

This thing's been busted for weeks.

Victor bumped shoulders with two passersby and nearly knocked one off their feet. "Sorry!" He decided not to walk and graft and turned his feed off. He forgot he told Innocius that he would stop by his place. It felt good to be walking these streets again. *They haven't changed much.* A cyberduel here and some propaganda posters there. *It could always be worse.*

It didn't take him on too long of a detour to get to Innocius' place on Jacobs Street. The kid was already waiting for him behind his screen door. "Hey, Victor!"

Victor opened up the door. "Hey man, how'd you sleep last night?"

"I just woke up a little bit ago. I'll be going to my mom's shop soon to help my sister. We own a voodoo shop…"

Victor couldn't resist a glance at his sociograft feed to check his latest messages as Innocius talked. He jumped up and threw his fist in the air. "Oh my God, Abiana sent me a sociograft message!"

"Who's Abiana? She your girlfriend? You know, before you went to Haiti," asked Innocius curiously. "I've never had a girlfriend before."

Victor paused his sociograft browsing and looked at Innocius. Here was a boy who had been beaten up, teased, abused. If Victor was honest with himself, he saw a lot of himself in Innocius. The kid just needed someone to help show him the ropes and find his voice. It was what Eli did for him when he was growing up.

"Abiana Earhart is her name. No, she wasn't my girlfriend. We were sort-of friends, but she was never…flirty with me. I never asked her out before." Victor was being generous in his recollections of himself. He was a scrawny punk in high school that was never in the 'in crowd.' "If I'm being brutally honest with you, she was a bit out of my league." Victor's inner monologue corrected him. *She was way out of your league.*

"How so?" asked Innocius as Victor began pushing his wheelchair down the sidewalk.

"I don't know, she was just the 'cool rich girl' who would always hang out with the older boys," said Victor, now rubbing his forehead, trying to recall his high school days. They seemed so long ago now. "Abiana was the type of girl who built her own circuit boards and rode them, wrote code probably better than Rocky, and listened to hardcore metal music. She was really intimidating. Not to mention, she has always been a complete smoke show."

The boys soon arrived at Innocius' stoop. Victor carried Innocius up the stairs to the door and then retrieved his chair from the curb. He didn't see it the last time he was at Innocius' house, because it was so dark out, but now he noticed that on the stairs leading up to the door were painted some strange markings.

A woman's booming voice called down to Innocius from the top of the stairs inside, "Innocius, is your new friend with you?"

"Yes, Mom, Victor is here," shouted Innocius. "Victor, you don't have to stay and talk if you don't want to," he said in a hushed tone.

"I can stay for a few minutes," said Victor, hoping to get back home soon so he could listen to Abiana's message.

Innocius' mother arrived to greet them at the door. He remembered her from Innocius' vision in the E.C.H.O. Chamber, and her resemblance to his own mother was even more uncanny in person. Her eclectic appearance was out of place in downtown Philly, though now the markings on the stairs made a little more sense. She was tall and, besides having a slightly crooked nose, was a beautiful middle-aged black woman. Her hair was done up in flowing serpentine locks that were tied high with a bright red bit of cloth. Her large, hooped gold earrings swayed as she situated herself on the couch. And as she motioned for Victor to take a seat his eyes were drawn to a lovely assortment of colorful talisman necklaces that rested on a purple silk gown.

When she spoke, it was softer than before and with an accent that

Victor immediately recognized as Haitian. "You just be Victor Gates. Would you like to come in for a drink of tea?"

"I would be grateful, ma'am."

"Please call me Vixama," she said as she motioned for Victor to enter the home.

Vixama's unconventional appearance was also captured in her home décor, which was a near-carbon copy of the layout of Carmenta's house. The stiff smell of burning incense permeated the small family room. The shutters and blinds on the windows were drawn, but wax candles placed on every flat surface gave the bottom floor of the house a soft glow. Stashed in the corner were picket signs that said in bright red lights things like, "End the Killing," "Stop the Mandate," and "Love not War." The only "normal" item in the room was a tellvision, and that was a bit abnormal because hardly anyone had tellvisions in their homes anymore. It had almost universally been replaced by the sociograft.

Vixama showed Victor a place to sit on one of the small plush couches placed in the living room. Vixama poured a small porcelain cup of chai tea for Victor. "Innocius has told me so much about you. Not that he needed to, I have seen your…exploits on the tellvision."

Victor could sense this conversation going downhill quickly. There weren't very many average Haitians, whether they emigrated to the US or not, who supported the occupation of their country. Despite despising small talk Victor decided that may be the appropriate topic to discuss. "I like your decorations…they remind me of some of the shops I visited when I was in Haiti." Victor could have just complimented the home, but somehow, he managed to steer the conversation back into dangerous waters by mentioning Haiti.

"Thank you. Unfortunately, I am unable to retrieve most things from my homeland now. The thing's you see, I have either made or…acquired." Vixama's eyes drifted to the shuttered windows, and

Victor gulped a long sip of tea. "I own a shop a few blocks from here called Madam Vixama's House of Voodoo. Quite a few Haitians are living in the Fair Heights neighborhood these days. It brings me so much joy to bring some of our homeland to my refugee brothers and sisters. This war, which has been prosecuted in my country, has devastated our community. I can hardly talk to any Haitian who hasn't had one of their family members killed or maimed. You would think that someone would stand up and stop the madness, the insanity, the killing."

Victor nodded and sipped tea, not trusting the words that would come out of his mouth.

Vixama sat her teacup on the table and flattened the wrinkles on her purple gown. "Mr. Gates, I must be frank with you. You stand for everything that I am against. You are part of a great killing machine that has ravaged my homeland and my people. For this, we can never reconcile our ideals with one another." She straightened herself higher in her seat and drew a long breath, exhaling deeply. "But you have befriended my son. The only kindness he has been shown by anyone in this world is by his sister and me. So if what you are offering my son is kindness and not your country's mayhem, then I can offer you a seat in my house." It took Vixama significant strength to say these words, words she probably never thought she would have with a soldier, but Victor knew they were coming from the heart.

Victor finished sipping his tea and told Vixama, "Your son is a friend of mine, ma'am. And I know he's been through a lot." He wanted to say more but always struggled to find the right words at the right moments.

Vixama could recognize the sincerity in his words. "Good, Mr. Gates. I invite you to our home and our family's shop."

"Thank you, ma'am. I'd like to visit sometime." There was an awkward pause. He rose to his feet. "I should be going." Before walking out the door, he stopped at the threshold. "Hey, kid, how would you like to do a few rounds on my buddy's practice power circuit board?"

"I'd love to!"

"Power circuit board? What is this Inno…is it dangerous?"

Victor and Innocius traded looks. "No, no, not really," they both muttered incoherently while shaking their heads dismissively.

"Pretty safe," said Victor, trying to inspire some degree of confidence. "I'll swing by tomorrow morning. See you, buddy."

"Bye, Victor!"

* * *

Victor flipped through incoming messages on his sociograft as he walked back home. Nothing too interesting. *Just a shitload of spam.* Now that his sociograft was fixed he was able to unlock the front door to his house. His eyes were immediately drawn to the bay window when he walked into the living room. Carmenta had patched the hole caused by the thrown rock with a few strips of duct tape. That, along with the bars on the windows, made the house look even more shabby than before. "Ma…are you home?" yelled Victor up the stairwell, with no reply. *She's probably working.*

He climbed the stairs to his bedroom and flung himself on the sheets. It was a warm day, even warmer on the second story of a brick-row home. The only relief was a cool breeze coming in through the open window. He was still a few hundred notifications short of catching up on his missed sociograft video messages. Most of the messages were annoying sales pitches. Many had scantily clad women dancing around the products being advertised: boats, cars, cars that turned into boats. There were ads for everything these days, and everyone's always trying to make a buck, thought Victor.

Some other messages were from real people, but ones he never met. "Victor the Victorious. We stand with you!" said some.

"Victor Gates, marry me!" said quite a few others.

Some others weren't so friendly.

"Fuck off, four-head," said a couple.

"Burn in hell, you fascist drone," said a fair amount.

Victor skipped to the ones that were from people he knew. His video message from Rocky was particularly entertaining. When Victor selected the video, a projection of Rocky wearing those ridiculous multi-layered Coke bottle glasses. "Hola, Vic-aroon. Hey buddy, something wacky is going on with me and my dad's project here at the shop." A cranking sputtery noise that sounded like a wrench being thrown into a wood chipper erupted from the sociograft. "I don't think I'm gonna be able to get you from the train station, my dude." The sound got significantly more wood-chippery, presumably why the transmission cut out a moment later.

"Oh, Rock." Victor laughed. "What are we gonna do with you?"

He scrolled some more and found Abiana's message. His heart fluttered a little bit when he clicked on it. When her video popped up, she appeared to be walking along the sidewalk with Stacy.

"Hey, Vicky! I just ran into you, and I wanted to let you know how excited I am to go to the power circuit with you. Mwah!"

Victor couldn't keep his mind off Abiana. She looked even sexier than he remembered, and that was saying something. He smacked his face in frustration. "Fuck this," he said drowsily. He couldn't wait for tomorrow night. The gentle breeze, warm room, and soft bed made prime conditions for an afternoon nap.

His thoughts became hazy and started to swirl together. Images of Abiana, Eli, Rocky, Innocius, and back to Abiana all started dreamily intertwining together. The sweet tune of a songbird singing on the power lines drifted through the window. Victor felt completely at ease. He had never fallen asleep this easily when he was in Haiti.

He was lying on a beautiful beach—the waves crashing gently on a snow-white sand. Abiana was a lifeguard there. She always had a lifeguard job during summer vacations. She wore a red two-piece bikini complete with a red visor and whistle dangling from her neck. She blew her whistle on the lifeguard chair, ran to Victor, and started giving him mouth-to-mouth. Victor closed his eyes, hoping this wouldn't stop. When he opened them, he was swimming in a pool of jello inside the E.C.H.O. Chamber.

He didn't remember there being a pool of jello when he and Innocius were there. Vixama was yelling at him not to jump in the pool, that it was dangerous. A man in black with a tattoo of a yin-yang on his forehead came up from behind him and pushed him into the pool. Tengo squad (Lewis, Rojas, Sullivan, Chan) all jumped in after him, but they too were soon drowning. A hooded, faceless man was in a school holding a voodoo doll that looked like a bruised version of Victor. He poked the doll's hands mercilessly, all while saying Omega, Omega, Omega.

Victor's sociograft was vibrating so hard that it was shaking his hand. He awoke in his room, sat up, and shut his window. The breeze now felt freezing against the cold sweat on his body. His sociograft read that it was five in the morning. "Holy shit, how have I been sleeping for fifteen hours!" To Victor, those disjointed dreams felt like they took place within a matter of minutes, definitely not hours.

There was an incoming message that he was trying to open to turn off the buzzing, but it wouldn't stop. "Why in the hell is this stupid thing not opening?" he said angrily, all while trying to get his eyes to adjust to the sociograft's blue holograph projection. A pop-up message appeared that said, "Encrypted—your eyes only. Scan needed."

Victor held the sociograft up to his face, allowing it to scan his eyes for a retinal signature. "Signature confirmed—incoming message from codename Omega."

"Omega," said Victor, petrified. He thought he was dreaming that. Whether he was awake or still dreaming, this had all taken a sharp turn into nightmare territory. Victor pressed the accept icon on his sociograft, and a hooded face appeared in the projection speaking with a deep synthetic voice.

"Victor Gates. Omega has found you. The gift of knowledge of good and evil is now yours. It's your job to decide who is who. In this message, you will find the schematic of the most dangerous device ever devised by man. Within the schematic is a partial program, procured at great cost, to destroy the device. You must find the other part of the code to destroy it. All are watching, and nothing is as it seems. End transmission."

7

Power Circuit Race

Victor walked to the bathroom that was shared between his and Carmenta's room and splashed cold water on his face. He looked at himself in the mirror. *This is gonna be a long morning.* He went downstairs to make a cup of coffee and paced around the living room. Daylight was only beginning to creep through the damaged bay window. Victor couldn't remember if he slept more than just a few hours a night. Sleeping more than a newborn baby was generally frowned upon when serving in the military. It may have been the longest he'd ever slept, but it was also his most restless night. Rarely did he remember his dreams, and yet the voodoo doll that the faceless man was holding seemed as real to Victor now as the cup of coffee in his hand.

There were too many other important things to worry about than a silly doll right now. "Omega," said Victor out loud. "Omega has found you," he whispered. *Notify me immediately.* Those were DeThroe's exact instructions to Victor should he be contacted by Omega. *Why would DeThroe assume that I would be contacted by Omega? That doesn't make any sense.*

Not much was known about the elusive band of rebels that called themselves Omega. Victor only knew that they were responsible for some of the most heinous terrorist acts of the twenty-first century. It was well known that Haitian terrorist groups had close ties to Omega, but how close was anybody's guess. Then there were other rumored sects that were rumored to be aligned with other nations. The bouncing ball of 'who is really Omega' was a riddle in constant motion.

Maybe that's why they're contacting me. That didn't make much sense because if that was the case, then why would they be giving me a schematic for a weapon? And what is the code they're talking about? What is the device, and why is it so damn dangerous? And most importantly, why in the hell do they think I would destroy it?

They did say that everyone is watching, maybe they're trying to blackmail me. But they would have to know that I would go straight to the police, or someone like DeThroe, with this.

None of this was adding up and was giving Victor a serious headache. He poured himself another cup of coffee and slumped on the couch. It was one thing that some mass murdering terrorist contacts him out of the blue. It was another thing entirely when the alleged leader of that band of loonies was your father.

Victor heard footsteps upstairs and knew Carmenta would soon be downstairs, making breakfast and probably asking if he was on drugs or something because of how long he slept. His mother always wore her emotions on her sleeve. She was affectionate to a fault. It had been an unwritten rule in the Gates household to *not* talk about Mobius Gates, that son-of-a-bitch.

He had abandoned them, casting them into destitution, not to mention being the most reviled man in the country. Even though he couldn't remember when the last time it was that he and Carmenta talked about Mobius, he knew that if anyone wanted to see Mobius brought to justice and put behind bars, it was her. *Could the faceless man in the dream stabbing a voodoo doll likeness of me be Mobius? Yeah, what in the hell is the deal with that voodoo doll? Maybe I am on drugs.*

He took the last swig of his coffee and got up to pour another cup.

I need to just stop thinking about this. It was all just a stupid dream. There are no voodoo dolls, no hooded, faceless people, swimming pools of jelly…okay, hopefully, there is Abiana in a two-piece somewhere. I'd be alright with that part.

He chuckled, yawned, and started to wargame how today was going to go. For starters, he was not going to discuss either the dream or the transmission with his mother. Victor would rather be dead than dump more problems or worries on that poor woman. He thought that maybe he should talk to Eli about the dream. Victor knew that he had some demons he was suppressing. He hadn't talked to anybody about the deaths of his friends in Haiti. Maybe now was the time to start deconstructing how jacked up things got down there. One thing he knew for certain, he needed to tell DeThroe about the Omega transmission. *That was crucial.* And time was of the essence. Victor knew that by telling DeThroe as soon as possible it could prevent whatever devious cataclysm Omega had planned from ever happening.

Victor heard her coming down the stairs. "Victor, are you awake down there, baby?"

"Yeah, I'm down here, Ma. Made some coffee already," Victor said, trying desperately hard to act normal. Victor just needed to play it cool and not admit knowledge of what an international terrorist organization was doing or what having voodoo dreams was like. *Easy.*

Carmenta walked downstairs and immediately kissed Victor on the cheek. "You fell asleep so early, Victor. Is everything alright?" She walked to the kitchen to start making breakfast.

Play it cool, Victor, just play it cool. "Oh yeah, no, everything is just great." Realizing he had never in his entire life said, "Everything is just great," he knew he sounded suspicious. He'd better spice things up a bit. "Well, I went over to my new friend Innocius' house. His mom seems like she's pretty heavy into the occult. She has all these skulls and talismans everywhere in her house, and…"

The sound of a shattered coffee cup hitting the floor made Victor jump a bit. "Hey, you okay, Ma? Let me help." Victor grabbed a broom and pan from the closet and started sweeping up the pieces.

"I'm fine. It just slipped right out of my hand, that's all. I'm getting clumsier by the day. What about today? Are you going to see your friends again?" said Carmenta, mopping up the spilled coffee with a rag.

"Yeah, I'll see Eli and Innocius this afternoon and Abiana later tonight."

"Abiana…do you mean Abiana Earhart? Oh, Victor, she's so pretty and rich! Are you two going on a date?"

"No, it's not a date, Ma. We're just meeting at the pow…er, the power, uh, power supply. It's one of those places where you can pick up spare robotics parts to build your machines. You know she's really into fixing up robots and drones and all that." Victor didn't want his mom to worry about racing in the power circuit tonight. And he'd read somewhere about a new store that really did open up downtown that sells mechanical and electronics parts.

"She's a keeper, Victor, but so is my handsome baby. Who else can say that they're dating a genuine war hero?" Carmenta said proudly, already well into making the first batch of scrambled eggs with toast and sausage. "Hey baby, if you're seeing Eli today, would you ask him if he'd stop over here sometime to take a look at the upstairs toilet? It's on the fritz again, and I think we need some new parts for it."

"Ma, don't worry about it, alright? I'm home now. Let me take a look." Victor scoffed indignantly. He had operated and maintained the world's most advanced drone hardware. Surely, he could fix a little plumbing problem.

"Okay, baby, I didn't want to trouble you with it. This happened while you were away, and he came over and fixed it in a jiff, so I know it'd be easy for him. Like you said, though, now my big man is home to take care of us. There are some tools in the closet. How about you go upstairs and turn some wrenches, and I'll finish up with breakfast?"

It was good to be needed. Victor grabbed the toolbox and went straight to work. *This is going to be a cinch,* thought Victor. *I'll be done in five minutes tops.*

About an hour later, a small pool of sweat and expletives known only to the most battle-hardened veterans, Victor had not even an inkling how to fix the running toilet. He swallowed his pride, tucked his tail between his legs, and resolved to ask Eli to stop over when he had a chance.

After a big breakfast and an even bigger lunch, Victor stopped by Innocius' house to pick him up before going to Eli's. Innocius was home alone and said his mother and sister were both at the store to assist "an important customer." Eli's place was on the edge of the Fair Heights neighborhood. "His house isn't a house at all. It was a converted fire station that he bought on a fire sale—no pun intended," said Victor to Innocius as they made their way through the hot mid-day streets. "He lives with his daughter, Jacky, but she spends most of her time at her mom's house. They divorced soon after Jacky was born."

"Jacky Abramson? I know her. She's in my class," said Innocius.

"Well, Jesus, isn't that a small world?" said Victor.

They had just arrived at Eli's nineteenth-century converted fire station turned house, complete with three enormous red wooden doors and all. Eli let them in through the normal-sized door on the corner of the house and showed them inside. The home had a large open bay style first level (where the firetrucks used to park), with a fireman's pole connecting the upstairs to the downstairs. The second level had two bedrooms, a living area, a kitchen, and a bathroom. Eli used the first level as a garage for his police car, decrepit Ford Bronco, and whatever side projects he was working on. Eli had a knack for tinkering with repossessed property he got on the cheap from public auctions. He made it a point to buy any kind of exotic tech he could get his hands on.

"Eli, don't let this guy fool you, okay? He single-handedly beat down five scumbags the other night," said Victor with a wink.

Eli took one look at Innocius and did the same leap backward that VanHeller did at the E.C.H.O. Chamber. "Blimey Victor, is this your little brother?"

Victor and Innocius laughed it off. "Yeah, I guess we do a bit," said Victor.

"A bit? Christ, you two could be twins." Eli extended his hand to Innocius. "The name's Eliazar. My friends call me Eli."

"Nice to meet you, Eli," said Innocius, shaking his hand.

"What…is that?" asked Innocius, pointing at a huge saucer-shaped metallic object in one of the garage bays.

"Ah, that, my little friend, is an oversized magnetosphere displacement device (MDD)," said Eli adoringly. It was a good thing that Eli's garage could fit three large firetrucks because that's about how big the MDD was.

"You never did tell me where you got that thing," said Victor with crossed arms.

"And you never will," snapped Eli. "My ability to tactically acquire valuable items through questionable means has always been a strength of mine, a discrete one at that," said Eli with a wink.

"Eli, you are, without a doubt, the worst cop ever. So what's Jacky up to these days?"

"With her poor excuse of a mother six out of seven days out of the week," Eli said sharply. "Hard to believe that woman birthed something so unlike herself. Equally hard to believe that Jacky's already almost fourteen. She almost a proper young lady already," he said proudly.

"Innocius just told me that he and Jacky are in the same class," said Victor, trying to preemptively diffuse Eli's short temper.

"Wouldn't know now, would I? Her mum goes to all the parent-teacher events. I only ever get to drop her off at school once in a blue moon." Eli sighed. "The only thing that brings us together anymore is this bucket of bolts, and it'll be your two's saving grace for tonight's festivities," said Eli, motioning to the MDD. "Jacky and I spend our one day a week surfing on this beauty," he droned on with a far-off stare.

Eli snapped out of it and struck a more formal, business-like tone. "Now, let's get right to it. MDD-101: it creates huge localized magnetic waves that allow certain craft, and those crazy enough to ride on top of them, to float. And through some subtle manipulations of the device, we are accurately able to replicate the conditions of the underground power circuit track. Once you don the..."

Before he could finish, Innocius interjected. "Um, excuse me, but I'm still not quite sure what the power circuit is exactly. I'd like to know what I'm getting myself into." Victor was by no means a power circuit pro, but tonight's race would be Innocius' first time on the board. Despite understandable apprehension, Innocius did not sound fearful when he spoke up.

"You'll need to see it to believe it," began Eli. "There's this fucked up underground cave of wonders that powers the E.C.H.O. Chamber. Not sure if anyone knows exactly what it is, to be honest, but what we do know is that there's enough exotic magnetism down there to allow some materials to levitate." Eli pulled a large metallic surfboard-looking apparatus from a nearby closet. "This circuit board is one such item that can float down in the tunnels. After you hop on the board, it's easy. Complete the 'circuit' (which forms a big figure-eight-shaped loop underground), and…don't fall off."

"How am I going to fall off? I can't even stand to begin with," said Innocius, motioning to his wheelchair with a hint of sarcasm.

"Oh, my little circuit boarder, you have so much to learn." Eli put the metallic circuit board on the MDD and pressed a few buttons on its control panel to activate it. Once its smooth whooping noise had stabilized, Eli walked into the middle of the MDD and laid the circuit board flat. Miraculously, the board began to levitate in thin air about six inches off the ground while Eli's shoes remained firmly planted on the ground. He walked over to Innocius' wheelchair and rolled it into the middle of the MDD. Eli picked Innocius up by the waist with one hand and gingerly placed his feet into two indentations on the board with the other hand. As soon as Innocius' feet made contact with these markings, bindings began to sliver up his legs, entombing them in a thick metallic wrapping from feet to lower back. He was standing.

The gravity of the moment wasn't lost on Innocius. He was not only standing, but he was also floating. "Looking fine, mate," said Eli. "There's just one more thing we need to get you started—the headset. This is going to be how you control the board. The tunnels you'll be in not only have an ass load of magnetism to make the board float, but they also have a metric fuck-ton of theta waves. The headset allows navigate those waves while you're on the board. Think of it like a surfboard. Where you see a theta wave start building up, feel your way into it and let the theta pull you in."

Victor and Innocius nodded like they clearly understood what Eli was talking about, but perhaps their vacant expressions gave them away.

"Magnets make it float. Theta waves allow you to control the board," he said loudly and slowly. "Now, unfortunately, I do not have theta waves in the quantity that are present in the tunnels. The only thing we have to work with here is a big magnet and a mock headset to help simulate the theta-rich environment you'll be in."

Maybe it was starting to sink in. Maybe it wasn't. Either way, Innocius looked rare and ready to go. Eli handed him the headset and pressed some more buttons on the control panel. "Alright, Innocius, put it on, and let's run some tests. Okay, do you see a little white ball resting on a horizontal line?" Innocius could see it. It looked like an old-school video game console. "Good, we're going to play a little game. I want you to make that ball move with nothing else other than your thoughts. I know that sounds a little ridiculous but give it a shot."

Eli had a screen on his control panel where he could monitor what the rider was seeing. He and Victor were monitoring the screen while Eli whispered, "Kick back and relax, Victor. This part usually takes forever, and…holy stinking dog shit. Look at that!" Not only was the ball on the screen moving off the line, it was bopping up and down, side to side, and everything in between. To top it off, Innocius split the ball into mini-balls and controlled them with the same ease as the one. "What in the actual fuck Innocius? Have you done this before?" Eli was flabbergasted at the spectacle in front of him.

"Mate, God as my witness, I've never seen anything like this," whispered Eli to Victor. "The kid is an absolute freak. A brilliant one. But a freak."

"You're telling me. Didn't it take me like four hours to get that stupid ball to move half an inch on the screen?"

Eli ignored him in a haste to see more of this spectacle. "Innocius, you're freakishly good at this. Let's see how you do with the real thing." Eli pressed some buttons on the control panel, and a thin purple road appeared on the screen. "Innocius, this is meant to replicate what the power circuit tunnels will look like when you're in them. Your board will be riding on top of these large power conduits down in the tunnels.

My simulator program is meant to help you control your board so you can balance and navigate it on these conduits. Let's see how you do. You ready?" Innocius nodded. "Good. Three, two, one…let's ride."

* * *

Victor and Eli couldn't stop gushing about how well Innocius did on the simulator. And there was no talking Innocius out of it when Eli mentioned he had a real chance at winning tonight's race. After about four more hours of relentless simulations and some BBQ ribs that Eli grilled up for the boys for dinner, he offered to drive them to the power circuit tunnels. An offer that Victor half-heartedly accepted, understanding that the Bronco was probably more dangerous than racing in the power circuit, but also knowing that he didn't want to transfer bus lines three times. Victor barely got any time to practice on the circuit board simulator, it was too much fun watching Innocius destroy the simulator program. While he and Eli were watching Innocius' progress on the control panel monitor, he did get a chance to tell him about his dream. Eli explained that he also had bad dreams after he returned from his tour in Haiti a few years ago and that they were almost to be expected after all the trauma they had seen. "The big green weenie of the Army will always get you, Victor, even in your sleep. Just lube up before bedtime."

* * *

After a hair-raising journey via the Ford Bronco, they arrived downtown. Before Eli drove off, Victor asked, "Hey man, would you be able to swing by the place tomorrow morning? Our toilet broke, and I…er, ran into some problems."

"You mean your mom can't do it? I thought she was able to fix it herself now after I showed her how. No big deal though, sure thing I'll see you in the AM," said Eli as he sped away, leaving Victor and Innocius in front of a derelict warehouse in a cloud of black smoke.

Victor saw Innocius frown at the cringeworthy rust bucket of a warehouse in front of them and assured him that they were in the right spot. "Yeah, looks about as shitty as I remember it. Power circuit racing isn't, strictly speaking, legal. So the entrances to the underground tunnels need to be hidden from the cops."

"Isn't Eli a cop?"

"He pushes the boundary of the word, but yes."

The two boys walked up to a large metal door, and Victor knocked on it in a rhythmic pattern.

"Wow, fancy," said Innocius with a snicker.

A slit in the metal door opened to a pair of dark-colored eyes on the other side. "Hold your sociografts up," said the owner of the eyes as he held a scanner up to the slit. Once the boys scanned their devices, the door opened to reveal a large crowd of people, all carrying on excitedly.

"This is like an Eagles game," said Innocius. He wasn't too far off the mark. The vendors, the crowd, and make-shift bleachers set up to accommodate the throngs of people now pouring through the checkpoint. There were vendors on the sides selling an assortment of circuit board headsets, circuit boards, and bindings, amongst others. "Five thousand credits for the gold board, ten thousand for a platinum!" the vendors called out to the crowd. A purplish-red glow was emanating from the center of the room.

"That's where the entrance to the power circuit tunnels is," Victor told Innocius.

Victor and Abiana spotted each other and exchanged enthusiastic waves. "Come on," said Victor to Innocius as the two boys began walking toward Abiana and Stacy. As they approached the girls, Victor saw that they were surrounded by a small crowd of onlookers as they crouched over to adjust their circuit board bindings with wrenches. Abiana jumped up onto Victor. "Vicky! I'm so glad you made it. This is going to be fun, fun, fun." Victor didn't know how, but Abiana was somehow able to pull off an oil-stained pair of coveralls nearly as well as the two-piece bikini she was wearing in his dream. "I've signed the three of us up already, so we're good to go. And I brought a few extra boards and headsets I had lying around at the house."

"No, I think we're okay." Victor motioned to Innocius. "Abiana, this is my friend Innocius. Not sure, but I think he was born to ride the power circuit."

"Really? Well, any friend of Victor's is a friend of mine," said Abiana with a curtsy of her overalls.

"Thanks, it's nice to meet you too. Victor's told me so much about you."

Abiana laughed and punched Victor in the arm. "Well, I hope it was all good things. You guys need to get any practice rounds in before we go?"

"If there's anybody who doesn't need practice, it's Innocius. This kid was tearing it up on Eli's MDD."

"Oh yeah? I refuse to fix it for him anymore. That crusty old fart. Now he just gets Rocky Rizal to fix it."

"What happened with you two?"

"Ever since he and his goons broke up our circuit race last year, I've wanted to cyberduel him, and he always refuses. Probably cause he knows I'll stomp his ass," she yelled over the dull roar of the now several-hundred-strong crowd. "You want to know why he broke it up? It's because he heard that Jacky had entered the race, so he came to shut it down."

"Yeah, I guess that explains it. I wouldn't want to fight you either."

"Oh, Vicky, I would never fight you. Unless you kept staring at

Stacy's ass, that is!"

"What? No, I wasn't!" said Victor defensively.

"I'm kidding, you big goof," she said with a giggle punch to the shoulder.

A man appeared on a stage of tough boxes in front of a large projector set up on the far side of the warehouse. "Ladies and gentlemen, we're about to get our race underway. I'm Jay Cromwell, and I'll be your MC for this evening's festivities. First, I'd like to thank our illustrious sponsor for today's event—Ms. Abiana Earhart!"

The crowd erupted in applause to a curtsying Abiana.

"Secondly, I don't need to remind anybody how dangerous riding the power circuit is. Exposure to (mostly harmless) amounts of theta waves and magnetism aside, if you lose your balance for a second, you could end up flatter than a pancake. And if you do, that is entirely on you. That said, we'll be monitoring your vitals from the command center here, and if you need extraction, hail us on your sociografts. You were given our code when you scanned in to the building. Alright now, enough of that bullshit—we've all traveled near and far for today's race. Let's get this show on the road!"

The crowd broke out in uproarious excitement.

"Can I have the contestants gather in the center of the building, please?"

About thirty or forty people started to converge together in the middle of the warehouse, where there was a deep shaft leading down to the tunnels that emanated a soft purple glow. As Victor pushed him, Innocius received no less than a hundred stairs from fellow contestants and spectators alike. People exchanged whispers and laughed as Victor pushed him to the shaft's edge. Victor stooped down to whisper to Innocius, "You know, you don't have to do this if you don't want to."

"I want to," said Innocius, quite sure of himself.

"I'll be right next to you the whole time, okay?"

"Gates, I didn't know that you were babysitting cripples nowadays," said a voice from behind Victor.

"You can go fuck right off, Falcone," said Abiana hotly.

"Wow, wow. You don't have to get all feisty now, Abiana. Victor, tell your girl to slow her roll, jeez," said Falcone.

"I guess not a lot has changed, eh Falcone? Still, the biggest asshole in the tri-state area, I see," said Victor cooly.

"I take that as a compliment, Gates." He lowered his voice to a whisper. "While you've been playing war in the jungle, I've been doing things that matter back here. You'd have to be able to afford this beast." Falcone motioned to his circuit board. "It's a top-of-the-line Lucier Corps series board, and it's going to wipe the board with your trash."

Victor could feel his face getting hot; he turned red pretty easily when he was either angry or embarrassed, and he happened to be both right now.

"Don't listen to him, Victor. He's just a bully," said Innocius.

"Yeah, I know he is," said Victor, trying to shake it off, adding, "He'll regret it."

"Ladies and gentlemen, just a quick reminder from our sponsor that the winner of today's race will take home a brand spanking new Lucier Corps series platinum board, with the second place winner taking five thousand credits, brought to you by our lovely sponsor," said Jay Cromwell as Abiana took another bow. "By way of introductory remarks to our thirty racers, I'd like to lay out a few ground rules before we get started. I know we have a very competitive bunch here today, but there is to be absolutely no physical contact among contestants while you are in the tunnels. Save those cyberduels for after the race. And that's pretty much the only rule we have. As always, the first one back to their starting mark will be declared the winner. Does everyone understand? Good. Contestants find your marks."

Around the shaft to the entrance of the tunnel, there were board launchers that formed a circle and held the boards to the floor. Each contestant stood on their board at the precipice to the tunnel shaft and donned their headsets. Victor brought Innocius to his mark and helped him initiate his circuit board bindings. Victor peered over the edge to see a purplish-red light emanating from the deep pit that led into the tunnels. "Racers have their marks? Good. Watch your step on the way down, in three, two, one…Go!"

The racers all leaned forward and began falling faster and faster. The wind whipped in their faces. Down the shaft, they twirled like they'd been shot out of a cannon down a great big mine shaft. One by one, their circuit boards began to make magnetic contact with the glowing twirl of the helix-shaped conduit cables, like skateboarders dropping into a half pike. The pack of circuit boarders was speeding deeper and deeper into the shaft until the glowing metal conduit began to level out into a large horizontal tunnel. All the racer's circuit boards had successfully made contact with the conduit and were now surfing atop its glowing surface.

Through the headset, Victor could see identity tags for each fellow racer speeding along in the tunnels, and even in what place they were in at any given moment. Abiana was two racers behind him, and Innocius was crushing it, three racers in front of him, in third place. He could also communicate with the other races using a mic in the headset.

"You're killing it, kid, don't get too cocky, though," said Victor to Innocius.

At each point where the helix converged, there was a danger of colliding with another racer. At speeds of over one hundred miles per hour, the racers twisted and turned around each other, careful to avoid starting a mid-air pileup. Avoiding a crash was one thing, but it took an enormous amount of concentration to navigate along the helix conduit by harnessing the theta waves into steering the circuit board. Any stray thought could send the rider tale-spinning toward the concrete walls that encased the conduit.

Victor sped past a few racers and was now right behind Innocius who was in second place behind Falcone. They were already quickly approaching where they started along the figure-eight-shaped circuit and would soon be traveling back up the shaft to the finish line. Innocius and Falcone were neck-and-neck. Victor got a front-row seat to the two twirling past each other as the helix converged, barely missing one another several times. "Careful, kid, I want to take you back to your mother in one piece, or she'll kill me!"

They began the ascent back up the shaft toward the finish line, with Falcone and Innocius competing for first place. Then, during one of the final convergences of the helix, Victor saw Falcone stick out his arm and clothes-lined Innocius in the neck. The boy was knocked right off his board and began falling straight down the shaft. Victor had no time to react. By the time he knew what was happening, Innocius was already speeding fifty feet below him toward the tunnels.

Through the headset intercom, Victor heard Abiana say, "Got ya, kid!"

"When I get up there, I'm going to beat the piss out of that guy."

Sure enough, once Victor and Falcone passed the threshold out of the shaft and back into the warehouse, Victor unstrapped his bindings and confronted Falcone. "You could have killed him, you asshole!"

"What are you talking about, dick? I didn't mean..." But before Falcone could get another word out, Victor cold-cocked him right in the face. Falcone landed a clean one right on Victor's eye and forehead.

The cheers the crowd had given the two upon their arrival turned into jeers and screams. Jay Cromwell tried to break up the crowd while Falcone's face began bleeding from both sides of his mouth. The cries for blood from the crowd were drowned out by the sound of police car sirens driving into the warehouse. The police began to part the crowd, and two officers grabbed both Victor and Falcone apart by the scruff of their necks. They asked them if the fight had been an agreed-upon cyberduel, and both of them said that it wasn't. "We're going to need you to come with us, son," said one of the officers to Victor. As Victor was being put into the back of the police car, he saw Abiana surface back into the warehouse, holding Innocius' small frame in her arms.

8

Jailbird Drip

The steel bars of the prison cell closed behind Victor with a deafening thud. The only thing he regretted was not tossing Falcone into the pit to finish the job. If anything had happened to Innocius, he wouldn't have been able to forgive himself. *Falcone only wanted to win. He didn't give two shits or not if he killed a kid in the process.* Victor balled up his fists. *Next time I see that guy, he's a dead man.*

His thoughts of kicking Falcone into the power circuit pit were distant fantasies now. Tonight, Victor's only company were those in the precinct drunk tank, an eclectic cobble of drunks, homeless, and people who needed to chill out.

"Hey kid, you got a smoke?" asked a man sitting across from him dressed in a disheveled blue suit with a welt on his eye that started to bruise the shade of his garments.

"You can't smoke in here," said Victor.

"I didn't ask you if we *can* smoke in here. I asked if you had one. What are you, my mother? What'd you do, kid?" The man had a New Jersey accent that was barely distinguishable from that of a Philly native.

"Got in a fight. You?"

The man just pointed to his cheek and winked. "Well, this and a few other things that I'd rather not incriminate myself on. Now that said, though, if you want to get wet, I'm your guy. If you know what I mean," he said with another greasy wink.

"No…I don't think I do."

"Christ, you really are a boy scout, aren't you?" He lowered his voice. "I'm talking about neuro-drip kid. I have the best neuroenhancements on the market. Anything you want. These things are out of control. Want to fly, fuck a supermodel, or fly while fucking a supermodel? The sky's the limit, kid, anything your little heart desires. These drugs can make it come true without ever leaving the comfort of your home or jail cell. Like Disney World for your cerebral cortex. The best part is that you never come down off of it."

"I'll pass, thanks."

There was a tellvision that the guards were watching outside the cell. Victor tried to pretend as though he were watching it to avoid engaging in more conversation with this sleazeball. The newscaster, who was speaking live from his newsroom, sounded quite alarmed. "The grand architect himself is planning on being in Philadelphia for the Fourth of July tri-centennial festivities. However, due to security concerns regarding the annual chant on the preceding day, it is expected that Grand Architect Lucier may make a televised appearance only from his office in Washington. Earlier today, we interviewed the grand architect, and he had this to say." The video cut to a clip of Valter Lucier addressing a few supporters in downtown Washington DC.

"The American people deserve strong, resolute leadership. Nothing on heaven, earth, or hell will keep me from being in Philadelphia on the Fourth of July to celebrate the tri-centennial of our nation's birth. I fully expect there to be some lively protest, cyberduels, and other frivolities to celebrate three hundred years of liberty."

"But Grand Architect, aren't you concerned that there may be some significant unrest during the annual chant on July third, and that it may continue into the tri-centennial celebrations?" asked the reporter.

"I am not concerned in the slightest. I challenge every red-blooded American to come to the chant and the tri-centennial celebrations ready to speak your mind. Our vigilance, vigor, and anger have sustained our democracy for three hundred glorious years. We mustn't cede our passions to the most moderate voices among us."

As Victor listened to the grand architect, he remembered VanHeller's proposal that Victor join him during the festivities on the Fourth of July. He knew things would be safe since the grand architect himself was planning on being there. But he couldn't shake the feeling that there were going to be some real radicals out and about during this chant and the tri-centennial. Usually, the chants got pretty heated, but there were some pretty controversial issues on the docket. Not to mention that this year's particular chant would be held the day before the tri-centennial celebrations. *It'd be the perfect time for someone to do something stupid.*

The image cut back to the newscaster delivering the nightly report. "The grand architect sounds optimistic about the annual chant going relatively smoothly. But, as we all know, polls suggest that one of the issues that will be voted on during the annual chant is whether or not a neurograft mandate should be imposed. This, of course, is a hotly contested issue, and one..."

One of the guards turned off the tellvision. "Enough fake news for one day. There's nothing 'hotly contested' about it. Everyone thinks we should get the mandate. It's a no-brainer."

"Yeah, I hope that mandate goes through," said the man in the blue suit. "Ever since people started getting the neurograft, my neuro-drip business has sky-rocketed. When people get that neurograft, they're able to tap into parts of their brains that they never thought were possible. And they get higher than a kite when they're on my stuff." The man took off his jacket, made a pillow out of it, and laid down on the cold metal bench. He crossed his hands behind his head and stared at the concrete slab above. "Everybody loves my stuff, kid. You would, too, if you gave it a chance."

Will this dufuss just shut his face and go to sleep.

"I'll give you a free sample. What do you think?"

This guy is so full of shit.

"You look exactly like the type of guy who would love it. Everyone ends up loving it. Especially the ones who think they won't and the ones you wouldn't think of. Like these guys out here." He pointed to the guards that were visible through the plate glass windows of the cell. "*Those* guys are the ones who love it the most. I probably sell to all those law-abiding citizens. And look what they do to me. They throw their buddy Lou in the slammer." He pulled a yellowed toothpick out of his jacket pocket and picked a piece of crud out of his mouth, spitting it across the cell onto the glass.

God, what a sleaze.

"I take care of them. They're like my little wayward children. Serve and Protect." He held up his hand to his forehead in a mock salute. "Who's gonna protect them, huh? Nobody. Nobody cares about them, 'cept Lou. There's one guy that comes to me at least once a week. Some fuzz with a British accent. Always giving me some sob story about his daughter."

Wait, what?

"Yeah. Jacky is her name." Lou balled up his hands, rubbed his eyes, and made fake pouty cries. "Ah. Jacky. I never see you. Boo hoo hoo.'"

Victor shoved a guy out of his way to make it over to where Lou was lying down and started wailing on him. The other prisoners started cheering and clanging their hands on the metal benches. Victor didn't stop punching until the guards came in and ripped him off of Lou.

"You piece of shit!" yelled Victor.

***

Victor got his own cell that night. He barely slept a wink and groggily awoke early the next morning to the sound of the cell door opening and Eli standing in the opening. "Wakey wakey, eggs and bakey. Get your stuff, I'm getting you out of here, and I have your winnings." He held a small bag that jingled when it shook.

As they were walking out of the police station, Victor started to stomp away. "I didn't need your help."

"Like hell, you didn't. You know, if I didn't sweet talk Falcone and his parents into not pressing charges, you'd be in front of a judge by day's end. And these precinct a-holes were going to hold you till later this morning." Eli grabbed Victor on the shoulder and spun him around. "Victor, mate. Did you want your mom to find out you got put in the slammer overnight? No, you don't. Now listen, I love getting into fights just as much as the next bloke. But you need to be smart about it. I mean, all you had to do was enter into a cyberduel with that idiot, and it wouldn't have been a problem at all."

"Right after his mom gave me the third degree about not putting him in danger. Like an idiot, I let him do the most dangerous thing he could've possibly wanted to do and then let some asswipe almost kill him."

"Falcone told me it was an accident, that he didn't do it on purpose, Victor. Shit happens down there, you know it does."

"That's some grade-A bullshit, Eli. Thanks for believing that scumbag over me."

"Hey. You crossed the line," said Eli, with a finger to Victor's chest. "It's not about believing or not believing. It's about me being here right now and taking care of my mate when he needs help. That's it."

"That's it?" Victor tried to stop the word vomit from coming up. "Well…you seem to have a lot of buddies, don't you? I met one of them in there, Lou. New Jersey guy. Biggest sleezeball east of the Delaware. You know him? Yeah, he and I had a fun chat about *you* last night."

Eli put his hand up to his forehead. "Fuck."

"Yeah, fuck. You're always talking so much shit about neuro-junkies, and you're one of them. Eli, how can you do that to yourself? To Jacky?"

"Not exactly proud of it. I'm trying, Victor, I really am. Now come on. Let me drive you home. You've had a long night. We'll get some breakfast in you, and I'll teach you how to turn a wrench to fix your mum's toilet, eh? Here, take your winnings, Mr. Second Place."

Victor grabbed the bag of credits from him and took a deep breath. "Whatever, let's just go."

The two arrived back at Victor's house at about six o'clock and were greeted at the door by the sound of sizzling bacon. "Good morning, Mama Gates. Mind if I hang around for breakfast?"

"Of course, dear, it's almost ready. How was the power supply?" asked Carmenta as she flipped the bacon.

"It was alright, Ma." He slumped into a seat at the kitchen table. "I asked Eli to stop by and see if we could fix the upstairs toilet."

"You look so tired. Let me take a look at you." She held his face in her hands. "Oh my word, Victor, what happened to your eye? Did someone hit you, baby?"

"It was just a little accident, Mama Gates…"

"Eli, I can speak for myself, man."

"Alright, I'll leave you both to it," said a dejected Eli, "and get upstairs to fix the necessities." Eli grabbed the toolbox that he brought and headed upstairs.

"You don't need to tell me everything that's going on with you, Victor, but I need you to know that I'm here for you whenever you need me," said Carmenta as she sat down next to Victor and put her arm around him. "I will love you no matter what's going on."

Victor drew himself up and took a deep breath. "I know that, Ma. I just don't want to get you worried about me, that's all. You've been through enough as it is, having to keep this place together without me. I won some credits for us." He placed the bag on the table.

Carmenta ignored the bag, straightened her hair, and folded her hands on the table. "Victor, your mother is not made out of glass. If something is on your mind, and there's something I can do to help you, I need you to tell me, you hear?"

"I don't know if there's anything you can do to help Ma. I've just been having these crazy dreams lately, and well…things just aren't how I pictured they would be when I came home. I thought things…would be different. I don't know if I'm ready to talk about everything that happened to me down there in Haiti, Ma. I thought coming home, I could escape it, but I can't. And…there's something else…" Victor was torn about whether or not to tell his mother about the Omega transmission. His mom was clearly on 'Team Victor,' and she only wanted to help him. And, he thought, this might cheer her up a bit. He would be able to tell her that he was going straight to DeThroe, and maybe that dirtball husband that left her and her small child would finally be found and made to pay for his crimes as a traitor.

"What is it?"

"I…I received a transmission a few nights ago. It was from Omega. They said they found me and…then they gave me instructions on how to destroy a device."

Carmenta stared into Victor's brown eyes for a moment; they were mirror images of her own. Then she gently pushed her seat from behind her and stood up, resting her hand on the kitchen countertop with her back facing Victor. "The device included in their instructions, what is it?"

This seemed like an odd question, and one Victor wasn't prepared to answer at all. "I have no idea. They sent a schematic of it, but I haven't even looked at it yet. Mom, I'm going to tell Colonel DeThroe. He should know that I might be able to find...Mobius."

Carmenta froze like a board, and then she started to tremble. "Victor, I don't think you should talk to DeThroe. There's so much that you just don't know, baby."

Victor stared at her with a puzzled expression. This was not going the way he thought it would go. "Why in the hell should I not tell DeThroe? Mom, Mobius, or one of his Omega cronies might be planning something."

Carmenta whispered low, "...he's found you. God in heaven, I don't believe it. I don't know how this could have possibly worked."

"Are you afraid that Mobius will find us if I go to DeThroe? Mom, he can't hurt us anymore. And what worked? You're being weird about all this, you know that?"

Carmenta turned around to face Victor again. Now she had a fervent, almost desperate expression as though she were pleading with him. "Victor, you need to promise me that you won't tell DeThroe or VanHeller or anyone in The Fourth Branch. Do you understand?"

"I absolutely do not understand!" shouted Victor. "You are making zero sense right now, Ma. Omega is pure evil!"

"You don't understand..."

"If I don't tell them, that makes me about as big a traitor as Mobius was. Is that what you're trying to make me?"

"Of course not Victor, but Mobius wasn't..."

"I just can't even believe you!" Victor shouted much louder than he meant to at his mother. She tried to say something again, but her voice couldn't break through the tears.

"Is everything alright down here?" Eli had come down the stairs without making a peep, or perhaps neither Carmenta nor Victor were blocking out the rest world right now. They were both pretty upset. "Well, the toilet is fixed. Just had to change out a part. I even gave it a trial run to make sure it worked alright," he added with an awkward giggle.

"Eli, is it alright if I hang out at your house?" asked Victor.

Eli looked at Carmenta, whose hands now covered her face, trying to hold back tears and hide them from the boys. He moved a little closer to Victor and whispered in his ear, "You're being an asshole, mate. Quit treating your mum like shit. I'm leaving, and you should apologize." He raised his voice. "Have a good evening, Mama Gates. Glad I could help."

Carmenta managed to get out a "thanks" between more tears and blowing her nose in tissues. Eli walked out of the house as Victor stomped up the stairs to his room. He slammed the door behind him and lay down.

It's hot as hell in here, he thought. His room didn't have an air conditioner in his room, and the morning sun was turning his room into an upstairs sauna. Victor wiped a bead of sweat already forming on his forehead and searched his sociograft to find DeThroe's contact information. He became distracted with some of the messages he'd gotten since last night. His sociograft was deactivated when he entered the police station, so he had no way of checking anything. He scrolled through the feed.

Advertisements, more advertisements. Jesus, everybody's always trying to sell you something. Hey, here's one from Innocius. Victor opened up the message, and a very small hologram version of Innocius appeared in his hand. "Hey Victor, I just wanted to call and let you know that I'm okay. Didn't get too banged up, and I almost won! That Falcone guy and I were neck and neck right up until the last second. Well, just wanted to say I had a great time. I hope I see you again soon. End transmission."

That kid's alright. Victor kept scrolling through the feed. *More advertisements, more advertisements. Ooh. A message from Abiana!* Victor clicked on the message, and a small hologram of Abiana appeared.

"Hey, Vicky. Falcone is the world's biggest asshole. I would've done the same thing to him if you hadn't gotten to him first. I managed to get in a few kicks to his sternum. Mwah. I'm going to the parade downtown tomorrow night. And if I have to break you out of the slammer with a key baked in a cake to make sure you go with me, you know I'll do it. See you then. End transmission."

"Tomorrow night? Jeez, she sent that last night, so that parade must be tonight. I'll text the guys and see if they want to go too." Victor sent a message to Rocky, Eli, and Innocius asking if they wanted to meet up at the parade, too. He had no idea what the parade was for, all he knew was he wanted to have an excuse to get out of the house as much as possible right now.

He stretched his arms and legs out. *That's enough sociograft for one day.* But he still had one transmission to send. DeThroe's contact information wasn't hard to find, and Victor rehearsed what he was going to say. He knew he had to tell him that Omega had contacted him. That was a no-brainer.

But maybe that's not enough info, right? Maybe I should just forward him the entire message that they sent me. Yeah, perfect. His feuding inner monologue wouldn't let him off that easy. *Well…there's a lot of stupid stuff in that message. Like, what's the deal with 'knowing good and evil? Yeah, what was all that about? Maybe I should listen to the whole transmission from Omega again, and I'll just send DeThroe the good parts.*

Victor looked back through his old transmissions and listened intently. *Omega has found you…*

So wait a second, they never came right out and said, 'We are Omega.' What if it wasn't Omega who sent this? An icy coil of anxiety started snaking its way around him. *That's ridiculous. If it wasn't Omega, then who could it have possibly been?*

"…the most dangerous device…"

Now what could be so dangerous about this device, exaggerate much? Victor looked through the transmission to find where he could view the schematic that was included. It was an old-style blueprint that had dark stains all over it, making it barely legible to begin with. At face value, it looked like one of those big floating balloons that people used to fly a long time ago. Except instead of flying horizontally, it looked like it was doing a nosedive. *What were those things called again?* Victor looked at a poster on his bedroom wall of one of his favorite bands—Led Zeppelin. *Zeppelin! That's what it looks like. What the hell is so dangerous about a big old floating balloon?*

"…destroy the device…"

What, with a Beebee gun? It's a balloon, for crying out loud, what's so damn dangerous about it? This was beginning to sound all too ridiculous. Maybe it was a hoax. At this point, that seemed to be the most plausible explanation. Even so, Victor thought it best to send DeThroe the message, the whole message, just to be safe. DeThroe was explicit with his order. *Any* communication from Omega (suspected or otherwise) should be reported. Plus, he'd already pissed his mom off, and at this point, there was no hopping off that hate train. Victor prepped the transmission and added a message to DeThroe that explained how he had unwittingly been sent this message in the first place.

He sent it. *Well, that was easy.* He wiped a bead of sweat from his forehead. *Jeez, how did it get even hotter in here all of a sudden?*

9

Spiders, Snakes, and Horsemen

There was hardly a nook, cubby, or hole to hide in. Victor didn't want to be found. He wanted to stay under the radar. Any sudden movement would be a lightning rod for the enemy to find him, resulting in getting obliterated or squashed. It was almost always best to stay in the shadows, never in the light where you were exposed and seen. Being seen as the ultimate danger and being heard was even worse. He didn't have to worry about either of those now. He learned certain survival techniques while fighting in Haiti, but this was the ultimate game of 'cat and mouse.' Though hopefully cats and mice would steer clear of this room, for now, they were the enemy. And he was so hungry, so very hungry. His web hadn't caught anything for days, so now he was forced to use his spindly eight legs to search for game.

He searched the corners of this spacious room for anything: flies, ants, maybe a centipede with a few missing limbs. Nothing, there was absolutely nothing living in here besides him. This place barely even had a speck of dust to speak of—it was immaculately clean. Victor always liked things tidy, but a little mess here and there might be helpful to aid his hunt. Oh, what he wouldn't give for a few spilled crumbs on the floor to entice some unwitting bugs to feast.

His eight tiny eyes peered all around this strange room. Strange for him but luxuriously decadent for its usual inhabitants. The ornate stonework was nice to grip his legs into, which was nice, but those damn stained glass windows always let in too much light. Though he greatly enjoyed the gentle pitter-patter of rain now rapping on the glass. No one was here for now, but they could be back any minute. Victor's favorite was the one with the cane that had a spider on it, for obvious reasons. There were two more who usually came into this strange room with four great wood doors but never more. Usually, they would all sit around the large stone casket in the center of the room with four seats around it. Unusual, thought Victor, always only three people but room for a fourth.

The door opened, and the man with the spider cane came limping in. Victor scurried back to his web, careful to not be seen. If he was lucky, the door opening would let in a tasty fly or two. This time, it was only him. He sat himself into one of the four chairs with a painful grunt. It must be tough having such fleshy legs with all those pesky nerves in them.

Once the man sat in his chair, something quite incredible happened. One other human appeared out of thin air in one of the other chairs, with the third and fourth remaining vacant. The humans who sat there were like glowing ghosts—see-through—even though they weren't there at all. Incredibly, one of them started speaking.

"Colonel, where are we in finding the intercepted plans? We need to know who took them and recover them immediately."

"Isn't this just the most pleasant coincidence," said the man with the spider cane. "I just received a transmission of unusually great import. It happens to be from our young Corporal Gates. And it just so happens that he has received a copy of the stolen plans."

"That is fortuitous, though not unexpected. Ever since the theta anomaly occurred a few days ago, we must assume that certain, undesirables, also detected its presence as well. Can we use the boy to recover the plans?"

"We'll get him. And if we play our cards right, we'll capture an even bigger fly in our web."

"Good. Proceed as planned. We cannot let the enemy gain operational control of the device. It will destroy years of well-laid plans. You would do well to exercise some caution regarding our two young friends. We are still unsure of how the energy anomaly has…affected them. And colonel, the grand developer has intimated that he wants no mistakes. Hail The Fourth Branch."

"Hail The Fourth Branch. End transmission."

The man with the spider cane began whistling, and the stone casket in the middle of the room erupted to life with intense flames.

* * *

Victor awoke in his bed from a dream that he couldn't remember. The sun was beginning to set, and he was nursing a throbbing headache from his mid-afternoon nap. It seemed these afternoon siestas were becoming a bit of a habit now, and he had no idea why. He tried to concentrate hard on what he had just dreamed. It was one of those that if you couldn't piece together a few bits within the first few minutes of waking up, you'd never remember the rest of it ever again. *Spiders. I know there was something about spiders. Shit. I need some Tylenol.* He rubbed the area between his eyes to try to coax the pain out of his cortex.

His stomach rumbled hard into a knot of hunger. Somehow, he'd managed to sleep through lunch and dinner. He hardly had anything for breakfast, even though his mother had cooked him some. *Maybe I was a little bit too hard on her. Eli sure thought so. Still, there was something that she was hiding or at least not being open about.*

Victor let out a tired sigh. Coming home so far had not been what he expected. His stomach rumbled like a geyser ready to surface. He stood up and put his ear to the door. He couldn't hear Carmenta downstairs. Maybe she went to her shift, he thought. He threw on a clean pair of jeans and a shirt after having sweated profusely during his sleep marathon.

When he got downstairs, there was a sandwich and some chips in a Tupperware on the counter with a note. "Love you so much. Had to go to work. I'll see you soon."

He finished scarfing down the last few crumbs and heard a car honk from right outside the row home. He opened the door to find Abiana, Rocky, and Innocius all waiting for him in the car.

Abiana was in the driver seat of a lipstick-red antique Chevy, wearing a matching red dress. "You look like you just ran a marathon, or got out of a sauna."

"No, but I just woke up. Where are we going again? And Jesus, where did you get this car?" asked Victor, running his hand through his hair once, trying to clean out the cobwebs that the strange dream implanted in his head.

"I rebuilt this hunk of junk from the ground up, and we're going to the parade, you goof. God, it's a good thing you're so cute. And this happens to be a 1976 limited edition Chevy Chevelle."

Rocky grabbed Victor's shoulder from the backseat. "Dude, you never told me how much this kid is like your mini-me. I feel like I'm sitting next to six-years-ago Victor."

Innocius and Rocky must have been discussing Vixama's voodoo shop before they picked Victor up because they dove headlong back into the conversation.

"So your mom's store is right across the street from the high school, right?"

"Yeah, she's owned it for a few years now. My sister and I help her run it."

"Little dude, you have to let me stop by sometime. I have a special machine that detects theta wave activity and the spot where your mom's store is always lights up on my screen like the fourth of July."

"I wonder what it could be," said Innocius curiously.

"No idea. I've never seen anything like it. But it's definitely emanating from your mom's corner store."

"Maybe it's voodoo," said Abiana with a spooky voice.

"Not likely. There must be a scientific explanation for it. I'll need to bring a tool with me to measure the energy waves. Is that okay?" said Rocky.

"Sure," said Innocius. "I bet my mom would love to see you all in the store. Maybe she could to Tarot card readings on you all."

Rocky clapped Innocius on the back. "That would be so cool! I don't believe in that stuff, but I love card games."

The three started a spirited discussion on everything from Tarot cards, poker, and a new sociograft game that Abiana's dad at Lucier Corps had invented.

Victor interrupted them. "Oh yeah, we're going to the parade." The brain fog was slowly lifting. "Isn't Eli coming? I asked—"

"Yeah, I know you did," said Abiana. "Thanks for hijacking my RSVP list by inviting that miserable old zealot. These two," she said, motioning to Innocius and Rocky in the back seat, "totally fine. I like you guys, but not Eli. He's a nark, and he smells. But—" she started begrudgingly, "I know he's your guys' friend so when I asked him if he wanted to come he said he had a shift tonight and couldn't make it. So he's someone else's problem now. Knowing my luck, though, we'll see his trifling ass doing crowd control or something. Would you get in already?"

Victor sat shotgun while they blasted 1980s music till they got downtown. Abiana never skipped an opportunity to rev the engine a bit at every red light. She was really in her element right now. Driving an old school car while serenading the boys to the best of the eighties hairband, Poison. Innocius thought this was somewhat peculiar. "You know, Abiana, if you like oldies so much, I would've had you pegged as a Taylor Swift or maybe Katy Perry fan."

Abiana chuckled good-naturedly. "Kid, next time you go falling down another well, you might have to ask someone else to save you." She turned around at Innocius, giving him a smile and a wink. They were almost to the parking garage after listening to Nothing But a Good Time for the fourth time when the engine started to sputter. "Damn, damn, damn, damn!" shouted Abiana while slamming her fist on the steering wheel. A puff of smoke billowed from the hood.

She pulled the car over, got out, and started kicking the hubcaps while shouting the most obscene expletives any of the boys had heard. After a few moments of venting, she grabbed a tool kit from the back, popped the hood, and went straight to work diagnosing the problem.

The boys stayed in the car until Innocius suggested, "Maybe we should go and help?" Abiana was still swearing a long stream of expletives laced with disturbing sexual imagery.

"I don't know guys, it might be safer if we stay in here. What do you think?" said Rocky. Victor had seen Abiana on a mechanically induced tirade before, and it never ended well for people who got in her way.

"Yeah, but I think Innocius is right. We could maybe, you know, hand her the tools or something?" said Victor.

"But do all three of us need to hand her tools? You know, she's your girlfriend, Victor. Maybe you could just go?"

"She's not my girlfriend, dude, at least I don't think she is…" Victor's thoughts drifted off as he began to feel his cheeks becoming red. "That doesn't have anything to do with anything, though. I don't know jack shit about cars."

"And you think I do?" asked Rocky.

"Well, yeah. I mean, you and your dad have a workshop and, you know, all that."

"It's a *cyber* parlor, Victor, not a classic car mechanic shop!"

Victor had enough bickering, and also Rocky made a pretty good point. Plus, it made him look pretty good in front of the guys to be the one to go out and help turn a wrench or two. He opened the door to go, and a screwdriver flew past him, barely missing his nose. "You know, on second thought, I'll just sit tight in here."

It was starting to get dark out, but thankfully, Abiana had fixed the problem. She closed the hood and threw the tools in the trunk. "Damn timing and choke. It's a good thing somebody brought along a few extra gauges, or we'd be sitting ducks out here." She cast them all a look before jumping back in the driver's seat.

They parked as far as their feet would permit them to from where the parade would begin near City Hall. Abiana knew it was going to be a complete mess, trying to leave downtown when the parade was over.

"Why didn't we just take the subway?" moaned Rocky as they started the trek.

"Because I wanted to get some windshield time on my baby."

"And why exactly are we doing this again?"

"Don't be such a party pooper, Rocky. Haven't you ever been to the Twenty-Eighth Amendment Parade?"

Rocky shook his head sheepishly. "I've never been to one. And I hope this is a good one. My dad wanted me at the shop tonight."

"Well, what about you two? Don't tell me Philly's greatest hero has never been to any of the Twenty-Eighth Amendment Parades." Both Victor and Innocius shook their heads.

"My mom wouldn't let me be caught dead going to one of these things," said Innocius. "I told her that we were out getting ice cream. I think she knew I wasn't telling the truth, but she'd have killed me if I told her the truth."

Abiana seemed horrified. "Why would you have to lie about coming to a parade?"

"My mom isn't exactly a 'fan' of politics, and you know…all that."

"But this isn't even remotely about politics. It's about celebrating coming out of the dark ages. I mean, just think what would've happened if the twenty-eighth amendment didn't get passed and we didn't have a fully functional cyberocracy? Well, I, for one, don't even want to think about it. When she was alive, my dad and my mom always talked about…the war."

"The War of the Moderates?" asked Rocky.

"Yeah, that one. My dad fought in it. Did I ever tell you that, Victor?"

"Umm, no, I don't think you did." Victor was being polite. The past few days were cumulatively more than Abiana had talked to him in his entire lifetime. It went without saying that he tried to hang on to every word she said. *She's hot, smart, and vivacious, so who cares if she's a little bit too into politics and history. It makes her sexier. And the red high-slit skirt helped a bit, too.*

It was clear the quartet was getting closer to the parade route since they now found themselves elbowing passersby for walking space. Most wore red, white, and blue or something else that screamed patriotism and love of country. This type of freedom-laced frivolity was something that Carmenta had never enjoyed very much herself.

Victor was sure she had her reasons, but he was also beginning to question how valid her intentions were. She couldn't stop herself from trying to convince Victor to do the right thing, which was telling DeThroe about the transmission. And after what Mobius did to her personally and what he did to the entire country, it was a damn wonder that she wasn't out here parading and skipping along to "Yankee Doodle." She wasn't, though; she never had, and she never will.

This was hardly the time to think about your parents, or anything serious for that matter. The four had just arrived on the parade route and were watching as big patriotic floats rolled by. Screens televising famous musicians and singers were plastered on every building's edifice. Fireworks lit up the night sky and illuminated the throngs of people below.

Everyone looked so happy to be there. Kids on their dad's shoulders, friends dancing together, and couples holding hands. Couples holding hands. *Maybe I should take Abiana's hand.* Victor had never actually held a girl's hand, much less had a girlfriend. Her spaghetti-strapped top revealed a strange tattoo on her shoulder. He didn't know what it was, but whatever it was, he loved it.

Abiana punched Victor in the arm. "Having fun, you big goof?" She rested her head on his shoulder. "I knew you would," she said with a bright smile, somehow showcasing every one of her exquisitely shaped teeth. Maybe it was the fireworks or brightly lit city streets, but Victor found it very difficult to hide a deep, rosy blush.

The large holograph projects that floated above the crowd now showed General VanHeller on a stage at the National Mall in Washington. There was an older man on the stage with him. He had a short and immaculately manicured beard and pulled a gold stopwatch out of his blazer pocket. *The man at the train station.* Victor was sure he was the same person who had sat down with him at the 30th Street Station and exchanged a few words. If that really was him, even from the holograph image, it looked like he really didn't want to be there.

"Hey, who's that guy behind VanHeller?" Victor asked Abiana.

Abiana squinted at the nearest holograph. "Thomas Locke. He's the Speaker of the House in Congress. And next to your dad, he's the biggest piece of shit this country's ever shat out."

Victor didn't know what she meant by comparing Locke to his father. Whatever her reasoning, she wasn't a fan of the man. VanHeller took to the podium and tapped on the mic to make sure it was working.

"Greetings, my fellow Americans and warriors for our eternal cause of freedom. It is a somber day." he paused for dramatic effect. "It's a somber day because twenty years ago on this date, our country was wrenched from its darkest point in history. Our determination remains as resolute today as it was then. Our vigilance to maintain a system whereby the people's voice is amplified by our cyberocracy will never be called into question. Ladies and gentlemen, the people spoke twenty years ago, and they speak again now in one unified voice. Never again shall we experience the tyranny of those masquerading to be for the people. Only the people can speak for themselves, and their voices will never be silenced!"

The crowd erupted in rapturous applause.

"Now comes the time when our uncompromising determination to maintain the voice of the people is again commemorated on this hallowed day. Twenty years ago today, we witnessed the birth of a new order of freedom. The twenty-eighth amendment ushered in this new era of freedom as a cyberocracy took the helm as its vessel. Our vigilance to defend this system and the chant of the people must never be called into question. We owe these freedoms, and the rights and liberties contained, to our great patriots. Patriots like Corporal Gates in Philadelphia. If it weren't for the likes of these heroes, we would have very little to celebrate and much less to give to one another. The grand architect and I look forward to seeing all of you in Philadelphia. The birthplace of our great

cyberocracy. God bless you all, and God bless the United States of America."

Rocky, Innocius, and Abiana all looked glowingly at Victor. Rocky couldn't stop shouting. "You're the man, this is Victor freaking Gates, this is him, this is the freaking man right here!" Innocius was pumping his fists up in the air furiously. 'Cyber festivals, which were the opposite of cyberduels, began breaking out spontaneously on the street. Strangers embracing and couples kissing could be seen as far as the eye could see. And Abiana looked like she could have devoured Victor whole. And maybe she would have, had it not been for who appeared on the screen next.

The tellvision screens went black, the fireworks stopped, and all the lights on the street went out. A face in a white mask appeared on the screen and used a deeply modulated voice to address the crowd.

"My fellow Americans, this is indeed a somber day. Omega will rise, and the place that offered the cradle of your cyberocracy will be your tomb."

An eerie and terrifyingly ominous tune started to play on all of the screens lining the streets. Everyone instantly started to panic and began sprinting in any direction they could to get away from the parade route and the horrible sounds now filling the streets. Abiana and Rocky seemed to be in shock. Victor grabbed their shoulders and said, "Follow me!"

Victor took Innocius by the wheelchair, and the four of them made a mad dash down a nearby street. Everyone else had the same basic idea, get as far away from those screens and that noise as possible. Unlike most people, though, Victor knew where he was running to. His mom's work was very close, and there was a place that Victor's mom always used to take him where he knew they'd be safe.

At this point, it was a miracle that the four of them were still together despite the jostling of the terrified crowd. They were so close to their refuge when they heard the explosion. It was so violent that Innocius' chair almost came loose from his grip. Now the crowd, if they weren't completely deafened or knocked down by the blast, were stricken with the fear of God. As hard as Abiana and Rocky tried to stay with Victor and Innocius, it was now impossible, and Victor soon lost sight of them. Victor and Innocius made a hard turn into a skinny little alleyway that the horde of passersby completely missed. There was a shabby wooden door leading into an equally shabby-looking building.

Victor threw the door open and pushed Innocius inside, yelling, "Stay here. I'll be back for you!"

Victor knew he'd be safe there. Now he had to find Rocky and Abiana and make sure they were okay. He ran out of the alleyway and back onto the street. They must have been pushed further down by the crowd. Victor hopped up on the hood of a nearby pickup truck to get a better view. He wished he hadn't. No one could have seen the second coming, and it threw him flying off the pickup and onto the pavement.

"Victor…Victor…"

It sounded so far away, yet so close.

"Victor…Victor!"

He looked up and could see Eli shouting at him. Eli picked him up by one arm and flung him over his shoulders. He carried him to that shabby-looking brick building in the back alleyway that Victor had dropped Innocius off in.

Victor's ears were still ringing, but he was now starting to come to his senses. "Where are we…what happened?"

"We're in St. Croix pub, mate," said Eli. Victor looked around at the familiar bar he hadn't been in for three years. *It hasn't changed much,* he thought, ears still ringing. It may have been shabby on the outside, but inside, it was quite warm and inviting. The bar had six seats, and there were a few custom-built wooden booths with cozy cushions. On the wall behind the bar area, there were a few dozen framed pictures, as well as American and Haitian flags hung prominently. It may have been small, but it was kept immaculately clean by its proprietor. It had been for years. "We're all here. Innocius, Rocky, and Abiana and we're all okay. Except you, of course. How's your head?"

All the noise and voices around him sounded as though he were listening to it underwater, but he understood Eli. "I'm alright, I think," he said, maybe a bit too loudly. They were all seated at a wooden booth next to a window. Eli had his arm around him, and Rocky was sitting across from him furiously checking his sociograft while Innocius looked despondently out the window. Abiana had just finished ordering drinks at the bar for the group.

She looked worried when she came to sit back down and saw Victor. "How is Vicky?"

He gave her a thumbs up.

She looked at him more closely. "Do you think we should take him to the hospital?"

"He's got his bell rung a few times before. He'll be fine. Just a bit concussed. Speaking of that, can you ask Ollie, the bartender, for a bag of ice? He's already getting a golfball-sized lump on his head."

The bartender was already walking toward them with their order of drinks, along with a bag full of ice. He looked at Victor, placed the bag of ice on him, and kissed his forehead. "It's good to see you again, Mr. Gates. You've grown up." When he spoke, it was with a low, deep voice laced with a strong Haitian accent.

Victor glanced up at him with a smile. "It's been too long, Ollie, and it's good to see you again too."

"And, of course, I am already familiar with Mr. Abramson. It is good to see you too again, sir. I never thought I would see you in a uniform again."

"That makes two of us, Ollie. I'll need to get running soon. I just needed to make sure these knuckleheads were safe."

"Well, I think it suits you. You will always be that punk rock kid from West Philly to me." He gave a polite nod to the group of friends. "You must be young Mr. Gates's friends. "It is an honor to meet you all," he said with a low bow.

"I'm Abiana, and this is Innocius and Rocky. How do you know each other?" asked Abiana.

"Ollie and Victor's parents go way back," said Eli. "When he was growing up, Carmenta would drop him off here while she went to work. Victor grew up in this booth we're sitting at."

"Oh wait, you're *that* Ollie!" said Rocky. "You know my dad too!"

"You must be Enrique Junior. Oh yes, I know him well. And did you say your name was Innocius, young man?" Innocius looked at Ollie and nodded. "So that must mean that you are Ms. Vixama's son then? I knew you looked familiar. I go to her shop once in a great while. It's been some time since I've been there lately." He paused for a moment and held his gaze on Victor. "It is shameful that a young hero returns from war only to be maimed by his countrymen. Have any of you heard anything more about these atrocities?"

Rocky was still fiddling with his sociograft. "Yeah, Omega took credit for the attack. And now," he continued scanning through his feed furiously, "The Fourth Branch is saying that it was a Haitian-backed syndicate of Omega."

Ollie hung his head down low. When he looked up, Victor was still nursing his head with the bag of ice. "You know, I can remember a time not too long ago when this booth sat another group of five very close friends. And they were friends at not very different times than the one we are in now; chaotic, divisive, and filled with cruelty. If you can imagine, though, it may have been even worse. We always had our fights, but they were petty. It wasn't until we allowed ourselves to be consumed by the world. We lost sight of what was important. The world will do everything it can to tear you apart and to make you care about things that hold no weight…things like acclaim and power. Don't drink from that poisonous chalice." Ollie cleaned a wet spot on the table with a white cloth, then threw it over his shoulder as he turned to leave.

"What happened to them, your friends?" asked Innocius.

Ollie turned around slowly. "We lost our souls a long time ago." When he got back behind the bar, he removed the American and Haitian flags that were hung there.

"And on that cheery note, we need to get going. I'm driving you all home in my patrol car, and I'm not taking no for an answer."

Victor's hand started to shake violently. He was receiving another encrypted message on his sociograft. "Wow, Victor! That's a Level Five transmission. Whoever that is, they must be pretty important.

This was the second time he'd gotten one of these 'Level 5' messages. It was becoming annoying. He held it up to his eyes to allow the retinal scan, and a small blue figure appeared on his hand.

"Holy shit, mate, that's General VanHeller. What in the fuck is that dickbag calling you for?"

Victor shrugged. "Corporal Gates, I hope this message finds you well. I hadn't planned on seeing you again until our little Fourth of July rendezvous. However, something quite urgent has arisen. I need to speak to you at The Fourth Branch Executive Suite in Washington DC. I'll be sending a car to pick you up tomorrow morning at 0800 hours. Have a pleasant evening. End transmission."

They all looked at Victor as though he had three heads.

"I bet it has something to do with all this!" said Rocky motioning out the window where people still walked in a panic. "But why would he want to talk to you about it, Victor? I mean, I know you're famous and all that, but how would you be able to help him?"

"I don't know."

Of course, Eli had to weigh in. "Victor, you know you don't have to do this. You're out of the military now. He has no authority to give you orders. And that twat is the last person you should be taking any orders from."

"I think it's great," said Abiana dreamily. "I mean, it's about time The Fourth Branch got some fresh blood. They're all just a bunch of old dudes."

"Abiana, don't even start," said Eli, rolling his eyes. "That's enough jawjacking for one night. Let's get you all home."

Innocius and Victor were Eli's last drop-offs that evening. The ride out of the center city was harrowing, to put it best. Apart from the near omnipresent police blockades (which they were able to skate right through thanks to being in Eli's patrol car), there were also protests, counterprotests, and opportunist vandals at every turn. Philadelphia wasn't a stranger to this unruly cocktail of unrest, but this time it was different. Victor couldn't remember the last time anything this big happened in his hometown, or even in the country for this matter, and he'd been at ground zero of it. They had all checked their sociografts while Eli drove. The death toll had risen to 229 people.

"I haven't seen that many people tits up in the street since the War of the Moderates. That includes you back there, handsome." Eli looked in the rearview mirror at Victor. "Civil unrest, domestic and foreign terror, bombings, shootings. People just can't stop being a bunch of miserable fucks can they?"

"Why would they do something like that? Killing so many innocent people?" asked Innocius, staring blankly out the window.

"Like the government would ever really tell us the truth. I reckon they would tell us how many aliens are in Area 51 before we get the real story about today."

Victor looked over at Innocius. No kid should have to see people get blown to pieces, not to mention getting blown up themselves. *It was one thing to see soldiers getting killed on some far-off battlefield, but it was another one entirely to see it down the street from your house.* Victor couldn't imagine having kids right now. Things were just way too messed up. "Have you talked to Jacky today, Eli? Is she okay?"

"Yeah, she's at her mum's house. Tomorrow should be my day with her, but my Chief is going to have us doing twelve-hour shifts for the next fucking moon."

They'd just arrived at Innocius' house, and Victor started helping Innocius into his wheelchair. "Hey, I can make it from here, Eli. Thanks for the ride, brother."

"You got it, kid."

"Stay safe out there, you hear?"

"Don't worry, I always carry a rubber," he said with a wink as he pulled a U-turn in the street and sped off.

Victor helped Innocius into the entryway, and the two boys said their rather exhausted goodbyes. As Victor walked down the stoop and onto the sidewalk, Innocius called down to him. "Are you excited for tomorrow?"

'Excited' wasn't the term he would describe for it. Clearly, VanHeller wanted something from Victor, and it was probably something that would cause his anxiety to spike through the roof. Though through the eyes of a young kid, he could see how it may be viewed as 'exciting.' He was going to the Executive Suite of The Fourth Branch. Not many people ever got the opportunity to go there. Maybe Innocius might cheer up a bit if he brought him down to DC. "Hey, how would you like to come down there with me tomorrow—as my guest?"

"What—no way! Down to The Fourth Branch? That would be so amazing! I'll tell my mom we're going to the zoo or something. Thanks, Victor!"

Victor walked back home to find some fried chicken and mashed potatoes in a Tupperware container on the counter with a note for re-heating instructions. It was signed, *"Love you, baby, from Ma."*

She's probably working the late shift again.

Still, he was surprised that she wasn't at the St. Croix bar. She usually went there to visit Ollie on her breaks. Victor hadn't eaten all day, but he just wasn't hungry right now. And even if he was, he wasn't sure whether he could since his stomach was in a tightly wound ball of nerves right now. It was the same kind of feeling that he would get the night before he and Tengo Squad did an early morning operation. His stomach would get all into knots, and he'd feel like garbage until after it was all over.

Then, he and the boys would cook a fattening breakfast on an open firepit. Usually that consisted of eggs they stole from a local farmer's chicken coop, with some wild rabbit or deer. But now, there was no Tengo Squad or operation for that matter. And the only barrel he'd be staring down wasn't even one on the battlefield. It was something much more frightening, the boardroom.

10

A Bloody Good Time

Morning came too quickly. It was one of those nights where Victor hardly knew if he slept at all. *I've slept like shit since Les Rouge.* Between bad dreams, urgent transmissions, and this God-awful heat, it was a wonder that he was able to get in more than a few hours. He threw on the least ripped pair of jeans that he owned and a collared shirt that he assumed belonged to his father.

Carmenta must have moved some of his clothes to his closet since she knew he might fit into them now. It was 7:30, and her bedroom door was closed. She must still be asleep, he thought. He didn't want to wake her before he left since she was probably tired from switching between day and night shifts so frequently. Cleaning hotel rooms was stable work, but the schedule was anything but predictable in today's market.

His Tupperware of chicken and mashed potatoes was replaced with a Tupperware of scrambled eggs and sausages. Despite his stomach groaning loudly, he felt no hunger pangs whatsoever. He'd trained his stomach to wait until he had overcome the day's most arduous task before it would succumb to eating itself as revenge for his neglect.

Plenty of coffee always helped satiate his metabolism, with the added benefit of kickstarting his brain into wake-up mode. He needed to be on his A-game in front of VanHeller. After all, he was the most senior ranking person in the entire military and effectively the second most powerful person in the country after the grand architect himself, Valter Lucier. The highest-ranking person he'd ever talked to on a semi-regular basis was a lieutenant, with maybe an occasional ass-chewing from a captain or major. In fact, before he talked to Colonel DeThroe on the train, he had never even seen a colonel before.

At precisely 8:00 AM, Victor had just finished his second cup of coffee and heard a knock at the door. A staff sergeant, dressed sharply in formal military attire, stood in the doorway. "Are you Corporal Victor Gates?" He spoke in a thick Southy Boston accent.

"Yes."

"Please hold your sociograft up to this scanner." Once the staff sergeant was satisfied, he lowered the device. "Just needed to be sure. My name is Staff Sergeant Anderson, and I'm one of General VanHeller's assistants assigned to bring you to his office this morning. The sergeant's left side of his face and neck were covered with burn marks that scarred his still chiseled features. Victor looked at the sergeant and, looking beyond the scars, there was something so familiar about him. He was quite certain that he had seen him before, but also sure he had never encountered anyone who had been disfigured like this before. "Please get in the backseat." He motioned to a black SUV parked on the street.

"Are we able to pick up a guest along the way?"

"Whatever you say, corporal. Where does he live?"

Victor was a bit surprised at the sergeant's agreeableness about his short-fuse request. Normally military types would be inclined to call up their superiors if deviating from the plan even slightly. Victor had thought that picking up an additional passenger may have triggered this type of 'mother may I' attitude. Anderson's flippant 'whatever you say, corporal,' was also highly unusual since sergeants outranked corporals and seldom 'did whatever they said.'

Once they reached Innocius' house, Anderson helped carry the wheelchair and Innocius into the SUV. Innocius thanked him for his help, and off they went down route I-95 toward Washington.

Typically, the drive to DC would have been a fairly uneventful three-hour or so trek. Had it not been for the police lights and sirens equipped on Anderson's SUV, it would have taken days just to get out of Philadelphia. People were lighting anything flammable on fire and stealing anything that wasn't bolted down. Several times, he had to swerve violently to avoid hitting protestors and use his car's bullhorn to disperse the crowds. "If you scratch this paint job, I will make you roadkill!"

"Jesus, you Philly boys know how to party, don't you?" Anderson said a few times to the boys in the backseat. "You would think those bombings would've, like, I don't know, brought you all closer together or something. City of brotherly love and all, right?"

Once they were outside the city limits and onto the highways, things started to clear up. And from then on, apart from the occasional act of road rage, it was pretty smooth sailing. Sergeant Anderson and Victor passed the time by arguing over who was going to going to make it into the NFL playoffs this upcoming season. Both Victor and Innocius were, naturally, diehard Eagles fans, and Sergeant Anderson took great enjoyment in getting them riled up. "I wouldn't have taken either of you for Eagles fans, you know that? You're actually kind of nice. All the Eagles fans I've ever met are total jerk-offs. And that coming from a Patriots fan. I'm probably the biggest mass-hole you'll ever meet."

"Mass-hole is short for somebody from Massachusetts who's an asshole," whispered Victor to Innocius.

"Well, apart from my cousin Tommy. But I mean that very affectionately. You two don't know how many people I have to drive that are complete toolbags. They're such big tools that they probably have a couple of little wrenches hanging from their dicks, instead of nuts. Sorry for the visual. I know you Eagles fans have virgin ears. I'm just messing with you. Quit being a couple of pussies."

It was hard not to like Sergeant Anderson after their long car ride, and as it turned out, he and Victor had a lot in common. They both loved football, hated the Jets, and both served in the Army. He had been stationed in the Philippines and Guam for a while and said he loved it there.

"I've never eaten so good in my life. I had three major food groups when I was there: adobo, pancit, and lumpia. And don't even get me started on the women there. Gorgeous," he said. "I didn't see any action in the Pacific, and the Philippines assignment was one of those times the Army gave me some 'free chicken,' the only better job I've ever gotten from them was this one."

As it turned out, Anderson had also been stationed in Haiti for a brief time. "Yeah, I was there…" It seemed like his train of thought had just been T-boned by an even bigger train. He went from lucid and chatty to as rigid as a brick wall.

"You want to talk about it at all, brother?"

"You know, maybe not right now." He took a stab at laughing it off by saying, "I didn't always have this pretty mug, you know? It used to be a lot uglier than this if you could believe it." Leave it to soldiers to make light of their own wounds, thought Victor. He had the good sense not to pursue the topic any further.

The last half-hour or so of the trip was uneventful and relatively quiet, apart from Sergeant Anderson rolling down the window to tell fellow motorists to "fuck yourself" and "suck my dick." They arrived at their destination at around eleven a.m. and were greeted on the sidewalk by another soldier, a female major with a stern expression and her hair done in a tight bun. They said goodbye to Sergeant Anderson, who said, "Oh, don't worry, you'll see me again," and they proceeded up the stairs of a very old and stately-looking building.

"We've been anxiously awaiting your arrival, Corporal Gates," said the major. She looked at Innocius. "And you are?"

"He's my guest," said Victor. "This is Innocius Rios."

"Very well. General VanHeller is expecting you. He's in a very important meeting at the moment, so he asked his Minister of Security to entertain you for a few moments. I will take you to him, his name is…

"Colonel DeThroe, yes, I've met him already, ma'am."

"Very well."

"Welcome to the Hall of The Fourth Branch. We affectionately call it the center of the universe," said the major with a dry laugh. They walked into the atrium of this grand old building with a stained-glass dome on the ceiling and stone columns that would've made Michelangelo blush. Incredibly, the artwork depicted on the stained-glass dome actually appeared to be in constant motion. "Did you know that before this building was repurposed as the headquarters for The Fourth Branch it had previously been the Library of Congress?"

Victor and Innocius nodded as though they were attentive students in class. After all, this factoid was something that was now taught to all grade school kids. Where there had once been bookshelves, there were now rows upon rows of office cubicles and small laboratories manned by diligent members of The Fourth Branch. And where there had been books on walls, there were now portraits of great Americans since the War of the Moderates had occurred. The most conspicuous of these was a large painting of none other than the grand architect himself, Valter Lucier. "The grand architect himself was the one who created the Sentients to enhance the cyberocracy's core programming

- the code. This artificial sentient intelligence is what breaths life into our cyberocracy."

In the labyrinth of cubicles and laboratory spaces, curious workers began poking their heads out to see who was walking by. One by one, fervent whispers of "he's here" and "it's Victor Gates" quickly turned into smiling faces coming out to greet Victor and Innocius. A small gaggle of folks next to a water cooler all burst into applause and shook Victor's hand vigorously as he walked by. Distracted by the waves and backslaps, Victor and a woman in a white lab coat collided with one another, causing her to fall down and the vase she was carrying to shatter.

"Oh dear me," said the woman, picking up the shattered pieces of the vase and the large flowering plant that had been contained in it.

"Dr. Desir, please watch where you're walking. You bumped into our guest, Corporal Gates," said the major.

Victor bent down to help the doctor collect the pieces of the vase. "No, it was my fault." Victor couldn't think of anything to say other than, "That's a lovely flower you have, doctor."

"Thank you…corporal. I should be getting it back into a new vase," said Desir softly.

"Yes, and we must be going. Looks like somebody is popular around here," said the major hurriedly with a smile. "You can't blame them, though. We don't get very many visitors to the Hall of The Fourth Branch, let alone someone as famous as you."

Victor looked over his shoulders to catch one last peak of Desir cleaning up the vase. They walked until they encountered a large marble staircase that started at two different points and converged into one at the second level. Before choosing which side of the staircase they wanted to go up, they were met by a massive inscription chiseled onto the wall directly in front of them. It was the twenty-eighth amendment to the Constitution. Victor had read this many times in school. In fact, in fifth grade, he had to memorize it. Still, he stood for a moment to read from the grand stone tablet in front of him.

28th Amendment: The sentient code, as facilitated by the will and chant of the people and the administration of The Fourth Branch, shall heretofore be the arbiter of decision-making for the federal government of the United States of America. Votes for the annual chant will be tabulated on the third day of the seventh month. Only the people can overturn the results of a previous chant. Congress and the Supreme Court shall, from time to time, inquire into the results of an annual chant by ensuring they are consistent and without error. Congress will appropriate funds for all chant legislation by the fifth day of the seventh month.

Heretofore, the President of the United States is no longer head of government. The office of the president shall retain the official title of Head of State and those powers thereto belonging. The power of the legislature is now vested with the people, and the powers of the executive branch are now vested in The Fourth Branch, led by the grand architect. The grand architect shall administer The Fourth Branch and maintain the sentient code and its infrastructure that facilitates decisions on a quantum level. The sentient code shall decide all cases brought before the Supreme Court. Hail the will of the people, hail the chant, hail The Fourth Branch.

Done in the city of Philadelphia on the twenty-third day of the sixth month in the year 2056.

"It's really something, isn't it? Almost like poetry. Imagine what would happen if we didn't have The Fourth Branch, the code, or the Sentients or any of it?" The reverence in the major's voice was more likely to be found in a church than in a hall of government. And it was hardly poetry. In fact, it was probably the driest bit in the entire Constitution. Though perhaps its poetry comes in the form of single-handedly upending every portion of the document that comes before it.

The major checked her sociograft for the time. "We should be going now." She started walking up the stairs, expecting them to follow.

Innocius looked up at her from his wheelchair, motioning instinctively to the immovable nature of his legs. It took her a few seconds to pick up on his non-verbal queues. "Oh goodness me, like I said, we don't get many visitors. Here, we'll take the elevator right this way."

They entered into an ornate late-nineteenth-century elevator and walked along the curved wall that wrapped around the beautiful rotunda above them. From here, the moving artwork on the stained glass windows of the dome was visible. On the lower edges, it depicted a great battle, complete with men on horseback slaying archers firing arrows into a fierce infantry melee. Around the middle section of the dome was a hazy red cloud that wrapped around the entirety of the rotunda. In the very center was a painting of a winged cherub entering a gate that was being opened by a fierce-looking warrior. Victor was hypnotized by the beauty of this moving feast for the eyes. "What is this meant to be?"

"You know, I'm not actually certain of that myself. I've actually heard a few different interpretations from several people. Some say it depicts the Sentients themselves, and others think that it is some version of the book of Revelation in the bible. And there are a few other explanations, but I apologize. I need to escort you both to Colonel DeThroe's office. I'm afraid I'm running a bit behind."

Down one of the long hallways leading from the center of the rotunda were offices, and the further they walked, the bigger offices became. They got about halfway down when they stopped at one with a large oak door that was propped open. The major knocked on the door, out of politeness, its occupants.

A voice with a thick Southern accent replied, "I will be with you presently, my dear major."

They heard another door in the office slam shut, and shortly afterward, Colonel DeThroe appeared with a broad smile.

"Thank you so kindly, Major Silver, I can look after our guests from here."

She nodded to the boys and hurried down the office the way they came.

"If this isn't the most special treat I've had all day. Not only do I get to catch up with our dear Corporal Gates, but I also get to make an acquaintance with his dear friend, Innocius. Oh, don't worry, I'm not telepathic. Sergeant Anderson informed me of your plus one, Corporal Gates. My ministerial duties dictate that I be kept thoroughly informed of all security-related matters within The Fourth Branch. Thankfully, I don't see any hiccups whatsoever in your friend joining us here today in our humble dwelling place." DeThroe's gaze lingered unbroken on Innocius for a long while and wasn't lifted until Victor interjected.

"Thank you, sir. It's good to see you again," said Victor.

Colonel DeThroe stretched out his hand that had the spider-topped cane into the office, gesturing for them to enter. Despite it being a balmy summer day in July, he was wearing his white overcoat indoors. And he definitely didn't have the AC running in here, thought Victor. All this, and DeThroe wasn't even breaking so much as breaking a sweat. Victor, on the other hand, felt like he just walked into a sauna. It was the same kind of hot that filled the train car on the day that he and Colonel DeThroe first met.

He looked around Colonel DeThroe's grandiose office. The sheer amount of dark mahogany that was so coated in the lacquer that it shined exuded tastefully gaudy overtones. There was a stone fireplace with a stately granite mantle. Hanging above the mantle was a painting of four men riding horses. Victor was so sure he'd seen it somewhere before.

"Are you a lover of the arts, corporal?"

"Uh, well, no, sir, not really. There's just something very familiar about your painting."

"It's really nothing special," he said with feigned modesty. "It's just a few college friends and I playing a spirited game of polo, is all." DeThroe limped over to Victor and rested his weight on his cane. He observed Victor carefully for a moment, then doubled over with uproarious laughter. He slapped Victor hard on the back with his free hand. "I'm just joshing you around, corporal, wanted to see if you still have the finely tuned sense of humor. Apparently not. This here is a painting of the Four Horsemen of the Apocalypse, Revelation Chapter 6, Verse 4: *'Then another horse came out, a fiery red one. Its rider was given the power to take peace from the earth and to make men slay each other. To him was given a large sword.'* That's my favorite one," he said with a grim smile. "You know what they say, 'people need killing.' Though not needlessly so. The four horsemen have a purpose and there is a methodology and a reason for their works."

"I don't fashion myself a Christian, at least not in the typical sense, but I am a great admirer of beautiful things. And this here, corporal, is one of the finest pieces of art that I own, absolutely chock full of spiritualism. And I can declare with great fidelity to you, and you, Mr. Rios, that I am a very spiritual man. New Orleans Voodoo is *my* perfect cup of tea. A splash of Christian dogma with gobfuls of malevolent and benign spirits; simply divine. Now, why don't you boys take a seat here? I'm already eating away too much of your well-earned time." He motioned to two chairs placed in front of his large oak desk. DeThroe's eclectic tastes carried over into the design of the desk—it was crawling with spiders engraved into its turned wood.

Victor tried not to stare too long for fear of being interrogated for it.

"I suppose now is as good as ever to talk business. Cigarette?" He offered one, maybe both of them, a stage from a tin case in his jacket pocket. The boys shook their heads politely. "Suit yourselves. So, corporal, about that transmission that you sent me." He crossed his legs and took a long drag of the cigarette, blowing smoke toward the paneled ceiling. "How about we refresh ourselves with the subject matter." He made a few hand gestures using his sociograft and a spotlight hologram shown down from the ceiling onto his desk. It was the hooded figure that Victor had seen before.

"Victor Gates. Omega has found you. The gift of knowledge of good and evil is now yours—it's your job to decide who is who. In this message, you will find the schematic of the most dangerous device ever devised by man. Within the schematic is a partial program, procured at great cost, to destroy the device. You must find the other part of the code to destroy it. All are watching, and nothing is as it seems. End transmission."

"Sir, how do we even know that it is Omega who sent the transmission? They don't come right out and say, we're Omega, and we found you. They just said that Omega has found you."

"Corporal, we know exactly who sent this message."

"Who?"

"Our cyber forensics team looked this transmission over, and it has your father's metaphorical fingerprints all over it. And that just makes perfect sense. After all, he is the head of the terrorist group known as Omega."

Victor's heart stopped, or at the very least tried to escape through his throat.

"We know he was looking for you. But what we're not sure about is he would risk coming out of the shadows to contact you."

"I…I have no idea, sir."

"I suspected not. The other mystery that we're grappling with is how, precisely, he found you. I have an unusual theory that, somehow, you and Mr. Rios here were the subject of a phenomenon that has only visited several other people in the past. The E.C.H.O. Chamber is a sobering, though usually unremarkable undertaking. For you both, it seems that something…changed when you underwent the neurograft procedure in the E.C.H.O. Chamber. Something rather unforeseen, though not unprecedented. Have both of you boys been feeling well the past few days? Run any fevers or anything peculiar happen that you can't quite explain?"

They both shook their heads, and Victor could not stop thinking of Carmenta. *She was so suspicious when I told her about the transmission. She said 'it worked.' Could she have somehow told Mobius how to find me? That was ridiculous, and there was absolutely no possible way Carmenta could have hacked the E.C.H.O. Chamber and created this anomaly that DeThroe was speaking of.* None of this was making any sense at all. "I couldn't begin to tell you, sir, I just have no idea."

"Of course, you don't, but then why would he ask you, of all people, to destroy it?"

"I sent the transmission to you. Why would I lie now?"

"Oh, is that what you think this is? Corporal Gates, this is not some kind of inquisition! General VanHeller and I called you here so you can help us. You boys are…special to us now. Well, of course, you were special before, but now you are special of a totally different variety. Corporal, do you remember when I asked you if you had Selena in your hand what you would do to that sack of shit traitor?"

"I said being shot would be too good for him…"

"Yes, but it would be so easy for you. You're a killer, Victor. You've killed in the name of a greater cause. And I need you to do it one more time for me. Selena here can go for six rounds without breaking a sweat. She's old-fashioned, but she's had some special cyberkinetic modifications to make her a really nasty bitch. Go ahead and give her a feel. I know you've been eye fucking her since day one." DeThroe slid the six-round revolver to Victor from across the desk, and Victor picked her up by the hand grip.

He opened the cylinder that would house six .45 caliber rounds in its chamber and saw that it was empty. He slides the revolver back to DeThroe. "Looks like she's empty."

"That's what you think, corporal," said DeThroe coyly. He picked up the revolver by the handle, and when he opened up the cylinder, it now revealed six .45 caliber rounds.

"Isn't she a special gal? Like I said, she's had some modifications. Only I can get her to scream if you know what I mean."

The door to the colonel's office flew open, and three men unceremoniously strutted right in, continuing a conversation that must have begun in the hallway. One of the men, who was more than a few years older than the other two, wore a familiar purple blazer with a crisply manicured white beard. It was the same man who he met at the train station and had seen on the stage during the parade. *Congressman Locke.* When he walked into the room, he pulled out a gold pocket watch from his jacket pocket and put his head down toward it. He wasn't checking the time. Instead, he stared directly at Victor, giving him an unmistakable wink.

"Jesus Christ, DeThroe, can you crack a window or something? I feel like I'm in the sixth ring of hell walking into this place. Is this him?" he asked excitedly, striding toward Victor with his black overcoat billowing behind him. Victor recognized the man immediately from all of the pictures and sociograft reels he had seen. His gold embossed undershirt, with an extravagant red silk cravat tie, belied a gaze of fierce determination and ambition. He placed both of his hands on Victor's shoulders and said somberly, "You indeed are a remarkable young man, truly. Your exploits have been told far and wide, and I will continue to sing your praises as America's greatest hero. There would be many sonless mothers if it weren't for you." He corrected himself. "Well, there are indeed many sonless mothers down in Haiti, thanks to you!" The four men all laughed and beamed at Victor while Lucier let go of his grip on Victor's shoulders. "My name is Valter Lucier, I am the Grand Architect of The Fourth Branch."

"I know who you are, sir. It's a great honor to meet you."

"The honor is all mine, I assure you. I believe you've already met our illustrious General VanHeller, but I'd like to introduce you to my greatest political opponent, who today, just so happens to be my best friend. Now, Thomas, don't go reporting me to your oversight committee on some trumped-up charge of trying to 'butter you up.' I'm just trying to be polite. Victor, this is Congressman Thomas Locke."

Locke pretended as though he had never seen Victor. "It's a pleasure to meet you, young man. As the grand architect said, many families owe you an unpayable debt of gratitude. The Congress is at your disposal." Locke extended a hand to Victor, who played along with Locke's charade.

"Honor to meet you, sir," said Victor. He extended his hand, not knowing what kind of game Locke was playing with him.

Immediately after their hands touched, Victor's ears started ringing loudly, and he began convulsing uncontrollably, falling to the floor. Locke attempted to catch Victor's head from crashing onto the ground with some degree of success.

As soon as it started, it felt like it stopped. When Victor woke up, the four men and Innocius were all looking down on him. There was also a Medic in the room now with his aid bag and a jug of water. Congressman Locke helped Victor sit up, and the medic began taking Victor's vital signs.

"Extraordinary," DeThroe whispered quietly while VanHeller and Lucier were speaking to one another in hushed voices.

Locke, on the other hand, looked absolutely petrified and was beside himself. "Dear Lord, Victor, are you alright?"

"Yes. I'm fine," he said with as steady of a voice he could muster. That wasn't even close to being true, though. He felt like his spine was removed from the tailbone to the brainstem and every nerve in between with a set of pliers. Powering through the excruciating pain, he managed to stand up under nearly his own power, with a bit of extra help from DeThroe and Locke. The pain was quickly subsiding, but now Victor had an unexplainable string of numbers and strange symbols streaming endlessly across his mind's eye. He had to focus hard to stay grounded in his present surroundings. Lucier and VanHeller had just finished their hushed murmurs and now shifted their full attention back to Victor.

"He's perfectly fine, Thomas. More than fine, aren't you, son? Probably just a bit too much excitement for one day, am I right? Though perhaps he caught wind of why you were here, Thomas, and feinted from pure astonishment. Why don't you deliver the good news to our newly conscious hero, Thomas? We were going to keep this a secret till the Fourth of July ceremony, but the congressman informed us there is a legal requirement to inform you ahead of time," patronized Lucier.

Locke fumbled through his green coat jacket and produced a crumpled-up bit of paper. He unfolded it hurriedly and adjusted his octagonal glasses to sit below the bridge of his nose. Looking up at Victor, he asked worriedly, "Are you sure you're alright, Victor? That was quite…unusual."

"He's fine, Locke. Now get on with it, please!"

"Very well." He cleared his throat and read from the paper verbatim.

"Attention to Orders: Victor Gates, by recommendation of your Chain of Command and with the endorsement of the Grand

Architect of The Fourth Branch, you are to be awarded the Congressional Medal of Honor for your actions at the Battle of Les Rouge, Haiti on December 24, 2075. The award ceremony shall be held in the City of Philadelphia on July 4, 2076. Will you accept this award by Congress on behalf of a grateful nation?"

The last time Victor was speechless was when he got his tonsils out when he was just a kid, and that was because it was just plain too difficult to speak at all. Maybe he was dreaming all of this. After all, his dreams had been absurdly surreal lately. Although the full-body pain that he had just experienced after shaking Locke's hand told him that this must be real, still, this reality was a very uncomfortable one. "I…I, uh, this is, really. It's really something."

"Such a modest boy," said Lucier. "Victor, you earned this son. It would be the highest honor to bestow such an award on you. Please, will you give me that honor?"

"I…uh, yes, yes, sir. Thank you." The four men and Innocius all broke into a very light applause.

"Wonderful, just wonderful." Lucier beamed. "Thomas, would you mind very much if I spoke to our hero in private for a short while? Just need to coordinate some specifics for the ceremony is all."

"Well, I may be able to help…" stammered Locke.

"Pss, watch this," DeThroe whispered to Victor. That same eerie tune that DeThroe whistled on the train poured from his pursed lips and filled the room. As Locke was carrying on about the arrangements for the Fourth of July he began tugging at his collar and sweating profusely. He fanned himself with some papers on DeThroe's desk and went from lucid to delirious in an instant.

Locke let out a short, dull yell of pain. "Is anyone else terribly warm in here?" He rushed toward the door and opened it while taking off his blazer.

Lucier smirked at DeThroe. "Sorry to see you leave so soon, Thomas. We shan't be long. I will see you momentarily in my office. And if you wouldn't mind taking Mr. Rios with you," said Lucier as he pushed Innocius out the door while ushering Locke out and closing the door behind him. When he left, DeThroe's pursed lips turned up into a devilish smirk.

Lucier breathed a sigh of exasperated relief. "'If you can't take the heat, get out of the kitchen,' I always say. Thomas means well, but he can be a real stick in the mud sometimes. Do you know people like that, Victor? People who either can't or simply refuse to see the grand vision?" He didn't let Victor speak and simply continued, "Sometimes I feel like the only people I can really trust are the ones in this room right now. In fact, the only ones who can ensure the survival of our experiment in cyberocracy are the ones standing in this room right now. That includes you, Victor. In time, you will come to see how very special you really are."

Lucier stared deep into Victor's dark brown eyes with penetrating precision. "Do you know who our enemy is? It's not men with guns, certainly not people with pitchforks and torches. Well, that's not entirely accurate. Sometimes, those folks can be a bit of a problem. Can you take a guess? No?" Lucier smiled a broad, toothless smile.

"Haitians?"

"Haitians, oh heavens no, my boy!" He laughed a hearty chuckle.

"Well, with a few notable exceptions, Grand Architect," interjected VanHeller. "The code derived from the labors of the Sentients and codified in the twenty-eighth amendment will soon be universal, implemented on a global scale. There are precious few hold-outs that remain. Haiti is, of course, one of those notable exceptions."

"Too right, General, but our enemy, Victor, the true enemy, is not even a person. Our enemy is contentment, and it is the most innocuous and insidious of enemies. We must be ever-guarded and vigilant against its sclerotic effects. Let me ask you something, how many people would come out to vote if they felt happy with everything life had to offer them? Forget about voting. If people were completely content with their lives, who would get breast implants or new lawn furniture or those little hoola girl dolls that dance on the dashboard in your car?"

"I'm afraid I don't understand, sir."

Lucier put his hand to his head to ponder a better explanation and bit his lip before continuing. "If they were in a state of constant bliss and enjoyment, how could there be any room for improving our society? We would atrophy, stagnate, become decadent, and wither away. Think about it in military terms, Victor. It's what happened to every great society that we have ever known: Rome, China, Persia. Their fate won't be ours, I assure you. All these bygone empires have one thing in common, decadent contentment. They all had these glorious militaries and they just decided one day to stop playing the game. They stopped being hungry. They were satisfied with their own pathetic little corners. Contentment is a horrible vessel for power to flow through. But when power has a chance to flow through passions like anger, well, then it's like Christmas for everyone."

Lucier reached into the air with his sociograft hand and began performing an intricate movement with his fingers. DeThroe's desk began to deconstruct into small blocks and reformed itself into the shape of a large stone casket. Instead of wood, it now appeared to be gray in color and as hard as a rock, other than some peculiar parts that glowed red and pulsated as though something was burning it.

The four men instinctively moved to the four sides of the rectangular casket, with Victor and Lucier on the short ends facing one another. And as they moved closer to the casket, it glowed brighter. Victor looked down upon the casket, which came up to his lower torso and could see his reflection staring back at him through it. It must be a trick of the light, Victor thought, because clearly, the top of the casket was constructed out of some kind of hard, porous stone. As he stared more intently at his reflection, he realized that it was no mirage and that, somehow, this stone was reflecting his image. What's more, the closer and harder he stared at it, the redder it became.

As Lucier began speaking, the casket continued to appear as though it were burning, though it didn't emanate any heat whatsoever. "We've found a way to calibrate our civilization's greatest passions to the beautiful point of near-constant agitation and make minor tweaks where we deem are necessary. There can be no other way to function. Our cyberocracy needs those passions to always be at a roiling simmer. This," he said, pointing to the casket, "is how we make sure the pot never boils over. The hard part now will be making this miracle of cyberocracy universal, but we are close."

The grand architect lowered his voice to barely a whisper. "We must be careful, Victor. Everyone is watching. And there are those who would see this great experiment in cyberocracy shuttered and torn asunder. We're within arm's reach of achieving something that no civilization has ever done. A true global order."

Lucier smiled at Victor. "We need young blood and a fresh platform to do the things we will soon need to do, Corporal Gates. The American public will rally behind their newest hero." He leaned in even closer to Victor, put his arm around his shoulder, and directed him to the stone casket glowing shades of red. "This is why the neurograft mandate is so very important, Victor, and it's also why we must guard ourselves against the misdeeds who seek to destroy this perfect order. People think that it is mind control because they are small-minded fools. It's so much more than that, it is an art form, and it is understanding intentions, emotions, and fears. Only through the neurograft infrastructure can we ever hope to achieve the optimal level of global governance that we need. Imagine a world where we *knew* the emotions of our society at any given moment. The neurograft will allow the Sentients to understand, not only the will of the people but also their *deepest* fears and desires."

With a flick of his wrist, a large holograph of the globe appeared above the casket. Small red dots speckled the Earth wherever there was a land mass and were connected by a thin red line. The largest dot was where Philadelphia is located. There were notable spots where there was no dot, such as where Haiti is located in the Caribbean.

Victor moved closer to the globe. "What are those?"

The red glow from this web of red nodes reflected in Lucier's dark eyes. "The cyberocracy's network comprising the seven E.C.H.O. Chambers scattered all over the world, and these little E.C.H.O. Boosters allow us to keep tabs on the theta wave levels. So before the kettle boils over, we always hear the whistle first."

VanHeller waved his hand and two shrouded figures appeared below the globe and supported it with outstretched arms. "This whole system allows the ecosystem of the cyberocracy to flourish precisely how it was intended. The people are the true governors of the nation. And the Sentients can sense when the public wants something brought to a chant vote. Without the neurograft mandate, they are forced to rely on secondhand data injects. But with the mandate, we give the Sentients a true sixth sense. It's *crucial* that the mandate passes. Our foes are many, but there can be no unforeseen interference in the passing of the mandate."

DeThroe motioned in the air with his sociograft hand, and the casket reconfigured itself once more. "Only you can get close to our vigilante without peaking his suspicion. It's why we need your help now." A strange-looking object emerged from where the desk had been, appearing to float soundlessly under its own power. It was the balloon-shaped object from the Omega schematic, but in real life, it looked more like a silver teardrop. "This is the 'most dangerous device devised by mankind.'"

Victor recognized it now as the device from the Omega transmission. "Sir, that is the device that Omega sent me the specification for."

"Yes, it would seem that our enemy has gotten hold of the specifications for this device to destroy, duplicate, or hijack." He stood up from his chair, and out of respect, Victor did the same. He came around the object to stand within inches of Victor. "Will you help us?"

"It would be an honor, sir," said Victor without hesitation, and for the briefest of moments, he thought he saw embers emanating from the device. If Lucier, VanHeller, and DeThroe saw the same apparition, Victor couldn't be sure, though for some reason, though looked at each other with the giddiness of a child finding candy in their pocket.

"Your path will be full of challenges, Victor, but also full of great rewards," said Lucier triumphantly. "I would like to use my powers as Grand Architect to welcome Corporal Gates to our special little club." Lucier made another odd motion with his left hand, and the device transfigured itself back into the burning casket. "Step forward, son. Hold your hand out above it."

Victor did as he was told. The instant he did, his sociograft hand was enveloped by the casket, which burned brightly with a fiery red glow along with Victor's neurograft.

"There you are, a new man, as they would say," Lucier said with a twisted smile. "This will help you channel your very special gifts. I dare say they will come in handy on the Fourth of July. Suffice to say, it will be a bloody good time!"

Lucier turned to VanHeller. "We should leave these two to it, General." Before Lucier and VanHeller reached the door, Lucier smacked his head dramatically and turned back to Victor. "I almost forgot! You know they had asked me to throw the first pitch at the Phillies game on the Fourth of July? Well, the grand architect may be a God at taming artificial intelligence, but I am but a mere mortal when it comes to sports. Not to mention, I think the people would much rather see this visage of vitality and heroism before me here. What say you, Victor? Will you be my champion on the field of friendly strife?"

"I played third base in high school, sir, I won't let you down."

"That, my boy! Colonel, make sure you show him the ropes with his new abilities." Lucier left the room humming "Take Me Out to the Ball Game," with VanHeller in tote, leaving the colonel to impart some important instructions to his new partner. Victor saw Locke and Innocius peering through the doors at him until DeThroe shut them again with a wave of his sociograft. This door may have been closed, but Victor knew that so many more had just opened for him.

"As it turns out, you really are quite special. Let's talk about what you can do for us and go over a few ground rules, too.

11

Madam Vixama's House of Voodoo

T he last week in June came and went faster than a power circuit race. Less breakneck twists and turns, yet still fast and furious. You couldn't swing a cat anywhere in Philly without hitting at least a handful of tri-centennial party goers getting into the patriotic groove of the holiday. The grand architect, along with the mayor of Philadelphia, had declared the entire week leading up to Independence Day to be a "Week of National Celebration." For a very brief time, it seemed as though the whole city was trying to forget the horrific bombings that had just occurred one week before.

The stars and stripes were flown on every street and outside of nearly every home. People would dress in flag-themed clothes from head to toe, undergarments included, and the streets were filled with every imaginable form of Americana-flavored music there is. People even seemed to hate each other just a little bit less for the time being. Victor had noticed an appreciable downturn in the number of cyberduels that would occur spontaneously. However, after it was announced that a militant Haitian spinoff of Omega was responsible for last week's attack, there were multiple beatings of Haitians reported by the news.

Victor had gotten used to at least one group of people being intensely hated by the rest of the country at any given time. Eli had always said that it was as 'American as apple pie.' However, it hit much harder when that particular group that was being singled out now was of your heritage. Both Victor's and Innocius' mothers were Haitian, and many people he knew growing up, like Ollie, were also Haitians.

Violence against Haitians aside, the apparent uptick of goodwill was likely owed, in large part, to the brigade of grill masters who showed up in the most unlikely of places at all hours of the day and night. Leading up to the Fourth of July festivities, the normally mean streets of Philly wafted with the smell of thousands upon thousands of grills firing up the most delicious BBQ you would ever taste. These savory aromas not only caused bellies to grumble with delight but also had the added effect of curbing the frenzy caused by Omega's cryptic message about the upcoming chant. On the surface, everyone was doing their best to enjoy the patriotic festivities, but underneath it all, there was a deep reservoir of fear.

Victor hadn't seen Rocky or Eli since the bombings. And Mr. Rizal put Rocky on lockdown at the workshop for some reason. Eli hadn't even stopped by the house once for breakfast, which was very unusual. He had always found some time between his shifts to stop in for a quick bite. But with the upcoming holiday festivities, and especially after the bombings, the city needed a round-the-clock police presence everywhere. Carmenta had grown all too willing to indulge her 'second son' and always made sure she made a few extra eggs and sausages just in case Eli stopped by. Though since he wasn't a regular anymore, she was absolutely thrilled when Innocius started coming around for breakfast. To try to patch things up with his mom, he did what every man who faces a problem they can't solve, suck it up and don't ever let them see you bleed. That and inviting Abiana for dinner one night, along with her bubbly personality, may have helped Victor repair a damaged bridge between him and his mom.

Victor woke up on the first day in July, finally feeling like things were starting to become a little more normal, never mind the fact that he now had a secret mission that may very well prevent a complete calamity from befalling his city. He'd finally gotten a decent night's sleep and was used to that particular kind of pressure anyway. No, the pain he felt now was physical, presumably the after-effects of his strange encounter with Thomas Locke during his visit to The Fourth Branch. Ever since then, he'd been waking up with these God-awful headaches. That wasn't the worst of it, though. Throughout the day, he would see a stream of unintelligible symbols and numbers streaming through his mind's eye. It would always end in the same three digits, "1-8-7." He knew this was the same gibberish that he experienced the moment he touched Locke's hand. He saw this vision most clearly right after he woke up. The other peculiarity he was now having to contend with, albeit a much more welcome one, was the ability to manipulate any bit of tech that had a Lucier Corps chip in it. It wasn't as easy as snapping your fingers to make something happen, though. After DeThroe gave him a crash course in how to use what he called 'theta cyberkinesis,' the best he was able to do was make his bedroom light flicker for a bit.

This morning, like most other mornings, he didn't have the brain power for "1-8-7" riddles or cyberkinetic mumbo jumbo at all. He slept like crap, and until he had his first cup of coffee, he was lucky if he remembered what his own name was. Thankfully, his mom had already made a fresh pot before she had to go in to work to cover somebody else's shift last minute. She didn't have much time to cook, but what she did make was also Victor's favorite. He called it 'Carmenta's kitchen sink,' a delicious mix of whatever meat was in the fridge, tater tots, eggs, and bread all mashed together in a pan and fried to perfection. Victor gulped down a few swigs of coffee and dished himself this Fair Heights delicacy.

He checked his sociograft feed for some updates, only to find this morning to be an uneventful one. The only things that were even remotely newsworthy were a series of power outages along the East Coast and that Philadelphia Mayor Goldie had declared the Fourth of July a Day of Brotherly Love. He asked for the normal things that politicians do when they make such grandiose proclamations: don't litter, be nice to everyone, enjoy the speeches and parades. However, there was one special request that he made that was quite unusual.

"Philadelphia's star will burn the brightest on our three hundredth Independence Day, folks, and we all expect everyone to behave themselves. Though, in light of recent events." Victor turned up the volume on his sociograft at this point. "In light of recent tragic events here in the cradle of our nation, we know that, unfortunately, there are some bad actors out there. These folks are sub-human scum, and I would cyberduel the shit out of them if given the chance. I'd curb stomp every last…" Victor could see one of Mayor Goldie's aides poke him in his golden colored blazer during the transmission to get him back on-message. "Well, you know what I mean. In light of that, I have decided that all children will need to stay off the streets during the parades and streetside festivities that are planned."

There was an audible exasperation and fevered murmurs at the venue where the mayor was announcing this.

"Folks, folks, please! As I said, no children under the age of eighteen are to be permitted in the streets during the time of the planned celebrations. We have arranged for school-aged children to watch celebrations on a live stream to be viewed in the safety of their school auditoriums."

There were no more gasps and a flurry of requests for questions coming from the reporters present. The mayor was starting to lose control of the rowdy crowd assembled before him. "The school staff will have a host of fun activities for the children to do…ladies and gentlemen, please, I'm going to need everyone to calm…just calm the hell down, please!"

At that, the transmission cut out. Just when it was starting to get good, he thought. Though, his amusement at Mayor Goldie getting worked up during a press conference that was supposed to calm people down quickly faded away. Victor understood that the only way the mayor would make such a hasty and unpopular decision would be because he had a credible reason to do so. He hoped he was wrong, but the tingly feeling running down his shoulders told him that this was a genuine concern.

Victor heard a light 'ping' sound coming from the front door. It didn't sound like a knock. It was more like someone was flicking the door with the tip of their finger. Victor opened the door to find Innocius sitting on the street holding a pebble and winding up to let it rip. He let out a chuckle. "I was wondering what that racket was!"

"Well, I kept yelling for you, but I guess you didn't hear me."

"Yeah, I was watching the news. Do you want to come in for some breakfast? You probably owe me a paint job on the door, by the way!

"Okay…okay to breakfast, not to painting!"

Victor helped Innocius in and made him a plate of 'Carmenta's kitchen sink,' which he seemed to inhale after just a few minutes. "I told you I was hungry! Are your headaches getting any better?" he said between chews.

"No, not really. They kind of come in waves, though. Usually, they're worse when I just wake up, which is shitty because ever since I've gotten back home, I hardly sleep worth a shit."

"What about those numbers you keep seeing. Still not making any sense?"

Victor saw them stream across his mind's eye again and disappear as fast as they came. "No, I still see them, and it's all just a bunch of gibberish. However, I can't shake the feeling that it was because I shook Locke's hand that I started seizing up the way I did. I know that sounds weird, but nothing else makes sense at this point."

"I think that actually makes a lot of sense," said Innocius curiously. "Don't you remember when you beat up those boys in the street the night that we met? You grabbed my hand to help me up, and we both got that…funny feeling."

Victor leaned back in his chair and took a finishing swig from his coffee mug. He looked around and whispered to Innocius, "DeThroe told me something strange last week. I don't think I should talk about it because it has to do with the mission they gave me, but there was one thing that I thought was a little off. He specifically told me not to make any physical contact with, you know, the terrorist." Victor had begun to refer to his father as 'the terrorist' or 'him' rather than anything remotely considered a term of endearment. "And he said under absolutely no circumstances should I shake his hand."

Innocius looked at Victor's hands with a fake dramatic expression. He slowly slid his hand toward Victor's, grabbed them, and started convulsing unconvincingly.

"Knock it off, you dweeb." Victor laughed.

"Well, here I was thinking you were going to have to get your hands licensed as deadly weapons or something." Victor chucked a tater tot left in his bowel at Innocius.

When they had both finished with their fits of laughter, Innocius asked, "How about you stop by my mom's shop later today?"

"Yeah, okay. Does she need help at all?"

"No, well, I'm heading over there to help, but she might be able to help you out?"

"You can't cure ugly," said Victor with a smile. "Is she going to cast a spell on me or maybe make a voodoo doll out of that Omega drone?"

"Sometimes she helps people who are going through some bad stuff and who have…pain."

"You're acting like I just got hit by a truck or something, kid, I'm fine."

"Well, you did just get back from a war, and you got rocked pretty hard by last week's bombing. Victor, you didn't even go to the hospital!"

"I don't know kid."

"You're not sleeping well, you're getting bad headaches, you're starting to…see things. You've been through a lot, Victor, more than anybody should have to."

"I'm not an invalid. I'm *fine*."

"Abiana will be there!"

Victor smirked and nudged Innocius playfully. "You two are getting pretty close, huh?"

"What, no way! She's *your* girlfriend," he said defensively. "But she's stopped at my mom's shop a few times now. She's bought some jewelry and some artwork there. I think Rocky is coming around, too."

"Abiana buying jewelry, was it made out of hardware from a hot rod?" Innocius folded his arms and rolled his eyes in his best attempt at indignation.

"You're not taking this seriously."

"Alright, alright! I'm just messing around, okay? I'll be around later this afternoon. I need to do some things around the house here, but let me walk you home first." Victor thought it best to make sure that Innocius got home safe. Fair Heights was the mecca of Caribbean American immigrants, and with all the anti-Haitian bullshit going on now, he didn't want to take any chances with the kid getting roughed up. He somehow managed to attract that all by himself with no added help. After dropping him off, Victor got back home and went straight to all the things he needed to do for the day, nap time.

* * *

Victor had decided to sleep on the couch in the living room since it wasn't so hot on the first floor. He woke up with the late afternoon sun in his eyes and groaned after he checked his sociograft for the time. *4:00 PM already? Jesus.*

Carmenta had made him a sandwich that she left in Tupperware on the kitchen counter with another note, *"I hope you had good dreams, baby. I love you!"* He was starved from skipping lunch and polished off the sandwich like it was the last one on Earth. Once he finished, he put a pair of shoes on and started walking. The hot afternoon air was still thick and oppressive, but afternoon shadows had already started to creep from the rows of townhouses, creating some cooler spaces to walk in. Victor groggily walked in a bit of a daze for the first few minutes, still trying to fully wake up after his long afternoon nap.

He hadn't been to Vixama's shop yet, but he knew where it was. Before he left on his deployment her shop used to be a convenience store that also sold some Haitian bread and meat patties. Even though it was a bit of a far walk, around thirty minutes from his house, it was a familiar one since it was right across the street from James Wilson High School. This was the last public high school still left in Philly, where Victor went to high school and where Innocius was now a freshman. On the way to the store, Victor dodged a group of kids who had games of stickball going and another who opened up fire hydrants to stay cool in the summer heat. He and his friends used to do the same. The best part was running from the cops if they were in a pissy mood and decided to break up the fun.

The street corner up ahead was deserted, except for one hooded bystander who had their hands in their hoodie pocket. It was way too hot to be wearing a hoodie. *Only someone who didn't want to be recognized would be wearing something like that on the hottest part of the day.* Victor approached the corner and kept his distance from the hooded figure whose back was turned to him. Without any warning, the stranger swung a crowbar at Victor's head who grabbed the bar mid-swing, spun the assailant around, and held him in a chokehold.

Victor unhooded a scared looking punk kid. "What the hell is wrong with you kid?" He tossed the crowbar to the ground. "You could've killed me with that thing."

The boy broke free of Victor's chokehold, and turned to him, panting with tears rolling down his cheeks. "You're the one who's done the most killing out of everyone on this street," he said with a thick Haitian accent. "You're a traitor to your own people, you four-head piece of shit!"

Victor moved closer to the boy and recognized him as one of Big-T's thugs who tried to jump Innocius and him a few weeks ago. *"You're* one to talk," he said sarcastically. "You just tried to kill me, and God only knows what you would've done to my friend if I hadn't been there."

"Omega doesn't want your friend. They want you. And when they have you, you'll be dead!" The boy shoved Victor and took off like a bolt of lightning in the other direction.

Victor stood on the corner for a moment, utterly stunned by what had just occurred. He couldn't shake the feeling that those thugs were after him, and not Innocius on that night after they walked back from the E.C.H.O. Chamber.

This uneasy feeling remained with him, until he arrived at the city block where James Wilson Highschool was. This is where he became good friends with Rocky and Eli and where he started crushing hard on Abiana. He also got more black eyes and broken ribs than he could count. One of them had hurt so bad that he had a phantom pain in his chest just thinking about it. This was where he came into his own, though, and that's something he wouldn't have traded for the world.

When he finally arrived at Vixama's store, he looked around as if he may have made a wrong turn somewhere. This was the right place, but it looked absolutely nothing like the old corner store he remembered. That store was run down and graffiti covered. Its cheap neon sign had multiple letters that no longer lit up. There were rusty pipes, carrying God knows what, strung all over the brick exterior of the building, and there were trash cans everywhere. Victor didn't know the previous owner, but apparently, he had gotten into some legal problems and had to leave in a hurry. One day, the store was stocked from floor to ceiling with food goods, and the next, there wasn't so much as a candy wrapper in it.

Saying that the corner store had taken on a new life was a gross understatement. The brick walls with rusty pipes were now painted into beautiful murals of colorful and intricate symbols that looked like they belonged in a museum. Creeping vines in planters covered the blank spaces where the murals ended. And a metallic sign in the shape of a wolf hung from a rod above the front door. It was embossed with "Madam Vixama's House of Voodoo" and "Readings Available Within," written in small print. There wasn't an ounce of shabbiness to this now stunning exterior; it was warm and inviting, with just the right amount of weirdness in all the right places.

The only thing that looked a little out of place was an old man sitting next to the entrance to the store on a bench. He looked like he could have been from Philadelphia but also from elsewhere. He dressed in shabby clothes and had his cane propped up against the bench. He was smoking a pipe from underneath a broad-brimmed straw hat that veiled most of his face. As Victor passed him to walk up to the door, he gave the old man a nod of respect which he seemed to reciprocate despite his eyes being hidden from under the hat. Just as he put his fist up to the door to knock, it opened, and Eli greeted his expression of surprise with, "Madam Vixama said you'd be here at exactly four-thirty-three PM. And can you believe it, that's when your ass showed up."

"Are you serious?" asked Victor, now both surprised and a bit stunned.

"No, of course not you twit. I saw you walking from the window." He grabbed Victor across the threshold into the shop. "You do know how late you are, right? I've got places to protect and people to serve," he said sarcastically. Before closing the door, he motioned with his chin. "Oi, didn't I pull some burly-looking fuck trying to put his boot up your ass right there?"

Victor looked across the street to the high school's front lawn. "Good thing you did. That guy almost destroyed me." Victor looked out the door. "Hey, I don't think we should leave that old guy sitting out front by himself. He looks pretty frail. Some dumb kid might try to rough him up."

Eli peered out the door. "What old man are you talking about, mate?" Now Victor looked out the door, too.

"What the hell, he was there a second ago. Sorry, I'm late, though, man. Didn't get much shut-eye last night."

"It shows. They've got all kinds of fuckery planned for you in there. If I were you, I would just go in for a CAT scan and get a proper head check, but that's just me. How've you been a hero?"

"At least I'm not in the Jungle Gym."

"That bad, huh? Come on in. We've been waiting for you."

Eli walked to the back of the shop, and Victor followed slowly, taking in the shop's eclectically macabre ambiance. This definitely isn't a quickie-mart anymore, he thought. A thick emerald curtain covered the windows. Candles from chandeliers and wall sconces cast a dim light, creating an intimate mystique. Some were burning incense, causing a perfumed cloud to waft throughout the room. Every inch of wall and table space was covered with the oddest assortment of merchandise Victor had ever seen. Eli couldn't stop tripping over stacks of books and credenzas where jewelry and incense in small glass bottles were stacked to eye level.

"Fucking hell!"

Skulls, masks, colorful paintings, and crucifixes hung on the walls, while menacing gargoyle eyes seemed to follow Victor as he walked. Animal statues, dolls, and books sat on fine wooden bookshelves placed between the patches of the wall where there was no merchandise hanging.

Eli limped over to the far corner of the shop where Vixama was seated at a small table in a jade green poof chair. She was shuffling Tarot cards in a deck and placing them on the table.

"Hi, Mrs. Rios. Good to see you again."

"Welcome, Victor. Innocius has told me that you are not feeling well. Is this true?"

"Well, no. I'm doing fine, er, mainly just feel tired a lot. Got a bit of a headache. Pretty normal stuff, though."

"Let's cut through the bullshit, Victor," she said matter-of-factly, laying down a few Tarot cards in a row on the table. "You have sustained traumatic injuries from the warfare you engaged in. War is unnatural. An abomination of the soul. I fear though, now, it is as commonplace as a stroll in the park. You have both experienced war, yes?" Her eyes darted between Eli and Victor, who both nodded. "Eli, how did you get better when you returned?"

"I didn't. I drowned myself in a bottle, was on drugs, my dog died, and then I got a divorce. Thought about ending it all for a while. It's been shit, really." Victor, who had never heard so much negativity from Eli about his own experiences before, started to feel tears welling. Eli saw Victor's discomfort and composed himself. "But I got through it, mate. We all do. I focused on what matters in life, like Jacky and you, and a few of those twits in the next room. That's what matters, and that's what you have to hold on to. Everything else is just noise, you hear? I was in a big hole, mate, and it took me a long time to turn my life around. I never turned to anyone to get help. And I'm going to tell you, we're not going to let that happen to you. Even if you say you don't need help, I'll drag you to it kicking and screaming if I have to, got it?"

Victor nodded, and Madam Vixama stared intently at the tarot cards laid on the table. "Ah. I know what you need." She turned around, grabbed a glass incense burner, and poured in a colorful mix of spices then lit it with a match. "Here," she said, wafting the fumes toward him. "Breath. Breathe deeply."

Victor did as he was told and took several lungfuls of the sweet fragrance.

"How does your head feel now?" said Vixama.

Victor raised his eyebrows in surprise. "Better. Wow. Is there crushed Advil in that bowl?"

She ignored his stab at humor. "Victor, for your body to heal, your mind has to heal. And for your mind to heal, your soul must heal. The Loa, or this spirits, can guide us in the path to healing." At this, Eli made a disapproving grunting noise and tried to mask it by clearing his throat—just making it worse. "Is there something wrong? Are you sick in the body or mind?"

"Well, neither. Or, well, both probably, if I'm being honest, I suppose. It's just I don't believe in all this Voodoo mambo-jumbo."

"I see you wear the crucifix of Christ. You don't know much about Voodoo, do you? I think you and I are more alike than different. Just as Voodoo and Christianity are more alike than you realize. They say that Voodoo is thirty percent Catholic, thirty percent Protestant, and one hundred percent Voodoo. For us, the Loa are like guides."

"Angels, you mean," said Eli.

"Sort of, but not really. They are divine spirits that can help us.

However, they are not always right, and they are not always good either. The spirits that I call upon the most are Erzulie Freda and Erzulie Dantor. They are the spirits of Love and Protection and are considered sisters in Haitian Vodou. One is unpredictable and powerful, and the other is fiercely loving. Like a mother. We sometimes are all these things, are we not? And though they may be at odds with one another, they can always be reconciled. When we allow them to be reconciled within us, then we find that they are not at odds with one another but reinforce each other. Your friends are waiting for us in the reading room, shall we?"

She opened a door behind her that led to a smaller room where Innocius, Abiana, Rocky, and a girl he had never met before were all seated around a circular table. They all greeted him with cheers and smiles as he, Vixama, and Eli took seats at the table. The room was dimly lit by candles and windowless. The intense smell of incense, coupled with the lack of ventilation, was already making Victor light-headed. The feeling was surprisingly relaxing. He just felt very loose and dreamy.

When he entered the room, his friends were already well into a spirited Tarot card reading by the girl he didn't recognize. She was a little younger looking than Victor and wore a colorful traditional Karabela dress with a twisted jade headband that pushed back her black hair to reveal alluring brown eyes. Perhaps Eli noticed him paying her just a bit too much attention and gave him a sharp elbow to the ribs. Sitting on the other side of him was Innocius who whispered. "That's my older sister, Somera."

"Oh, okay, good to know," said Victor. He was seated next to Rocky and noticed a strange-looking device with two antennas in front of him on the table. "Hey man, what's that thing?"

"It's a Theta Wave Detector," said Rocky as though it were obvious.

"Rocky says there's an insane amount of 'Theta' in my mom's shop.

I still don't really get what it is," said Innocius.

"Check this out," said Rocky, turning on the device that hummed to life. The needle jumped all the way to the right side of the gauge. "See, this measures the amount of theta particulate, and it is off the charts. I've never seen anything like it! When Innocius sent me the address for the shop, my jaw dropped. Remember when we looked at the E.C.H.O. Booster and saw all that anomaly of energy build-up? It was coming from this exact spot, and it still is. I've never seen anything like it. If I didn't know any better, I'd say it had something to do with all this voodoo stuff."

"Who says it doesn't? Shall we continue," said Somera slowly. She gave Rocky and Eli readings, and when she did, it was in the most tender of voices. It was so melodic and hypnotizing that Victor was paying much more attention to Somera than to her interpretation of the cards. Evidently, and according to the cards, Rocky needed to break the chains that bound him, and Eli should definitely avoid eating spinach for at least the next six months.

Abiana's card had a picture of a chariot on fire, and riding atop it were a man and a woman who were both completely unclothed. Somera smiled wide before saying, "Oftentimes, there is a spiritual interpretation to these cards, and other times, the meaning can be quite…sexual. In the case of this card, it has a very, uh, specific sexual interpretation. It says that you will dominate someone while riding on some type of transportation." At this reading, though probably more from Somera's bashfully modest demeanor, everyone burst out laughing. Even Madam Vixama, who seemed to always maintain a stern countenance, couldn't help but crack a smile.

Abiana didn't even attempt to hold back her laughter and could hardly string three words together. "So you're saying…I'm going to… fuck on a bus?" The whole room laughed even louder. "Oh God…this is too much," she said, wiping joyful tears off her cheeks. "Oh, this is so inappropriate, I love it. You next, Vicky!"

At this, Madam Vixama took the deck of cards from Somera, who left the room, likely to regain some composure. "Let us be calm and allow the Loa's presence to wash over us." She spoke with the same tenderness as Somera though with much greater authority. She shuffled them several times in her hands and told Victor, "Breathe deeply and close your eyes. I want you to focus. Focus on your intention, but allow the Loa to guide you." Victor inhaled thick, perfume-laced air. He did this a few times until Vixama told him, "Stop, now open your eyes. And pick a card from the deck." Victor reached out to grab the card and turned it over right side up on the table to reveal a spider in its web.

She couldn't hide her immense intrigue as she picked up the card to examine it. "Normally, if there were not multiple people in the room, I would tell you that this is a sign of danger. That you will be caught, and like a fly in a web, not in a very pleasant way. However," she raised herself upright in her chair, "there are six people in this room. The rarest spiders are those with six eyes. The Tiphereth is the sixth branch and at the center of the kabbalistic tree of life. It is the gateway to other worlds and to a harmonic balance that we all seek. Most spiders have eight legs, just as there are eight paths, or journeys, to the Tiphereth at the center of the tree. I can feel passion, fire, and anger in your spirit. You will be given a choice, Victor. You can either journey along the spider's web to unlock this balance, or you can burn it and watch everyone fall. Only you can take the journey, only you can see the gate, and only you can open it."

"You have the sight, Victor." Vixama suddenly grabbed Victor by the hands and he collapsed in his chair, with his head swinging backward to reveal his eyes rolling.

Victor felt like he had been sucked into a vacuum that pulled him from the reading room where his friends were to a dark and tranquil place. His ears rang loudly and he could see the discombobulated numbers and symbols that he first saw when he saw in DeThroe's office, clear as day. They appeared to him now in vivid detail, so vivid it felt that he could reach out and touch him. He noticed that there were spots between the symbols that looked empty, as though letters were missing from a word. He still had no idea what they all meant, but now that he could see them clearly it was evident that they were identical in shape and syntax to the symbols that he saw from the Omega transmission. When this revelation occurred to him that they may be the same, the 'empty' spots between the letters began to fill themselves in. "Wow," he whispered to his subconscious self.

He reached out to touch the symbols, and when he did, they all came crashing to the floor as though they were made of glass. In their place appeared the numbers 1-8-7, red and quivering as though someone was shaking them. He heard a footstep behind him and turned to see Thomas Locke by his side. Locke walked over to him, put his hand on his shoulder, and said, "Protect the boy."

When Victor awoke in the reading room, he was still in the same chair he was sitting in, but now Somera and Eli were holding onto his legs. The lights were flickering, and they both looked as if they'd seen a ghost.

"Why are you looking at me like that," he said in a daze.

"You started shaking," said Somera, herself shaking a bit.

"Yeah, mate. We thought you were going to slip right off the end of the chair."

Vixama came into the reading room with a cold towel, a glass of water, and some incense. "I'm alright, just have a bit of a headache, that's all," said Victor.

"They all do after they have the vision," said Vixama as she placed the cold towel on Victor's head. "Though I can't remember any reading where my lights started to flicker."

"You think I had a vision?"

"Where are your brains, boy? What else could it be?" she said, forcing some wafting incense into his nostrils and putting the glass of water up to his lips. "It's a good thing you are so handsome. Drink." The bell at the front desk chimed, and Vixama left to tend to her customer, leaving everyone in the reading room to stare blankly at Victor.

"What's the deal, guys?" he asked them, trying to break them out of their gazing stupor. They all flinched except Eli.

"Yeah, Victor, *what the fuck* is the deal?" he said.

"What are you talking about?"

"Listen, you twat, I don't believe in all this mumbo jumbo, no offense Somera, but I know when you're scared shitless. I know you didn't have a 'vision,' but I know you saw something. Tell us."

"I'm not scared. I just can't explain what I saw…"

"Can you start from the beginning?" asked Somera softly.

Victor cleared his throat and began telling them about the Omega transmission, the device, the symbols he saw, and the strange dreams he has but can never remember when he awakens. He told them about how when he shook Locke's hand, he started seeing numbers and symbols and that he now just realized that when the symbols he saw from Omega and Locke were combined, they formed a complete list. Finally, he told them about how Locke, or his imagination of Locke, had told him, "Protect the boy."

"Who's the boy?" asked Somera. Victor's eyes, along with everyone else's, began to settle on Innocius.

"Do you think Locke is in on it?" snapped Abiana. "I told you, Victor, he's a scumbag, trying to drag us back to what things were like before the cyberocracy."

"Why would he, though? He's the one who is saying to 'protect the boy.' Doesn't exactly sound like a bad guy to me," said Victor.

"What the hell do you think one hundred eighty-seven could mean?"

asked Eli. They all pondered for a moment, but none of them could come up with a reasonable explanation beyond it being the name of an old movie made in the 1990s.

"What about those symbols?" asked Victor. "I feel like I've solved some kind of puzzle, but I'm nowhere closer to knowing what it looks like than when I started. When I had…the episode a few minutes ago, it's like the symbols from the Omega transmission filled in the spaces to the ones I saw when I shook Locke's hand."

"What did the symbols look like?" asked Rocky. Victor used an app on his sociograft to draw a hologram of what a few of them looked like. "I've seen those before. They're a programming language and one that not many people know, not even my dad."

"But you've seen them before," said Victor.

"Yeah, I have, but there's a lot of mystery around it, Victor. I even told my dad that some people think it's an alien language, and he just laughed. Most believe it's the language of the 'Sentients.'"

"The Sentients?" murmured more than one person in the room.

"They write the code that governs the cyberocracy, and The Fourth Branch is there to just make sure they have what they need to do their job. The code is the language of the Sentients, what did you think they spoke English?" Rocky laughed a loud, snorty kind of laugh and saw that no one else was reciprocating. "Well, of course, it speaks English. It is kind of all-knowing. But to get it to do things, you have to speak its language, right? Like getting an old-school computer to follow your commands. You need to have the right programming language to speak to it. The code is how the Sentients speak to us. And judging by the looks on your faces, you guys have no idea what I'm talking about."

"It must have something to do with the device…" Victor thought back to the Omega transmission. "Of course! The Omega transmission said that I would need to find the other half of the code. The Locke code is the other half! And it said that it could be used to destroy the device..."

"At the end of the day, it's just the code, Victor. The language would need hardware, a vessel, to actually manifest. You wouldn't be able to upload the programming just by thinking about it. He flesh and blood, not a machine." He snorted loudly again.

The cogs in everyone's minds began getting gunked up by the late hour and the now stale smell of incense in the room. Half of them began bickering about how absurd a notion all of this sounded, and the other half thought that a giant conspiracy was afoot. Undoubtedly, if Madam Vixama were in the room she would suggest that all these happenings were the result of some arcane battle being waged by spirits in some magical realm. Victor chuckled to himself. *If only I did have a bit of magic.* He couldn't stop staring at the light above the table while the rowdy bunch around him continued to string wild theories.

"Magic," he whispered. He stood up, still looking intently at the light, and when he did, the spectators began to hush. He reached his hand up and began focusing intently on the chandelier above him. It started flickering and, after a moment, extinguished its light entirely.

"Cyberkinesis," whispered Rocky. "Holy shit Victor!"

Victor relaxed his concentration on the chandelier, and the lights popped back on. "DeThroe's plan is for me to meet with Omega and deliver the device to them."

Abiana gasped. "Victor, that's so dangerous."

"They'll never actually get it. DeThroe chose the rendezvous point, and his plan is to bait them with the device, bring the cavalry in, and arrest every Omega drone they can get their hands on."

"For once, I agree with this she-devil. You're talking about that VanHeller goon that is always dressed in white?" asked Eli with raised eyebrows. "Victor, how many times do I have to tell you not to trust anybody who only wears white?"

"There is military man that comes into the shop sometimes," said Vixama strolling back into the reading room. "He's dressed all in white and has a cane with a spider topper on it."

"You and he have a lot in common, Victor," said Vixama as he walked past. "I am quite sure he would also draw the spider card if given a reading."

DeThroe.

12

In Good Hands

Eli insisted on driving everyone home again, except for Abiana, who wouldn't be caught dead in his dilapidated Bronco. He really didn't mind her refusing the offer of a ride.

"She's a flaming four-head fuck, Victor. I say this from a place of love, keep your dick out of that. I know she gets your jollies going, but if you are thinking about following through with DeThroe's plan just to impress her, I'll knock you flat out, mate. I saw how hot and bothered she was getting when you told her about his plan. She's a drone and not worth it. Neither is he."

Victor was the last person to be dropped off, and Eli couldn't help but drive the point home one more time before Victor shut the car door. "Mate, I will run you over with this car. Do *not* do anything rash, you hear?"

"Alright, man, I get it."

"Do you? You're being honey-potted. Don't let her use her she-devil magic on you. And DeThroe? That guy is the biggest, most murdery piece of shit that The Fourth Branch ever spawned."

"I'm not being 'honey potted' Eli. And if I want to follow through with DeThroe's plan, that's my business." He lowered his voice, "we shouldn't be talking about this in public," he said while looking up and down the street.

"Just trying to protect you, mate. Even heroes need it every now and then."

"Thanks, Eli but I'm fine, okay? You coming to Abiana's chant get-together tomorrow?"

Eli just stared unblinkingly at him with the most vacant of expressions he could muster.

"I'll take that as a no."

"Yeah, but I'm letting Jacky go. She told me it's supposed to be 'the biggest party of the year,' and I would be the 'worst father in the world' if I didn't let her go. Teenagers, they got to be all fucking dramatic and shit, am I right?"

Victor smirked. "Wouldn't know anything about that."

"Yeah, you would you twat. Hey, make sure you keep an eye on Jacky for me tomorrow, alright? Don't want some greasy-haired four-head fucker getting his mitts on her."

"You got it. Stay safe, alright?"

"You do the same. And tell your mum I say hi."

Eli sped off into the evening, the Bronco sputtering audibly for at least five blocks. Victor walked inside the row home and noticed the lights were still on. Sure enough, when he entered the house, his mother was busy trimming and watering her plants. He was hungry and tired after what happened at Vixama's. Plus, he felt that he and his mom were still on shaky ground after their last little blowout. Since then, she'd been pretending everything was fine, and he'd just been too exhausted to address things head-on. Maybe everything really was fine, though, and he was just overthinking things as usual. Right now, he knew he wanted a sandwich and some shut-eye.

"Baby, come here and give your mama some sugar!" She put down her watering can and walked with a slight limp to greet him at the door.

"You okay, Ma?"

"I'm fine, sweetie. Why do you ask?"

"You look like you're hobbling on your leg a bit."

"I'm as right as rain, son. Just been on my feet all day, that's all. Are you hungry? Let me fix you something up." She walked slowly to the kitchen and reached inside the fridge for some lasagna, which she immediately put into the oven to warm up. She set the stove timer and walked past him to continue watering her plants, all the while humming sweet tunes to them. It wasn't the type of humming that was for her or Victor that perhaps sought to fill in dead air or keep a mind from becoming idle. On the contrary, it was very intentional. Meant for the plants and the plants alone.

Victor had never thought to ask his mother why she did this. "It's like you're talking to them, Ma."

"Oh, to my babies? Well, they are as sentient as you and I, and they need love, just like you and I."

"They can't think, they're just plants."

"You're not wrong. But they can *feel* just as you and I can. Maybe even more so." She touched an odd-looking tall plant that resembled a white umbrella. When the plant felt her touch it retracted its umbrella and collapsed into a barely visible nub above its soil. "*Feeling* is far more powerful than thinking." She began to hum again the plant uncoiled itself upwards back into its true form.

Victor rolled his eyes.

Undeterred, Carmenta continued watering her babies. "There's been many experiments over the years where science has proven that plants thrive in environments where positive emotions are abundant and wither away at negativity. Just like people do. It was about thirty years ago that science discovered that the theta wave of emotions behaves like light, as both a particle and a wave. It didn't take long for them to use quantum mechanics to harness theta into more novel forms."

"What do you know about quantum mechanics, Ma? You clean rooms for a living." Victor couldn't catch himself and knew immediately he sounded like a giant asshole.

There was an awkward pause, and Carmenta was the first to break the silence. "So, how's Eli doing these days? I feel like I haven't seen him in so long."

"He's okay, I was just with him. He says hello, by the way."

Another awkward silence broken with, "What about your new friend? What's his name again, Innocence?"

"No, Ma, it's Innocius."

"Hmm, such an odd name. Well, anyway, how is he? He seems sweet."

"He's fine. I was just with him, too. Actually, at his mother's place. Her name is Vixama, and she owns that new Voodoo shop across the street from the high school."

At this, Carmenta began to cough uncontrollably and started patting her chest in a vain effort to dislodge the saliva that went down the wrong pipe. Victor quickly retrieved a glass of water at the sink which she sipped slowly, appearing to try to calm herself.

"Thanks, baby, I don't know what came over me."

"It's okay. Her shop is really something. There's all kinds of…strange things inside."

The kitchen timer went off, and Carmenta walked past Victor to open the oven door—releasing a flavorful aroma across the house. She wordlessly removed it from the oven and placed a large slice of lasagna on a paper plate.

"She even does Tarot card readings there. She did a reading for all of us, and me too."

"Now, baby, you shouldn't be getting yourself tangled up in those ways. This Vixama isn't someone you should be getting mixed up with. All that 'voodoo' nonsense is just a superstitious bunch of mumbo-jumbo if you ask me." She seemed to be getting a little more defensive than what was called for.

"Why are you getting like this, Mom? It's just a store."

"It is a store, but she is representing the Haitian community, baby. People see that kind of stuff, and they just go right ahead and stereotype us. I bet this Vixama's store is totally intact, though. Can't say the same for Ollie's right now."

Victor remembered how Ollie had taken down the Haitian flag behind his bar the last time he saw him. "What do you mean you can't say the same for him?"

"You haven't heard yet, baby? I figured Eli would've told you. His shop got ransacked a few days ago. Some hooligans broke the window and sprayed graffiti all over the walls inside. Stole all his inventory, broke the chairs and tables…" Her voice started breaking and she grabbed a napkin from off the counter to blow her nose.

Tears were now streaming down her cheeks. "I stopped in a few days ago to say hi, and he was there mopping up." She stammered over her words to fight to get them out. "They hate us, Victor, now more than ever, for reasons that they'll never understand, like voodoo."

"That's not true, Ma. They hate us cause these Haitian terrorists are blowing up bombs in the middle of crowded streets."

"They hate us for whatever reasons they tell themselves, honey. They always have, and they always will."

"It doesn't always have to be like that, Ma, and it won't. Just look at us—I'm the son of a Haitian immigrant, and they are going to give me the Congressional Medal of Honor in two days, for crying out loud! The grand architect, General VanHeller, Colonel DeThroe— these are all people who I respect, and who can help us. They are the ones who can take the stain off of our family's name, once and for all!" Victor could feel his face starting to get red with anger mingled with embarrassment. He couldn't help but wonder why he felt the need to defend himself in front of his mother. This should all be as intuitive for her as it is for him.

"You're never going to be like them, Victor. You're a good boy. The ones who are giving you praise and acclaim—they're only using you. That's all you'll ever be to them, Victor, just a tool."

"Why are you acting like this? Why can't you be happy for me?"

"Victor baby, I am happy for you, and I am more proud of you than you will ever know. I just need you to understand that the people who you're getting messed up with…" She took a deep breath. "All you're ever know with them is pain and suffering. Sure, they'll give you medals, and they'll make you important. They'll do all these nice things up until the moment they don't have to anymore. And after they've squeezed out every once of decency from you and no longer have any more use for you, they'll…they'll put you in the ground, Victor." Her sobs were more than Victor could bear anymore. He was tired and just plain confused about what had gotten into his mother.

Victor began walking toward the stairs and chose his words carefully, all while trying to regain some composure. "Ever since I've told you about the Omega transmission—it's like I don't even know you anymore." Victor took a step up the stairs, not wanting to continue this back and forth any longer. Something had been eating away at him since he spilled the beans to his mom about the Omega transmission.

He grabbed the handrail firmly and gave his mother, that same five-mile stare that he had given the enemy in Haiti. The type of piercing gaze that he reserved only for those whose fate would be decided in their next few words. "When I told you about the transmission, you told me that something 'worked' and that you 'couldn't believe it.' You've been working the strangest hours you've ever worked in your life. To top it all off, you start acting so weird whenever we start talking about Innocius or his mother. And now you accuse me of hanging out with the wrong crowd. I think maybe it's you that needs to take your own advice."

Carmenta stood in the living room and covered her eyes with her hands. Through the slits in her fingers and over muffled cries, she said, "Victor, baby, you've been through so much already. I wish I could tell you more now, but it would only hurt you." She walked up to Victor and put her hand on his heart. "You just need to promise me that you will stay away from The Fourth Branch." She now sounded desperate, even a little deranged. "You don't need to work with them. You can do anything else you want, baby, anything in the world. They won't take you like they…took him! I won't let them, they can't!"

"Who…what are you talking about, Ma?"

"I've already said too much. You just need to promise…"

Victor wretched his hands away from his mother's. "Are you talking about…*Mobius*?" Victor spat every syllable of the traitor's name. "Ma, what are you not telling me? Whatever happened to *him*, he had coming to him! He is the world's biggest dirtball. I'm not like him, and I never will be like him."

There was a knock at the door.

"Victor, you just need to promise me that you won't accept anything from them," said Carmenta frantically. "The Fourth Branch is not what they seem, and neither is your father."

Victor struggled to find his next words as the knocks on the door grew louder and more forceful. "Ma…what do you want me to do, turn down getting a medal? I don't understand what you want me to do."

His eyes fleeted toward the door. "Who the hell needs to see us this badly," he said as he moved toward the door.

His mother pulled him back as the knocks turned into a pounding.

The voice of a man with a thick Boston accent came from the other side of the door.

Carmenta began to compose herself. "They're going to take me now, Victor. I don't know what they'll do with me." She grabbed him by the cheeks, looked him in the eyes, and said, "They can't win unless they have the both of you."

"Both of us…?"

"You need to protect him. You need to protect Innocius."

Suddenly, the door creaked open to reveal Sergeant Anderson and two women who were dressed in the same all-white outfits that Victor recalled seeing in the E.C.H.O. Chamber.

Sergeant Anderson smiled and said calmly, "Corporal Gates, your mother has an appointment with us. Mrs. Gates, would you please come with us?"

Carmenta turn from anguished to enraged instantaneously. "How'd you open my door? I don't have any appointment with any of you!"

"Ma'am, you should have received letters from The Fourth Branch over the past several weeks. Your neurograft procedure is scheduled to begin this evening. As one of the selected beta-testers, you will receive the agreed-upon sum of forty-thousand credits for your troubles following the end of the procedure."

"I didn't agree to anything, and I don't want your money," said Carmenta.

"Ma'am, if you refuse to come with us today then you will be brought into the E.C.H.O. Chamber by the authorities, potentially against your will, and will forfeit the agreed-upon sum of forty thousand credits."

Victor tried to dismiss the bewildered expression he knew dawned on his face. "Sergeant, I believe there may have been some kind of mistake. My mother didn't receive any letters from your office."

"There's been no mistake, corporal. Either your mother comes with us now, willingly, or she will be forced to later, against her will."

"Ma…I think you'll need to go with them. I've gotten it before. It's really not bad at all. I'll be waiting here for you when you get back, okay?"

"Victor baby, just remember what I told you, you hear?"

Sergeant Anderson stepped between them. "That will be all now, ma'am. You're in good hands with our capable attendants here." The two women in white who accompanied him took Carmenta by the arms and sat her in the back seat of a large SUV. Sergeant Anderson tipped his hat toward Victor. "She's in good hands, corporal. We'll be seeing you again soon."

Victor stood in the doorway till he could no longer see the SUV driving toward downtown. He stepped inside and couldn't shake off how rotten all this seemed. His mother didn't have an appointment to get the neurograft procedure. Though perhaps she just wasn't checking her mail carefully enough. She had been working very odd hours, after all. Even more worrying, though. was how this turn of events seemed to be timed perfectly with their discussion about him. The one person in the world that seemed to trigger Victor now more than anyone else. *He* was behind all this. Somehow, Mobius Gates was the puppet master of this circus. At this point, Victor's only hope was that that man would cease to be a problem the day after tomorrow.

Carmenta didn't know how Victor was involved in DeThroe's plan, or anything about the plan for that matter, though he could understand her motherly intuition in being concerned for his well-being. DeThroe's plan was risky, and if Victor was being honest with himself he was the one who would be incurring most of the risk. It was a good plan, though, especially from a military perspective, and one that he was proud to be taking part in. In fact, the plan probably didn't go far enough, thought Victor. Perhaps there was a way he could enhance it somehow. And then there was the strange coincidence of DeThroe apparently frequenting Vixama's shop. Victor didn't think much about it, it was probably all part of the plan, and in any case, he did actually say to Victor that he was big into Voodoo.

He was tired now, though. Between Madam Vixama's and the fight with his mom, not to mention her impromptu appointment at the E.C.H.O. Chamber, Victor was totally spent. He had one more important thing to do before he could relax. According to DeThroe's plan, he needed to make contact with Omega tonight to let them know he had the device and that he was ready to meet in the early morning of the fourth of July for a rendezvous. He programmed his sociograft for a special transmission that DeThroe instructed him to send on this very evening. Once he had programmed the instructions, he simply pressed send.

His sociograft immediately notified him that there was an incoming transmission. It contained a very cryptic message. "Remember, everyone is watching. End transmission."

He sent a reply transmission with just two words. "Fuck off."

Hearing no reply, Victor cracked the window, undressed down to his boxers, and laid on his bed. His plan was to wait up for Carmenta. He played some music on a retro-looking speaker box that Eli had got him one Christmas. That should keep him up for a while.

There was a surprisingly cool breeze coming through the window. The kind of summer night where it's a struggle to decide whether to use a blanket or not. Victor opted for the latter and simply enjoyed the cool breeze wafting over him.

Tomorrow should be one of the best days of the summer, he thought. It was the day of Abiana's chant party, and it would be his first time going to one. It was well known that her parents threw the most out-of-this-world chant parties in all of Philadelphia. And with this one bumping up against the Fourth of July, it was sure to be a total blowout. With enough luck, maybe he might even be able to sneak a kiss with Abiana. God, she looked so good today, he thought. She let out a sexy sigh of approval in the reading room when Victor told them his part in DeThroe's plan. Victor rolled over to his stomach and felt the cool breeze and sleep come over him.

13

The Chant

Victor bolted upright from his bed in a cold sweat. His hands were waving wildly in front of him as though fighting off some unseen assailant. He fought this midnight assailant and struggled to open his eyes to see who it was until he realized that he had been torn out of his nightmare into the waking world. There was no one there. He was fighting a phantom.

His speaker box was still playing music at a low volume. He shut it off and massaged a throbbing migraine with his fingertips. *The dream was so vivid.* He quietly walked downstairs in his boxers to get a glass of water. It must have still been late; the usually rowdy streets were so silent you could hear the hum of the street lamp outside the door. He tried to remember his dream as the water splashed into the glass.

Water, it was the beach again. Victor's mind returned to one of the beaches at the battle of Les Rouge, where Tengo Squad had been pinned down. It looked identical to that horrible place, but this particular location was much less rocky than the one his squad had been on. Bodies of soldiers were strewn as far as the eye could see, many being washed out to sea by the tide. The jungle that lined the coast burned with colorless phosphorous flames. The smell of smoke, burning flesh, and death littered the rocky beach. He saw someone he recognized, though it wasn't anyone from Tengo Squad. *Sergeant Anderson.*

Victor gulped down the whole glass to wet a serious case of nighttime dry mouth. He put the cool glass up to his eye to calm the pulsating headache. He squinted and thought hard.

Sergeant Anderson was lying with the right side of his face buried in the sand, screaming in pain. The flames from the chemical fire were licking his body wherever the sand didn't sheath him.

If Victor concentrated hard enough, he imagined that he could almost walk amongst the flames right up to the burning soldier. A swarm of crawling spiders enveloped the sergeant's body. He reached up and screamed, "Protect the boy!"

Victor twitched so violently that the glass in his hand shattered on the floor with a loud crash. He walked to the closet to grab the broom and dustpan to begin sweeping up the shards that spread from one end of the kitchen to the other.

The shards of glass screeched across the tile floor. Victor didn't think to slow the motion of the broom into the pan so as not to wake his mother. But his subconscious wasn't remotely close to the kitchen in Fair Heights. *It felt like I was right there. Like I was right next to him again.* It was more than a dream. *It had to be a memory. It had to be.* He had saved the lives of dozens of fellow soldiers that day on the beach. Sergeant Anderson might have been one of those 'lucky survivors,' as some called them. Victor laughed at the irony and wondered how any one of those poor bastards could be called anything other than unlucky, especially Anderson. If the sergeant really was one of the soldiers that was on the beach that day, that would mean he would owe Victor an uncomfortable debt of gratitude. His scarred face would be a reminder of that debt for the rest of his life.

Victor swept up the rest of the pieces of the broken glass and threw them in the trash can. He didn't have to wonder very hard why Sergeant Anderson wouldn't thank him for saving his life when he had driven him and Innocius to Washington. Victor thought it was a bit unusual that he had pretended they had never even met. "Dude, what the fuck are you talking about?" Victor asked aloud to an empty kitchen. *It was just a stupid dream, I've never met that guy before in my entire life up until a few weeks ago, he thought. It was just a stupid dream.*

He walked to the living room with a new glass of water and slumped onto the couch. It was still far too early to do anything meaningful, but Victor was not even remotely tired anymore. He began scrolling through his sociograft feed to see what the latest news was. The feed was chock full of stories about the upcoming annual chant occurring later today.

There were all kinds of things that the people would be expected to vote for during the chant. Then there were the usual subjects like who would be voted for in Congress, the president, and the grand architect. It was no one's surprise that Valter Lucier would be voted in for the twentieth year in a row. Most of the chant was filled with petty issues like how much tax rates were going to be and other snooze fests like how much money would be needed to fund schools and the military. Beyond the typical humdrum, there was also a bevy of unique topics that the cyberocracy's code generated for voting. Everything ranging from who the US should go to war with to whether people are permitted to take certain neuroenhancement drugs. One of the biggest chant votes in recent years was whether or not to permit cyberduels in public. That passed unsurprisingly with overwhelming approval.

There were a few important issues on the chopping block this year, the most controversial of which was, was whether to impose a nationwide neurograft mandate. In one of the local news reports that Victor was watching, the female reporter was being jostled violently by swarms of protestors. The report had aired yesterday evening, and he was forced to isolate the volume on his sociograft to hear anything she had to say over the din of the crowd.

"The mood in Philly seems to reflect the mood in the rest of the country. That is to say, the upcoming chant could become a complete blowout. Some are even starting to speculate that there could be a re-chant following the initial tabulation of votes. While the twenty-eighth amendment does provide for a re-chant, there has never actually been one since the amendment was enacted twenty years ago. Protestors against the mandate argue that it is a form of mind control, while counter-protestors say that it is ridiculous and that neurograft has increased their quality of life tenfold. While the two groups differ enormously in their ideology, they have unanimous consensus that there will be a, and I quote, 'blood bath' during the chant vote on the third of July."

The reporter and her cameraman became overwhelmed by a rowdy bunch wearing animal costumes. "...that's all for us here on the ground. Back to you in the studio, John!"

Victor didn't know and really didn't care why people were so against the mandate. Rocky said that it was just some kind of fancy mood ring, and Valter Lucier himself gave a lot of great reasons why it should be enacted. Though, for people who were against the mandate, the hate was palpable. Victor knew that Eli was one such individual. His motivations for despising the mandate seemed to be both religious as well as political. He was vehemently anti-government and thought that The Fourth Branch was somehow using the neurograft as mind control. Victor watched some more news reports, a few funny sketch comedy shows, and some of the latest coverage on a few baseball games.

Early morning birds were starting to tweet softly, and a faint glow was beginning to overtake the dark sky. Victor knew that today would be a dangerous day for Eli since he'd be out on patrol or manning a checkpoint somewhere. If Eli had it his way, he'd probably rather be at Abiana's chant party where his daughter Jacky would be. He would never admit to it, but Eli would much rather be with his daughter, even though she'd be at a chant party, than walking a beat on the mean streets of Philadelphia.

Victor's glass of cold water was now gone, and the headache emanating from his bottom brow now seemed to be migrating to his upper neck. He yawned and began rolling his head from side to side to relieve some pressure. Today was going to be a long day, so he popped a few Advil and decided to get some more shut-eye for a few more hours.

He quietly walked up the stairs and straight past his mother's room. For some reason, he turned around when he got to his bedroom door and noticed that the door to his mother's room was slightly cracked. That was a bit unusual. Usually, she slept with her door closed. Out of sheer curiosity, Victor went and slowly pushed her door open to find that she wasn't in her bed. *Maybe she went straight to her shift after her neurograft procedure, or perhaps the staff at the E.C.H.O. Chamber were just running a bit behind.* What was even stranger than his absent mother was the state of her bedroom. It looked much the same as the first floor, as well as how Victor remembered it; with plants and herbs growing on nearly every surface. He and Eli would joke with her that her dream house was inside of a terrarium. It wasn't too far off the mark from reality.

Her room still looked like the inside of a greenhouse. That wasn't the strange part. It was the thick stacks of bio-engineering schematics, government reports, and paper maps that were strewn about the floor of the usually tidy room that gave him pause.

Upon more careful inspection, Victor saw that many of these

documents had copious notes on them or were tabbed for cataloging. The most unsettling part was the subjects of these papers. Some of them talked about Victor's heroic exploits in Haiti, while others, more ominously, discussed Omega. Her closet was stacked with boxes of information on everything from what the Sentients are to the source code of the cyberocracy.

Several boxes under her bed revealed in-depth system diagrams on theta wave emitters and receiving mechanisms. There were official pamphlets on the topic of theta waves and their effects on the human body and plant life. Upon closer inspection, these documents were all stamped with the Lucier Corps trademark and authored by one of three people: 'C. Gates, V. Gates, or A. Lucier.' *Carmenta, Mobius, and the grand architect.*

He kept peeling through the documents and discovered an old photograph of the three of them grinning in front of a large bush of red roses. Victor ran his hand through his hair and squeezed the back of his neck to help alleviate the pressure that was building up. *They worked together. Why in the hell would Mom be looking at paper documents that talked about Omega? And what's worse, why are all these conspiratorial-looking documents mingled with information about me and the grand architect.*

While Victor could not think of any logical explanation, he was sure that one existed and was now too tired to try to get inside his mom's head. He closed his mother's door and walked into his own room. The sun was now starting to pour into his small room. He closed the ripped-up curtains, laid down in his bed, and waited for sleep to come.

* * *

He was woken by two equally annoying sources, the vibrating of his sociograft and the beeping of a car outside his window. His eyes failing

182

to open, he began poking his sociograft control panel absent-mindedly to get it to turn off or answer the call. He was okay with either one at the former at this point.

Somehow, he managed to pick up the call and heard Rocky say, "We're out front, bro. Let's go!"

Victor threw on some clothes and, before walking downstairs, peeped into his mother's room again to see if she was back—she still wasn't. Still, no reason to worry, Victor thought. He'd give her a call on the way to Abiana's and probably find out she was stuck in traffic or something. He went to the kitchen, popped a few more Advil, and walked out to an expensive-looking SUV where Rocky and Innocius were already waiting inside. Victor hopped in the back with Innocius, and Rocky was sitting in the front seat next to a driver.

"Dude, what took you so long?" asked Rocky, turning up the car radio.

"Eh, just taking a nap."

"My man, you are missing valuable time at the party of the year with the world's hottest girl because you're…napping? You're killing me, man. Hey, check out this sick SUV. It's got free snacks!" He opened up some compartments, revealing a mini-fridge and a well-stocked cubby full of sweet and salty goodies. It was already one o'clock, and having not eaten breakfast or lunch, Victor stuffed his face with everything he could get his hands on. Innocius could not stop laughing at the 'explosion of wrappers' in the backseat, along with Victor and Rocky arguing over who got to eat the last giant Reese's cup. In the end, they settled it over a 'wrapper' rap battle, which Innocius decided they both lost miserably and *he* should be the one who gets it. The three began speculating that if the car ride was this gaudy, then the actual party at Abiana's house must be incredible.

"Have either of you guys been to her house yet. I've heard it's got two swimming pools. Two!" clamored Rocky excitedly.

Victor shrugged. "Neither have I. Just heard rumors."

"But you're her boyfriend, Victor. You mean to tell me you haven't met her parents yet?" asked Innocius.

"We're not really, er, boyfriend and girlfriend. I think at this point, I'm just crushing pretty hard," said Victor, trying to look away to avoid the other two seeing his cheeks turn bright red. His 'crush' wasn't a secret and, at this point, had only manifested itself through obvious pent-up angst between the two.

"I think she's throwing down some pretty obvious signals, though Vic," said Rocky. He wasn't wrong. Victor had been picking up on those signals for a while but just kept kicking the can down the road. *Or maybe I'm just more scared of girls than I am going into battle.*

"Yeah, you need to ask her out! She's going to say yes. You are Victor *freaking* Gates, for crying out loud," said Innocius, and he also wasn't wrong. *I just have to take a deep breath, stop being such a scaredy cat, and ask her out already.*

"It's not rocket science, champ," said Rocky. "Although, now that I think about it, love is way more complex than rocket science," he added pensively. "Speaking of science, I talked to my dad about your fainting spell and voodoo trance at Madam Vixamas. He said it's got nothing to do with voodoo and everything to do with your relationship to do with 'the theta wave phenomenon.'"

"The what?" asked Innocius.

Rocky put up his forefingers in air quotes. "'The Theta Wave Phenomenon.' It's a super rare side effect of the E.C.H.O. Chamber. No one is even sure if it exists."

Now both Innocius and Victor were waiting for Rocky's next words with baited breath. He looked out the window at some of the big houses starting to line the road.

"And...?" said Victor and Innocius in unison.

Rocky shrugged. "Most people just think it's rumors. But the theory is supposedly based on a few early test subjects where experiments with theta backfired. Living things shouldn't be able to store large amounts of theta. But, for whatever reason, some people can not only store a buttload of it, but they can also even manipulate it. At least, that's how the theory goes. So when I told my dad about your visions, when Innocius' mom touched your hands, he knew it was the Theta Wave Phenomenon. Before you were in the E.C.H.O. Chamber, you didn't have visions, did you?"

Victor shook his head no.

"Then that has to be it," said Rocky.

"Is that why I can make lights turn on and off?"

"If the theory holds up, anything that emits or receives theta would be controllable."

"But…lightbulbs don't emit theta."

Rocky turned around to face Victor. "You're right. Only living things have a theta signature. But lightbulbs, like most things these days, have Lucier Corps chips in them, which are synthetic mini-theta factories."

The frequency of the song on the radio started to pitch high and low. Rocky and the driver started to both give it gentle taps with their fists. Without them even touching it, the station changed. Victor looked over at Innocius who was staring intently at the radio and had his sociograft hand raised slightly to it. The boys locked their eyes, and the radio returned to normal.

* * *

It was a surprisingly fast drive from the Fair Heights neighborhood to the New Franklin Estates community. All the boys marveled as they drove through a large cast iron gate into what looked like a forest in the middle of downtown Philadelphia. As they drove along the access road, they could only see long driveways that quickly disappeared into a thick tree line.

The driver, who hadn't said a word the entire trip, pointed with his chin and, with a snooty voice, said, "We've arrived."

And boy, had they. Even from the bottom of the hill, the stone house made most mansions look like a lakeside shanty. Even the enormous pillars that supported the front portico were made of stone. From the backseat, Victor could see Innocius staring at the estate through his thumb and index finger as though to size it up. "Even from here, it's still *this* big!"

The car curved along beside a large circular fountain that led to the majestic front entry portico supported by huge stone pillars. When they exited the car, and were greeted by a member of the house staff in a black suit and tie who escorted them inside and told them that "all of the guests are in the courtyard." He guided them through an ornate maze of artwork and hand-crafted moldings that would have made the Mona Lisa blush. They reached what was presumably the back of the house, Victor wasn't sure at this point because of how many twists and turns they made. "You can change into your bathing garments here," said the staff member in the suite, motioning to a door next to them.

"I don't think we brought bathing garments," said Victor, turning to Rocky and Innocius, who also shook their heads.

"Not to worry, sir, there are a variety of sizes in the dressing chamber for you to choose from," said the nasally suit. "Or if you choose not to swim," he said looking nodding to Innocius, "there are other activities in the courtyard that may suit you." He really didn't need to tell them that since the doors were made of glass and they could see the pool on the other side. As he walked outside, he said, "I will let Ms. Erhardt know that you've arrived."

Victor waited till the butler was out of earshot. "I'm cool with not swimming. How about you guys?"

The boys nodded, and they opened the double doors that led to a large cobblestone patio. There had to be hundreds of people there. There was indeed a large pool, with a swim-up style tiki bar and a water slide. There were projector screens set up at various points around the yard that were all livestreaming the chant.

For the most part, the party guests were all wearing pretty formal-looking attire, so it was even easier to spot Abiana strolling up to them. Even if she wasn't wearing a scandalous two-piece swimsuit, Victor would've spotted her a mile away. She gave Victor a hug and a peck on the cheek. "Vicky, you made it, finally! Happy Chant Day, guys! Where's your swim trunks?"

"We were just gonna chill," said Victor.

"Chill? Guy's, you can't leave me and Jacky alone in the pool with all these old suits. Innocius, *you* have to go in. I had my dad install this space-age chair lift in the pool just for you."

"Really, that sounds cool!"

"And Vicky, you're jumping in there whether you're wearing swim trunks or nothing." She leaned in for a whisper, "Preferably nothing."

"Abiana, jeez!" They both laughed while Victor began going extremely red in the face.

"What, come on, guys. Jacky and I are basically the only ones wearing a swimsuit in this whole dusty place. Look at all these museum pieces." They all surveyed the crowd. The men were dressed in slacks, bowling shirts, and penny loafers, while the women wore colorful button-down dresses or swing skirts. "It's like they're still living in the 2050s or something. My mom and dad's friends mostly. I barely know half of them. Do you want to know what they all have in common? They all love money. You could love worse things, I suppose."

"Did you say Jacky was here?" asked Innocius.

"Yeah, and looking super cute in her bikini, too, by the way," said

Abiana with a wink.

A tall man with curly blonde hair wearing an all-white Cuban-collared shirt walked up from behind Abiana and said, "Abi, aren't you going to introduce me to your friends?"

"Guys, this is Daddy. Daddy, this is Victor, Rocky, and Innocius."

"So nice to meet you all, especially you, Mr. Gates," he said with an outstretched hand to Victor. Victor tensed up at the gesture. Flashbacks of him convulsing on DeThroe's office floor and Madam Vixama's tarot card table came rushing back in an instant. The last thing he wanted was for anyone here, especially Abiana's dad, to see him like that. Instead of a handshake, he swung an arm around and slapped him on the shoulder a few times. It was awkward, but the alternative would have ruined the party for everyone and made Abiana's father think he was a circus freak.

"Well, glad to meet you too young man," said her father jovially. I'm Richard, just call me Rich. Abi's told me so much about you. Not that she needed to. I've read all about your heroics down in Haiti. You really are the man who needs no introduction," he said, beaming.

"Thanks, sir, and thanks for inviting us today. Your home is spectacular."

"Ah, she does the trick, I guess," he said dismissively. "Abi, why don't you take your friends near the pool and games while Victor and I grab a drink?"

"Okay, Daddy. Come on you two, let's go hang out with Jacky." She gave her dad a hug, raised a pointed finger between his eyes, and said, "Behave," with a playful yet slightly demonic expression.

"You don't have to worry about a thing. We'll just have a little guy chat."

Richard had to wade through a sea of guests on the way to the tiki bar, all vying for his attention. A few guests began to realize who Victor was, and they began to cheer and pat him on the back. After just a few moments, it seemed Victor was marching in his own parade amongst the throngs of people trying to crane their necks to catch a glimpse of him.

Fervent whispers of, "That's Victor Gates," and yells of "hero, hero, hero" began emanating from the crowd while Victor just tried to stay in Richard's wake through the throngs of guests. Once Richard and Victor sat down at the tiki bar, the crowd seemed to dissipate on its own to give the two men some space. The live results of the ongoing chant were being screened on several large tellvision screens above the bar. Every few seconds, the people at the bar would cease their conversations and cast their votes using their sociografts for the issues under consideration.

"What will you have to drink Victor?"

"Rum and Coke, sir."

Richard motioned to the bartender and shouted over the crowd, "Two rum and Cokes, please!" He turned to Victor. "And no more of that sir stuff. My daddy was 'sir.' Please call me Rich."

"It's a force of habit."

"Oh, you don't have to explain it to me. I don't know if Abiana's told you, but I also served, too. I was in the Battle of Guam in fifty-two—even got the Distinguished Service Cross for it." He gave Victor a stern punch on the shoulder, chuckled, and said, "Not that I can hold a candle next to you. Oh yes, I've heard. Medal of Honor? Your mom must be very proud of you."

"Yeah, I guess she is." Victor had completely forgotten about calling his mother to check in on her and make sure she made it home alright.

"Guess? Victor this is the highest honor that our country has for its fighting men and women. I'm sure she's ecstatic!"

"She just has a funny way of showing it, that's all." The whole time Victor was talking he got the impression that this is how his own mother should be treating him. Like he had really earned something to be celebrated for. Instead, she was...*I even know what she's doing.*

The bartender brought their drinks to them. Richard raised his glass. "To you," he shouted above the music playing and the dull roar of the crowd, "to Victor Gates. If it wasn't for him, The Fourth Branch would be weaker." The guests raised their glasses and cheered for a very red-faced Victor.

Maybe Richard saw him get a little uncomfortable with all the attention. "You know, when I came back from Guam, I had a pretty hard time fitting in. We all did, then. I couldn't get a job, had to move back in with my parents, I didn't have a pot to piss in. I was just kind of disillusioned with it all, you know? Then I met Catherine, and somehow things just started to click for me."

From where he was sitting at the bar, Victor caught a glimpse of Abiana pushing Innocius in his wheelchair as the leader of a conga line that was starting to wrap around the courtyard. "She's your better half, right?"

"I'll drink to that."

"So, before she came along, you didn't have all *this*," said Victor, waving his hand at the luxurious backyard retreat.

Richard chucked. "Oh no, certainly not."

"What is it that you do again, sir?"

"Oh, I'm a bit of a dabbler." He took a long swig from his drink. "I'm President and Chairman of the Board at Lucier Corps. We manufacture all the biotech involved in creating sociografts and the new neurograft, amongst many other product lines. We're even to branched into the defense industry quite a bit."

"Oh, I knew it had something to do with Lucier Corps," said Victor, a bit embarrassed he didn't already know the answer to that question. Richard was one of the most well-known businessmen in the country. He tried to take a stab at sounding a little more informed. "So you and the grand architect must be pretty close?"

"Oh, Valter and I? Yes, we go way back. As a matter of fact, he is the Godfather to Abiana. He's a great man, Valter. He needed to divest most of his interests in his company when he became grand architect. I don't expect him to return to the company, though. He sees himself as more of a servant of the people than a businessman now. Valter's always trying to give back. I can't say he's removed himself entirely from the business. He's still involved with some of our charitable giving. His charity is going to donate over one hundred million credits to privatize your old school, James Wilson High School. When you and Abiana went there, that place was a God-awful dump, to put it delicately. It's one of the last public schools in the city. They're even going to change the name, 'Private School one-seventy' or something like that." Richard finished his rum and Coke and signaled to the bartender for one more. "Suffice to say Valter is a better man than I. Now here I am blathering on about us old geezers. What about you, Victor? Tell me a bit about Philly's greatest hero."

"Well, I suppose there's not too much to say, really. I'm getting out of the military, which I think is the right move. I want to be close to home, my mom, and friends. And, er, I guess I'm still looking for work right now." Victor hadn't been looking for jobs, but clearly, work was very important to Richard. Victor wanted to make sure he made a good impression.

"Well, don't be in too big of a rush. You practically just got off the plane! And I wouldn't be too worried about finding something. I mean, worst case scenario you come and work for me! I could use a man like you in our defense branch. We're really coming out with some cutting-edge weaponry, and I think it'd be right up your alley."

Victor was at a loss for words. *Was this guy offering me a job? And not only that but probably a high-paying job.* Victor came back from Haiti thinking he would just clean rooms with his mom at the hotel for a while till he got on his feet at least. "Umm, are you serious?"

"Of course I'm serious. Abiana would tell you I'm the worst practical joker you'll ever meet. Let me have our HR department draft up something befitting a man of your skills. Then you can look over it and see if you'd be interested. How does that sound?"

Victor held his drink up. "Cheers."

"Good man."

Victor hadn't really noticed, but now most of the crowd had become silent and were either glued to their sociograft or the tellvision screens. An eccentrically dressed government official with The Fourth Branch seemed to be playing MC for Chant Day. He was calling out what issues would be voted upon, and all respondents had a few minutes to cast their vote via sociograft. After the time to cast a vote had elapsed, the official would read the results of the vote and display them on the screen. When he spoke, it was with the spontaneity of a gameshow host rather than the sobriety of a government employee.

> *"Ladies and gentlemen, Cliff Mifflin here, and welcome back from the thirty-minute comfort break. We will now resume our day's grand festivities with part two of the chant. And if you skipped the first half, that's okay because this is where things get really good. Our next chant vote will be for that of the next Speaker of the House of Representatives. The incumbent is Mr. Thomas Locke, and the challenger is Ms. Michelle Phillips. Folks, you are now free to cast your votes. You have five minutes to do so."*

"Locke, he's such a cunt, am I right?" said Richard, chortling into his rum and Coke. "What do you think?"

"Oh yeah, I met him a few days ago. There's something fishy about him," said Victor, trying to agree with Richard's unveiled dislike for Locke.

"Exactly! We're on the same page, you and I." Richard started a chant amongst the crowd, "Phillips, Phillips, Phillips," slamming his fist on the bar with every syllable.

More of the party guests joined in until everyone in the courtyard was chanting, "Phillips, Phillips, Phillips," louder and louder. Everyone began entering.

Cliff Mifflin came back on the tellvision screen. He never left, actually. He had just been doing a little dance to the elevator music that was playing while the votes were being tabulated. "We're back, folks, and are you ready for the results? The winner of the race for Speaker of the House is…drum roll please…Mr. Thomas Locke!"

Everyone at the tiki bar moaned, with many throwing peanuts at the tellvision screens.

"Damn it!" shouted Richard. "That fuck is why things are so awful right now. Phillips was a shew in!" Richard wasn't talking to Victor. He wasn't even talking to the tellvision screens. He was just yelling. A few minutes ago, he had been a mild-mannered, charismatic host. Now, he had a manic look in his eyes. The mania increased throughout the next few votes for Vice President and President. Richard and his party guests were beside themselves with rage mingled with manic depression. Some people walked away from the tellvision screens, unable to stomach looking at the close-up images of the winners of these races. "Ridiculous, absolutely ridiculous," said Richard with his forehead in his hands.

"Our next chant vote will be for that of grand architect. The incumbent is Mr. Valter Lucier, and Mr. Lucier is running for office uncontested. The winner of the race for grand architect is, our very own modern-day George Washington, Grand Architect Valter Lucier!"

The mood of the crowd improved immediately, and they broke out in deafening applause, and chants of "Lucier, Lucier, Lucier" filled the courtyard.

"Thank God," said Richard. "That was the only race that really mattered. Imagine if anyone but Valter was the grand architect, I shudder to think."

"Folks, we're going to take another quick commercial comfort break, but don't go anywhere. When we return with today's chant, it's the main event. We'll be voting for a select group of issues that *you*, the voter, have told the cyberocracy's programming is so important that you feel a decision needs to be made."

Once Cliff finished his monologue, the crowd went silent with anxious anticipation of the upcoming chant vote. Richard hopped off the bar stool and gave Victor a pat on the shoulder. "It's game time," he said to Victor as he stood up and walked to a central point in the courtyard. "Hey everyone, can you all bring it in for a moment," he said loud enough for everyone to hear and begin gaggling around him.

Abiana, Rocky, Innocius, and Jacky came over to where Victor was sitting at the bar and sat beside him. Abiana gave him a kiss and wrapped her arms around his neck from behind. "Looks like this is the kids' table," she said.

"I just want to say a few words before the next chant vote gets started. First of all, thanks for coming to our annual party. It's for you, it's always been for you. It's the most important day of the year. The day when we get to decide how our cyberocracy is run and make decisions for the better. I don't have to tell you that the next few votes here today are vital. I'm not going to mince words, folks. We need the neurograft mandate. And no, it has nothing to do with Lucier Corps being the one who manufactures the device…though that certainly helps."

The crowd of, presumably, Lucier Corps employees began chanting, "Mandate, mandate, mandate!"

A single drunk man in the back chanted, "Bonus, bonus, bonus!"

Richard raised his hand with a laugh to quiet them down again. "Today wouldn't be made possible without the likes of people like

Corporal Victor Gates. He's a hero, folks, and he's sitting right there next to my daughter." Richard pointed to a blushing Victor. "Let's give him a big round of applause, please."

The crowd, if they weren't already, rose to their feet and gave Victor a resounding applause.

"The neurograft mandate." He waited for the applause to die down. "The neurograft mandate is so much more than commercial opportunity. It is the keystone to our society being able to truly become united. It offers the best solution to improving our cyberocracy and making sure that the United States of America remains the greatest country in the history of mankind!"

If Richard's goal was to over-excite his guests with his speech, then he succeeded spectacularly. Somehow, in unison, they all began chanting, "Neur-o-graft, neur-o-graft, neur-o-graft!" It was as though they were in a stadium cheering for their favorite football team. The finely dressed party guests again burst into rapturous, gleeful shouting and, generally speaking, making complete buffoons out of themselves. What was once an upscale garden party for business types now turned into a shot glass tossing, dancefloor groping spectacle of pure debauchery.

Victor and the others at the kid's table looked on with mingled feelings of amusement and horror. "What's wrong with them?" asked Jacky, as though they were at a zoo looking into a diorama exhibit of wild animals.

"I think they've all had a little too much to drink," said Abiana.

A nearby guest, who began trying his hand at break-dancing, ran headlong into Jacky, knocking her off of her bar stool and nearly onto the floor. Had Victor not caught her mid-fall, she would have gone face-first into the cobblestone ground. To prevent her from falling, he grabbed her arms firmly with both his hands. That's when he felt it. It was happening again. That same feeling he felt when he touched

Innocius, Locke, and Vixama. If he had to describe the sensation, it was what he felt when he pulled Innocius up off of the ground after Big T's gang of thugs had knocked him over. The music and noise of the crowd faded away, and he was left staring into Jacky's eyes with an overwhelming sense of peace.

Victor's ears began ringing that familiar high-pitched chord again. The tiki bar, courtyard, mansion, and warm summer day all began pulling out of focus. The images that replaced them were of a park in the Fair Heights neighborhood that Victor remembered going to when he was little. It was a cloudy day, and he could sense that it was cool outside. He wasn't able to walk in this dreamlike state he found himself in, but he could still somehow choose what he wanted to see. There was a little stream, a gravel pathway, and a children's playground with swings and a Jungle Gym. Victor could see a young boy and girl swinging there. The girl had black pigtails and was fit to burst with laughter as Eli, her father, pushed her back and forth. Victor never saw Eli happier than when he was with Jacky. The boy next to her looked like he was also having the time of his life and was being pushed by Mobius, his father.

Victor snapped out of the dream he was having and returned to kneeling on the floor of the tiki bar with Jacky. She looked only a little bit terrified but more surprised than anything else.

"Are you two okay?" asked Innocius.

"Yeah, we're fine. I'm fine, are you fine?" Victor rambled on, still trying to get his bearings.

"Yeah, totally. Just got a little lightheaded there for a minute," said Jacky, standing up and trying to balance herself.

"You guys okay? Jacky, I told the jerkoff who fell into you to f-off. Jesus, what is with these drunk assholes?" said Abiana.

Cliff Mifflin's eccentric face appeared once again on all of the tellvision screens around the courtyard and bar. Everyone began to hush one another out of their temporary stupor to now pay very close attention to Cliff's next words.

"Folks, we're back with your regularly scheduled programming. Before we begin casting our votes for this chant, I think we all need to reflect for a moment on how far we've come as a nation. The War of the Moderates ended twenty short years ago. How very, very far we've come, indeed. Who would have predicted that our cyberocracy would be so advanced that, through some social handy devices like the sociograft and neurograft, our Sentients would be able to distill untold amounts of data to give us the decisions that we need to make to make our country function? For twenty peaceful and blissful years, we have experienced peace and prosperity that is not diminished by our passions but enhanced by them. And on this, the nearly three-hundredth anniversary of our nation, we have only to thank The Fourth Branch, led by our intrepid grand architect, for these prosperous times. Hail The Fourth Branch!"

The partygoers dutifully echoed in unison, "Hail The Fourth Branch!"

"Mmm, that just rolls off the tongue, doesn't it?" Cliff said with a smattering of his lips. "Now we have some business to tend to."

Once the votes for this part of the chant began, the mood at the party again returned to a state of primal frivolity. The issues themselves weren't very salacious. In fact, they appeared to be god-awfully mundane. Issues such as waging war, bio-medical research, space exploration, and intellectual property were evidently hotly contested. On the tellvisions, the primal circus occurring in the courtyard seemed to be mirrored across the rest of the country. Protesting wasn't really the right word for it. People were just freaking the fuck out.

"I really love the energy I'm seeing people. It shows you care!"

Cliff just seemed to be feeding into everyone's carnal impulses. "And you've all waited long enough. It's time for the last issue of our chant in the year 2076. The next issue that is up for vote is whether or not you believe that a neurograft mandate should be imposed on all citizens. You have five minutes to cast your votes, starting now!" He disappeared from the tellvision, and a clock counting down from five minutes appeared. People were now carefully casting their votes using their sociografts. As more time began to elapse, and it was clear that few people still had their noses stuck in their devices, a low chant began, "Neurograft, neurograft, neurograft," with each syllable being enunciated by fists banging on tables. When they were about one minute away from five minutes being up, the chant was now deafening. "NEUROGRAFT, NEUROGRAFT, NEUROGRAFT, NEUROGRAFT, NEUROGRAFT!"

Cliff Mifflin appeared back on the screen. "Ladies and gentlemen, the final tally of the vote will now be displayed. This issue is decided… in favor of a neurograft mandate! The ayes have it, everyone—we will have the mandate!"

All of the partygoers gave celebratory cheers and cries of joy. A few of them placed Richard on their shoulders and began carrying him around the courtyard as though he were taking some kind of victory lap.

Cliff continued addressing the watchers by saying, "Now we understand that not everyone will be thrilled with this outcome."

The partygoers began chanting, "NEUROGRAFT, NEUROGRAFT, NEUROGRAFT, NEUROGRAFT, NEUROGRAFT!"

The tellvision coverage briefly showed some pockets of mass unrest breaking out around the country. "We need to remember that not only did the cyberocracy independently identify this issue for a vote by the people, but it was also *decided* by the people. We need to respect the wisdom of the independent wisdom of the cyberocracy and the will of the people."

"They're just a bunch of sore losers!" shouted some rabble-rousers in the courtyard.

"Yeah, they don't know what's good for them," said others.

"Drones, they're all mindless drones," yelled a few.

Amidst the joyous frivolity, the tellvisions all began glitching and, after a few seconds, cut out entirely. The image changed from that of Cliff Mifflin to a very harried and disheveled-looking Thomas Locke at his desk. He quickly ran a few hands through his wavy hair to straighten it as some of his staff members placed a script in front of him and then disappeared from view.

"My fellow Americans," he began. "As you all must know by now, the chant votes for the day have recently concluded. As the Speaker of the House, it is my duty, under the twenty-eighth amendment, to serve as an auditing agent for all issues related to The Fourth Branch. This includes the issues brought to a chant vote by the sentient programming of the cyberocracy. Nearly all of the issues brought to a vote and voted upon show no irregularity. However, there is one inconsistency that has been discovered by our experts and pertains to the vote for the neurograft mandate."

"Oh, what the fuck," moaned the partiers.

"This can't be happening," sighed others.

Locke continued, "After reviewing the programming logs from the neurograft mandate vote, the auditing committee for Congress has determined that a thorough investigation needs to be completed."

"Here we go, what a giant freaking drone that Locke is," cried a man wearing a gold embroidered suit jacket.

"We anticipate that our investigation will take no longer than twenty-four hours. We will announce the results of the investigation at five o'clock tomorrow, the Fourth of July. We appreciate your patience in the democratic process. God bless you, and God bless America."

"It's not a democracy, dickhead. It's a cyberocracy," shouted a woman wearing a large pearl necklace with matching earrings.

The mood had shifted starkly from exuberant to a brooding, contemptuous simmer. A few were crying into their hands, while others downed multiple shots of liquor in quick succession. Some collected their belongings, wished Richard goodbye, and mournfully traipsed out of the courtyard.

"I don't think I've ever seen grown-ups this sad before," said Innocius innocently.

"Psh, all my dad's friends are a bunch of big babies," said Abiana dismissively.

"All of a sudden, I don't feel so good," said Innocius. "My head just feels all funny."

"I'll take you home," said Victor.

"No!" said Abiana. "I mean, sorry, Victor, I thought you could maybe stay a while?"

"Oh, uh, sure," said Victor sheepishly.

"Don't worry about me, Victor," said Innocius. "Rocky and Jacky can take me back, right guys?"

Rocky looked a little dejected. "Actually, I was kind of hoping to stick around too. Abiana's place has so much cool tech, and I...ouch!"

Jacky elbowed Rocky straight in the ribs and shot him a dirty look. "We'll leave you two to it, won't we guys?"

Victor started to turn red. "You sure you're okay? Can I swing by your house tomorrow?"

"Well, my mom said she wanted me to go to my school tomorrow. She said that it'd probably be safer to be at the school while the parades take place than being at home. I think she thinks her shop is going to get ransacked."

"Why on Earth would she think that?" inquired Abiana, folding her arms.

"It's happened to friends of hers before, during a big protest, so she's just a little worried."

"There's no reason for anyone to target just her store. But depending on how the investigation into the neurograft mandate goes, it could be anybody's guess on how violent things get. I half hope that the anti-mandate crowd wins out. They're even bigger babies than my dad's friends. They'd boohoo about it till kingdom comes if they don't get their way."

"Yeah, I guess so," said Innocius, rubbing his forehead. "We should get going."

"Innocius, call me tomorrow if you want me to walk you to the school, alright?" said Victor. Rocky, Jacky, and Innocius made their way back into the house leaving Victor and Abiana to their own devices.

14

Under the Hood

The groundskeepers at Abiana's family estate were cleaning up after most of the chant partiers departed to sulk at their own homes following the results of the neuromandate vote. Many left with their tails between their legs, unable to fully celebrate the decadent frivolities that their host provided them for the afternoon.

Abiana and Victor lounged around the pool, basking in the heat of the early afternoon sun. When the heat was too much to bear, Abiana strong-armed Victor, quite literally, into finally donning a pair of swim trunks to take a dip in the pool.

After a while of playfully splashing, they lounged on the poolside chairs talking about everything from 1980s hair bands, Abiana's favorite topic, to power circuit racing and fixing up old cars, her second favorite topic.

Victor couldn't help but appreciate the surrealness of the moment. Just a few short weeks ago, he was on that beach in Haiti with Tengo Squad, ready to make an assault on their objective. Now he was at a gorgeous stone home, talking with a beautiful bikini-clad woman. Perhaps Abiana could see Victor becoming distant as he tried to reconcile these two counterpoints in his mind. She recommended they go somewhere else, which also coincided with one of the pool cleaners dropping a large vat of chlorine on Victor's foot by mistake.

They put their dry clothes back on and went into the pool house, where they were shooed away by someone vacuuming. Then they tried to go into several of the rooms inside the main house, where some party lingerers continued to drunkenly argue about the chant.

"Oh my God, can't these people just leave already!" Abiana whispered loudly past a group of them as she and Victor stormed out of yet another room. "Let's just go to the garage, and there better not be anybody in there!" she said angrily.

They walked through the maze of corridors until they reached what Abiana called, 'the garage.' Victor thought it looked more like a plush living room with about thirty cars and motorcycles parked in the middle of it.

"You know I'm not religious, but this here is my sanctuary. Well, apart from maybe the power circuit," said Abiana grinning from ear to ear.

"Do you have a favorite one?" asked Victor, surveying the exquisite selection of mostly twentieth-century vintage cars.

"Oh yeah, I'll show you one that'll knock your socks off." Abiana walked about halfway down the lineup and stopped at an ancient sedan that was painted lipstick red. "1957 Chevy. She doesn't look like much, but she's a real smooth ride," she said with a wink. "Wanna see what's under the hood?"

Even Victor could decipher what she was getting at. She was asking what Victor wanted, but it had nothing to do with opening the hood of a car. "I sure do," he said, playing along and walking closer to her.

As she propped the hood up, Victor peeked inside and wasn't expecting what he saw. The original engine block was gone, and what was in its place appeared to be a cylinder of red-purplish-colored goo.

"What the hell is that?" he said, bending down to get a closer look.

"It's my new project. Combining a little bit of new with the old is kind of my love language. That red goop you see in there is what powers this beauty, or at least will power her once I tinker with it a bit more. It's a reverse theta wave plasma converter."

"A theta…say what now?"

"A reverse theta wave plasma converter. You're not really supposed to be able to get your hands on this stuff, but I know some people. Do you know how you can control a circuit board with your headset while you're in the power circuit tunnels? Well, this works on that same principle, except you don't need to be in the tunnels to get it to work." She sighed. "But I haven't been able to get it to work. I'm not sure if anybody has." Abiana then went into great detail about how a series of electrical sparks from the ignition should cause a chain reaction within the plasma vessel. "And once that happens, the pistons would start to fire up, and Bob's your uncle. I've tried all kinds of Lucier Corps chips to get the reaction just right, but nothing is working. I'm about to march over to my dad's factory and give them a piece of my mind."

"Maybe the chip is bad," said Victor, trying to troubleshoot what the problem might be. "Or maybe it just needs a little convincing." Victor held his arm up toward the engine and closed his eyes. He tried to imagine he was in the power circuit tunnels piloting the circuit board. He focused all of his concentration on the engine block, the same way he was able to turn the lights in his bedroom on and off. After a few seconds of Abiana thinking he had just gone a little loco, something in that vat of red goo began to swirl. Then, it started pulsating a light that timed in sequence with the slow start of the pistons.

"Holy shit, you got it to start!" said Abiana jumping up and down with excitement.

Her shouting and continuous punching in the arm broke his

concentration, and when it did, the engine turned off.

"Vicky, that was incredible. You're incredible!"

"Well, now you can't say I never got your engine going," said Victor with a coy smirk.

"Do I hear some presumptuousness in your voice, Victor Gates? What exactly are you thinking is going to happen hear? We haven't even been on a date yet."

"Wouldn't you call this a date?" he said, moving a little closer to her.

She put her hand on his shoulder, stood up on her tippy toes, and looked deep into Victor's brown eyes.

At that, each of the garage doors opened up, and a band of lingering drunken partygoers came strutting in.

Victor watched in real-time as Abiana flipped the switch from sensual to murderous instantaneously. "Honest...to...God! Get the fuck out of my house! *Out, out, out, OUT!*" They began leaving the garage, snickering with a mixture of confusion and amusement at what they had just walked in on. They began corralling in the driveway to get a pick-up game of basketball going at a nearby hoop.

"Christ almighty, we are leaving!" Abiana grabbed Victor by the hand and marched over to a sleek-looking motorcycle. She handed him a helmet. "Hop on." Victor put the helmet on, straddled the cycle, and barely had time to hold onto Abiana's hips before she revved the engine and peeled out of the garage, narrowly hitting several stupefied partygoers.

It was nearly rush hour now, but that didn't deter Abiana from weaving and bobbing through traffic like she was riding a motorcycle in a video game. She laid on the gas even as they got closer to downtown and the streets narrowed. Victor tried not to squeeze Abiana by the hips too hard. It would have been a dead giveaway that he was overly concerned with falling off. Abiana must have known because the harder he squeezed, the faster and more erratic she piloted the motorcycle.

They sped alongside rows upon rows of warehouses. They looked familiar to Victor. It dawned on him this was where the dilapidated warehouse that contained the entrance to the power circuit. Victor could see that warehouse a few hundred feet straight ahead, but instead of slowing down, Abiana started to speed up. She was going so fast now that there was absolutely no way she would be able to slow down in time to avoid crashing headlong into the front of the warehouse. By some miracle, the large metal door of the warehouse opened just in the nick of time.

"Jeez, Vicky, I think you almost broke one of my ribs. Could you have been squeezing any harder?" Abiana said playfully.

"I'm just surprised you got us here in one piece. Hopefully, I'll get some payback."

"Oh, you will," she said. "Now, let's get us situated." She whistled loudly and yelled, "Come on out, Jay!"

A man crawled out from the center of the warehouse, where an unnaturally red glow emanated from the floor. Victor recognized him as Jay Cromwell, the MC from the power circuit race.

"There's some really strange stuff going on down there," he said as he approached the pair.

"What kind of strange stuff?" asked Abiana.

"I don't know, it's just more red than usual. And brighter."

"That's illuminating. Thanks for that in-depth description, Dr. Cromwell," she added sarcastically. He wasn't really a doctor. "All I want to know is if it's safe to go into."

"Well, the theta readings are off the charts, but a bit of extra theta never hurt anybody."

"Good, are the boards ready?" she asked.

"At the edge of the tunnel, dear," said Jay.

"Anybody else down there?"

"You got the whole place to yourselves."

"Great. Just make sure nobody comes in behind us," said Abiana grabbing Victor by the hand and walking toward the chasm in the floor that led to the power circuit tunnels. He and Abiana found their boards and headsets at the edge of the gaping precipice. They initiated their bindings, which wrapped snugly around their legs. Victor peered into the deep abyss. The glow from the conduit cables below pulsated ominous red light with flashes of purle every few seconds. "I've never seen it look so red before, looks like it could get pretty rough down there. Think you can keep up?" Abiana asked with a wink before putting on her headset.

"Oh, so did this just become a race?"

"Only one way to find out." She dove headlong into the tunnels. Victor quickly donned his own headset, pushed off the ground, and began plummeting down after her.

His magnetized circuit board immediately latched onto the helix-shaped conduit cables that made up the power circuit. Somehow, it felt like he was going faster than usual. He checked the settings in his headset, and sure enough, he was going about thirty miles per hour over what he normally raced at. He could see Abiana was a few hundred feet in front of him already. The red glow was pulsating so brightly, that he could barely see her at all. Had it not been for the filtered lenses of his headset, she would have been impossible to see. Victor remembered when he was a little kid going sledding down the hill at Fair Heights Park during blizzards. The snow would whip past his face as though he were traveling at light speed across a galaxy of stars. This felt a little like that, though much more dangerous. If he broke concentration from sledding, he would still end up at the bottom of the hill. If he tried that while piloting his circuit board, he would be a splat of pink mist on the ground hundreds of feet below.

He could see Abiana up ahead, already nearing the first turn of the power circuit. However, instead of making the turn and staying on the conduit cables, she flew straight ahead, clear off the track!

Victor was stunned. He was sure she had made a dire error and accidentally de-magnetized her board, sending her plummeting to her doom. He had to make a split-second decision, either stay on the track or try to go on after her. He chose the latter, and when the time came to stay on the helix cables, he instead demagnetized his board and went flying off course.

He was suspended momentarily in mid-air until his board came in contact with some of the super-structure that supported the power circuit. It didn't glow like the power circuit cables did, but it was made out of metal. Victor re-magnetized his board and began floating aimlessly to the edge of the tunnel cavern, where he was surely going to meet his death. Instead, he careened gently into a small cave that was nestled into the walls of the cavern.

Abiana was there unlatching herself from her board's bindings. It was dark in the cave, but he could make out her mischievous smile from the nearby light of the power circuit.

Victor took off his headset and shouted, "Are you out of your mind," half angry but half amused.

"What, you didn't think I wasn't going to make you earn it," she said, walking toward him.

"Earn what?"

"This," she said, throwing her hands around his neck and kissing him passionately.

It wasn't how Victor expected his first kiss with Abiana to be. Instead of allowing himself to be in the moment, he was struck by another one of his visions. This time, it was of a golden circle with two small lights illuminating its center. One of them glowed as bright as the sun, and the other sparkled with a dark lights menacing as it was beautiful. Victor pulled himself away from Abiana's embrace, which caused her to step back.

"Sorry," she said a little sheepishly. "I know I'm moving fast. I like you, Victor."

"No, it's not that," said Victor. "I loved it. I just had one of my weird daydreams again all of a sudden. They seem to hit me whenever I…whenever I touch someone."

"What was it about?" she asked, stepping forward again.

"It was just a big golden circle with two little circles inside of it. One was bright, and one was dark. It kind of looked like a yin-yang, now that I think about it."

Abiana held her hand up to her mouth and started giggling madly.

"I know it's stupid. You don't have to tease," said Victor, embarrassed.

"No! Don't be silly, you big goof. I'm not laughing at you." She composed herself. "I'm in awe of you, Victor Gates. You know, I don't believe in Madam Vixama's voodoo mumbo-jumbo or Eli's religious fanaticism, which is another reason why I despise that guy, but I do believe in something. And now I believe in you. You really are special, you know that?"

"What are you talking about?" said Victor.

"You really do have the 'sight,' like Vixama said. It doesn't have anything to do with voodoo, though."

In the middle of the darkened cave, Abiana unzipped her pants and pulled them down slightly. The purple light from the power circuit cast a light on all of her spell-binding contours. "What you saw was this," she said, lowering her panties a few inches. The golden circle he had just seen in his vision was tattooed, with uncanny similarity, on Abiana's lower pelvis. Victor bent low so he could see it better and touched the tattoo with his fingers. It had the same two dots as his vision, one black and one white.

"What is it?" Victor asked, wondering if he was dreaming all of this. The vision, the cave, Abiana - all of it.

"It goes by a few names," said Abiana. "In my sect, we call it the Grand Developers Entombed."

"Sect?" asked Victor, scratching his head in confusion. "Like a religious sect?" Victor sat down on his still magnetized circuit board that was hovering above the metal underneath it. Abiana followed suit and held Victor's hand in both of hers.

"I told you that I hated religion, but I didn't say all religion," she said, running her fingers across his. "We worship the sentient intelligence that forms the basis of the cyberocracy. Our sect is small, though there are bigger ones out there. One thing we all believe in, though, is that the cyberocracy and the source code of its sentience needs to be preserved. And anyone opposing it, like Omega, must be destroyed. DeThroe wants you to fight them, right? You need to make sure you kick their asses. And come back to me in one piece."

"I will. They won't know what hit 'em," said Victor.

"You better," she said, resting her head on his shoulder. "We believe the Sentients possess a spark of the divine and that there are those who can communicate with them."

"Them...? There's more than one Sentient?"

"No one is sure how many sentient beings were created by the cyberocracy. But we are certain there are more than one." Abiana continued to crawl her fingers like a spider up Victor's forearm. The ethereal light emanating from the power circuit seemed to pulsate with even greater intensity. "Some say that the power circuits glow brighter when the Sentients feel a particular emotion strongly—usually anger."

"Who can communicate with them?" said Victor. He could feel his face getting redder as Abiana began resting her other hand on his knee. She opened and closed her fingers on his lower thigh longingly, sending a tingling sensation throughout his body.

"Not many. I've never met one until now. You see things, Victor, things that others either can't see or won't see. They're trying to speak to you through your visions and maybe even your dreams. If you listen, they'll give you power." She rested her one hand on his neck, and the other was beginning to travel slowly up his thigh.

"Like the power to turn on a fifty-five Chevy?"

"No." Abiana laughed. "Though that is a pretty cool trick if something has a Lucier Corps chip in it. Speaking of that…my new piercing has one in it."She pulled her panties a bit lower, and made sure Victor's eyes followed them down her thighs. "Vixama's tarot card prediction is about to come true."

"What do you mean?"

"Don't you remember? She said I'd 'fuck someone on something you can ride on." She placed her hand around his head and drew him in for a kiss. "I think a circuit board will do the trick."

Victor lifted Abiana with the backs of her thighs and laid her on the circuit board. He pulled her panties around her ankles, concentrated hard on her piercing, and discovered a whole new way to use the new cyberkinetic skills that Valter Lucier gave him. Her screams of pleasure echoed to every cave in the power circuit tunnel.

15

Hanging by a Thread

Victor woke up lying on his hovering circuit board. He was still in the secluded cave deep within the power circuit tunnels. He looked around the cave and didn't see either Abiana or her circuit board.

She must have got up and left already. He looked out of the cave opening to the far-off power circuit cables still emanating a menacing purplish red light. It looked even more ominous now than it did when he and Abiana arrived here a few hours ago. Even so, Victor felt lighter than a feather. He couldn't remember the last time he slept so well, and although he couldn't be sure, he knew his night with Abiana had something to do with that.

He checked his sociograft. It was nearly midnight on the evening of the third. In a few hours, it would be time to confront Omega. Not to mention that the findings from the investigation into the chant's legitimacy would be presented too. On top of all that, Victor would be awarded the Medal of Honor during an official ceremony. He sat up from laying on the motionless, yet still levitating, circuit board. He rubbed his eyes and yawned loudly. *I'm too lax, I need to get my head in the game.*

For whatever reason, though, he felt calm. Too calm. You could almost say, downright peaceful. Now *that* was something that made his hair stand on end. He'd been through enough firefights in the Jungle Gym to know that the 'calm before the storm' was a very real concept. He probably owed a debt of gratitude to that heightened sense of awareness that sends shivers down his spine. It likely kept him alive these past years. He'd come to know that feeling as an overly concerned friend who, despite being a bit of a nag, was always welcome. If nothing else, it gave him the presence of mind to interrogate his surroundings and see them for what they really were. The lights from the power circuit swirled malevolently. But there was a beauty in the malevolence. Victor didn't know how or why it was all at once scary and serene.

Victor's stomach rumbled loudly. He wanted to stay in this cave a little longer. If nothing else, then to appreciate that he had finally had a decent night's sleep. Though nothing gets him out of bed faster than a well-cooked meal, especially one from his mother. "Shit, I forgot to call and check on her," he said out loud, the echo of his voice carrying outside of the cave.

He quickly put his clothes on and donned the headset to his circuit board. He hopped on the board and expected it to do his bidding and dart toward the power circuit cables. This part of the track was not part of the power circuit, though. It was just a long beam of metal. The board's magnetism allowed it to float, but it was about as useless as a car with no gas. It was all well and good that you could have sex on a gasless car, but Victor needed this thing to do its actual job at this point. He needed the theta wave energy from the helix-shaped power conduit to navigate the board.

So he did the only thing you can do when a circuit board doesn't have theta waves to power it. You push it. Victor had never tried this before, but he was pretty sure that if he pushed the board to where the metal beam sloped downward. At that point, gravity should take its course, and he could ride the metal beam until it made contact with the power circuit cables. It seemed logical, and it must have been what Abiana had done to get her board out of the power tunnels. So that's exactly what he did. He pushed the board right up to the edge of the slope and hopped on the board to strap in. Then he did a swaying back-and-forth motion, sort of like coaxing a stubborn sled to start its glide down a gradual hill. He knew if anybody was watching this ridiculous spectacle, they would either be laughing at him or covering their eyes at what was about to happen next. The slope of the metal beam leveled out after about one hundred feet, where it then connected with a nearby circuit cable.

With a few dozen sways back and forth, he was able to build up enough momentum to propel the board forward. At first, it moved slowly, but that turned into an outright freefall within seconds. With no way to control the board, he was at the mercy of gravity and began spinning down the beam. It was a very good thing that there was no one else in the power tunnels, as his screams were more than a little embarrassing.

Once his board reached the point where the metal beam connected to the power cables, he was able to instantly gain control. Within a few minutes, he was flying back up the shaft that led to the inside of the dilapidated warehouse. Since there was no one around, he thought he would turn up the juice on his board so that when he exited the shaft, it would propel him above the floor of the warehouse, where he could do a 360-degree spin with a grab. At least, that was the plan.

As the light at the end of the tunnel approached, he sped up and catapulted out of the opening on the warehouse floor. He did a very bad pirouette-type move in mid-air and came crashing flat on his ass—laughing like a lunatic the whole time.

He looked up at the ceiling of the warehouse and didn't expect Eli to walk into his line of sight. "The fuck are you laughing about?"

Victor sat up and undid his bindings. "Nothing just had a fun night, that's all."

"You've got a funny look on your face. Kind of like a 'just been fucked,' face." Eli interrogated Victor's goofy expression a little more closely. "Oh my God, you did! You did just fuck. Who was…" Eli's arms crossed about as quickly as his thick eyebrows furrowed. "It was Abiana, wasn't it? You two fucked didn't you?"

Victor picked up his board and started walking toward the door. "What are you doing here, Eli?"

"I told you to keep your dick out of that, and what do you do five fucking hours later? You fuck her. You fuck."

"Have you come here just to give me the third degree, man? What's the deal?"

"No. I haven't, even though someone obviously needs to. I need to talk to you." Victor kept walking toward the warehouse door. Eli grabbed him by the shoulder and spun him around. "I need to talk to you…"

"Something I can help you out with, officer?" Jay Cromwell had just come crawling out from the hole leading to the power circuit tunnels. He walked over to the pair, dusted himself off, and tried to muster as innocent a smile as he could.

"Nothing you could help me out with. Ever," growled Eli.

"Well, if that changes, you know where to find me. And Mr. Gates, is everything alright? I thought I heard some loud screaming down there a few minutes ago."

"Er, yeah. Everything was fine," said Victor, trying to pretend as though 'spinning out' in the power circuit tunnels and not losing your shit in the process was perfectly normal.

"Glad to hear it," said Jay. "Ms. Earhart took off about an hour ago.

She said to tell you that she'll see you during the parades tomorrow—or, er, today…" he glanced down at his sociograft. "Look at that, it's already twelve-o-three AM on the Fourth. Happy Tricentennial. Hail the fourth…"

"Fuck off," said Eli grabbing Victor by the sleeve and walking toward the warehouse door. They walked toward Eli's patrol car and got in.

"What is it you need to tell me?" asked Victor.

"Maybe I should wait till you're sitting down," said Eli.

"Eli, I am sitting down," said Victor as he strapped himself into the passenger seat.

Eli made a phone motion with his hand up to his face and pointed to his dispatcher console on the car dashboard. He then mouthed, "T-h-e-y-r-e l-i-s-t-e-n-i-n-g."

"Fine, where to?"

"I'll take you somewhere you can think."

Eli and Victor tried to make small talk as they drove through the city. Victor could tell that Eli didn't want to take any part of it. He seemed on edge, even more so than usual. Victor thought maybe he was still pissed about how he and Abiana had hooked up. Maybe he was stressed about the prospect of patrolling during tomorrow's Fourth of July festivities and investigation. It could have been that he had a blow-out with his ex-wife about Jacky. At this point, there were any number of things that could have been going through Eli's mind that would throw him off. After the first few minutes of forced small talk, the remainder of the trip was made in silence.

Eli parked his patrol car at Fair Heights Park, and the two stepped out into the night air. It was one of those rare nights where, even with the city's light pollution, a dazzling array of stars were visible. It was so late, or so early, that they were the only two people in the park. Victor could hear passing cars from the nearby freeway as they entered the park.

As they silently walked the winding path deeper into the park's interior, they came upon an old, rickety swing set and jungle gym. *The same ones that I saw in my vision when I touched Jacky's hand.* They sat on an old wooden bench that faced the children's play area. Victor couldn't hear the freeway anymore. Now, it was just the creeky sound of the swaying swings in the breeze and the occasional song of a stray midnight whip-poor-will.

"Why did you bring me *here?*"

"This is one of the few places in this dump where I can hear myself think. Why? You don't like it?"

"No. It's just strange that, of all the places you could have taken me, it was here."

"It's just a park."

"Yeah, I've had some more weird dreams lately. And…er, this was one I had a bit ago."

"You want to tell me about it?"

Victor looked at the swings swaying gently in the cool evening breeze. They were rusted over, and each swing looked as though it were hanging by just a few stubborn threads. "I saw you pushing Jacky on the swings, and I…" Victor paused to take a deep breath. "I saw…*him* swinging me too?"

"You mean Mobius?"

"Yes," said Victor, trying to already wipe the images of his young self in fits of laughter at being pushed higher against the backdrop of a crystal blue sky.

Eli rested his chin on his hand and stared blankly at the play area. "What I wouldn't give for those days again. I can blame a lot of what happened on Jacky's mom, but I wouldn't be honest with myself if I did." Eli sat up and rested both his arms on the back of the bench. "I can't really remember why I started taking hits of neuro-drip, but I remember what it did to me. I would give literally anything to have those days back with Jacky. When she was taken from me—it hurt. It hurt really bad. I became so angry, and bitter, and…small. Family is everything, and you're like a brother to me, Victor." Eli blinked quickly and rubbed his hand along his face. He looked at Victor with tears welling up in his eyes. "I shouldn't be telling you this, but I need to."

"What is it, Eli?"

Eli snorted and swallowed hard. "They have your mum, mate. They have Carmenta."

Victor's eyes widened, and he was struck with guilt-ridden fear. "What? Who, who has her?"

"The goons from The Fourth Branch issued a warrant. She's being held without bail."

Victor stood up and started pacing back and forth. "No. No, that can't be right. She was just at the E.C.H.O. Chamber. She was about to miss her appointment, and they came to pick her up."

"All I know is that when she underwent the neurograft procedure, they saw something…"

I was going to check up on her.

"It must have been something they didn't like…"

How could I forget to call?

"They've detained her…"

Eli stood up and grabbed Victor by the shoulders. "They have her on charges for crimes against The Fourth Branch."

"Crimes against The Fourth Branch?"

"Yeah, mate."

"What crimes?"

Eli let his hands down and shook his head. "I know it's ridiculous, Victor. Those fourth branch pricks are so full of it. We'll get her back, though, mate, alright? With your star power, there's no way they'll hold her for long. Can you call one of your buddies up there? This is probably just a big misunderstanding."

Victor's pacing became faster and more manic by the second. "He must have gotten to her somehow. It's because of him. I know it is!"

Eli's eyebrows furrowed. "Who got to her mate? What are you on about now?"

"*Him.* Mobius, I know it was him."

"Victor, you're talking like a nutter. Mobius is dead, or on the run in some country that doesn't have extradition to the United States. Like Haiti, or more likely Jupiter."

Victor was now fuming. "No. This is because of him. I just know it. I can feel it. And ever since I told her about the Omega transmission, she's been acting so strange and distant. Like she knows what's going on but is keeping it a secret for some reason. I didn't tell you this, but yesterday, I found all these weird documents in my mom's room. They were about Omega and *him.*"

Eli tried his best to speak as slowly and softly as his raspy voice would allow. "Victor, it wasn't Mobius or Omega that took your mum. It was The Fourth Branch. *They're* the ones that have her detained."

"They're just doing their job to protect the rest of us, Eli. Who knows how many people they've got to and how many of those have become their unwilling pawns. What do you expect The Fourth Branch to do once they know Omega's gotten to someone? Sit down with their thumb up their ass?"

"Well, no, of course not, but…"

"And you weren't there, Eli. You didn't get blown up by Omega downtown a few weeks ago. Your father isn't the leader of the world's biggest terrorist organization or the most wanted man. And he isn't the same man who walked out on his family just to be a traitorous scumbag." Victor tried to wipe the tears welling up in his eyes. "Do you have any idea how many times I had to sleep on a bench in Ollie's bar because my mom pulled a double at the hotel, and there was no one else to come home to?"

"Maybe your mum is right, Victor. There could be things that you just don't know about. With your dad, with Omega. You need to at least acknowledge that possibility."

"I don't have to acknowledge jack shit, Eli. He has taken everything from me, from us!"

Victor broke down in tears, and Eli wrapped his arms around him.

Victor shoved him away. "If I come face to face with that man, I'll kill him." He took one more menacing look at the swing set. The wind had stopped blowing, and they now hung lifelessly by only a few threads.

16

Zero Dark Thirty

Victor walked away from Eli, out of the park, and far beyond the streets of Fair Heights. The thought of going back to his mom's house and waiting for the day's events to start was unthinkable. He was dog-tired and needed a full night's sleep, but that was also inconceivable at this point. In just a few short hours, he would be confronting Omega.

Whenever he was about to go on a dangerous operation, he found that it helped to be in a state of agitation and discontent. This was the perfect mindset to have to confront an enemy. He'd rather be hyper-alert, angry, and paranoid than be perfectly content. There was nothing more dangerous than not being on your game right before you walked into the lion's den. *If I was more alert Tengo Squad would still be around.*

Victor soon found himself walking on a path that hugged the shores of the Delaware River. He kept walking, not knowing exactly how this impending battle would play out. If it all went to plan the way Colonel DeThroe described it, there wouldn't really be a battle at all. DeThroe made it sound like this would be a walk in the park. The

221

exact words he said were, 'shooting fish in a barrel.' What scared Victor the most was that he didn't know every savory detail of the battle plan. Perhaps Colonel DeThroe had left him out of certain specifics of the plan purposely, but even so, it was unsettling.

On the other hand, Victor knew that the first plan never survived first contact anyway. Once the bullets started flying, all hell would break loose no matter what. By the way the colonel described it, this would be less of a battle of bullets and more of a battle of wills. If Victor got his way, he would love to put a bullet in each Omega drone he could find, and one in particular.

He heard the great boom of the foghorns, warning the ships not to get too close to the coast. The lights of a large shipyard shone brightly in the distance. He was getting close to his destination. DeThroe had given him an address where he needed to meet up with him at 3:00 AM. '0-Dark-Thirty' in military speak.

The meet-up location with DeThroe turned out to be a towering, abandoned warehouse building. It was a perfect perch to observe the nearby shipyard where the operation with Omega would take place. The warehouse looked completely abandoned. The windows were all boarded up with not a sliver of light escaping from the inside. The large metal door had huge chunks of rust built up on it from its many years of being just a few feet from the Delaware River's brackish waters.

DeThroe must have given him the wrong address. The door was locked with a thick rusty chain and padlock. There was clearly no way he was getting inside unless he had an enormous set of bolt cutters or maybe some plastic explosives.

He paced back and forth at the door for a few moments. "There's no way I'm getting in this thing." After a moment of standing at the entrance, he noticed a narrow slit of light appear at about face height. He got closer to it and recognized what it was immediately. A retinal scanner.

After placing his face up to the scanner, the effect was immediate. The piece of sidewalk that Victor stood on began to rotate into the warehouse. It was as though he were standing on an enormous, and exquisitely well-hidden, revolving door. Once the rotation was complete, Victor was now inside. He was expecting the interior to match the derelict and shabby exterior. His mouth dropped at where he now found himself.

Hundreds of men and women wearing either uniforms or lab coats marched among dozens of armored vehicles and specialized communications equipment. There was no graffitied brick, rust, or even a speck of dust for that matter in here. It was as though it were a building within a building. The entire structure appeared to be made out of concrete that was coated in sterile white paint.

A silky smooth Southern accent surprised Victor from behind. "Well, well, well, corporal. You're nearly late for our little rendezvous."

Victor turned around while checking his sociograft. "I'm still a few minutes early," he said, locking eyes with Colonel DeThroe. He had traded in his white dress uniform for camouflage fatigues, complete with dark leather boots and a belt.

DeThroe furrowed his eyebrows and feinted a serious look. "Corporal, now you know as well as I do that if you're not fifteen minutes early, you're late." He broke his stern expression immediately and smiled. "You sure are brave for coming here tonight, I hope you know that. There aren't many who would volunteer to do what you're about to do, not least because it is before the ass crack of dawn."

"I want to do it. Omega needs to be destroyed."

"I second that emotion, corporal. Walk with me."

DeThroe led Victor deeper into the interior of the warehouse. The waves of military members snapped quickly to attention when Colonel DeThroe walked past them. "General VanHeller sends his regards. As does the grand architect. They very much look forward to seeing you today during your ceremony." DeThroe stopped mid-stride and looked at Victor. "Do you think your mother will be in attendance?"

"I wanted to talk to you about that, sir. I've, er…I've been told that she has been arrested."

"Ah yes, I have heard of the pickle that your mother now finds herself in. And really, I think it is all just a great big misunderstanding."

"So she'll be let go?"

"Well, when I say 'misunderstanding,' it means she is guilty as sin. Our findings are very clear. Your mother divulged a very disturbing string of memories during her procedure at the E.C.H.O. Chamber. She is our suspect numero uno for having intercepted highly classified plans relating to the device."

Victor found himself going red in the face - gripped with fear. "What? No…that can't be. Sir, my mother cleans hotel rooms for a living. There is no possible way that she could've done anything like that."

"There's likely a great many things you don't know about your mother, corporal. You have to remember that she lived her whole life well before you came along. And in my line of work, I see many people who get caught up in the wrong crowd. Usually well-meaning and innocent folks, just like your mother." DeThroe leaned toward Victor and spoke in a hushed tone. "Corporal Gates, you are a valued addition to The Fourth Branch's upper echelon, and there is not a snowball's chance in hell that we would want to see you unhappy. When you complete your mission here today, I'm sure that some sort of accord can be reached." He leaned in even closer. "I daresay that your unique skills and heroic repertoire make you a prized member of our exclusive little club."

"Sir?"

"All I'll say is that if you pull this operation off here tonight, you'll be able to write your own ticket, corporal. That, and so much more. For now, we have a mission briefing to get to."

They continued their walk toward the center of the warehouse-disguised bunker. Ahead of them was a large concrete dome that stretched almost to the ceiling. They were greeted by a guard who stood sentinel in front of a thick blast door. The guard scanned their sociografts with a device and the door slid inside of the wall to allow them passage into the dome's anti-chamber. A decontamination shower stood beside the doorway that led into the inner portion of the dome.

They walked through it and were now in a bunker within a bunker. Exotic communications and weapons equipment were stacked neatly on the sterile white door. In the center of the circular shape was a cluster of scientists in lab coats and military officers, all huddled around a large holograph table.

When Colonel DeThroe and Victor approached the table, the group snapped to attention.

"As you were," said DeThroe. "I believe a few introductions are in order. Folks, this here is our resident hero and the main effort for tonight's festivities. I'd like you all to meet Corporal Victor Gates. Everything about tonight is about him and his safety. Corporal Gates, these folks here will be your eyes in the sky, the birdy in your ear, and the proverbial pain in your ass." Everyone laughed except for a very serious and familiar-looking major. "Major Silver is our planning officer and she will be briefing us today. The floor is yours, major."

Once she began talking, Victor recognized her as the major who greeted him and Innocius at The Fourth Branch Headquarters. "Corporal Gates, your mission is to bait Omega into our kill zone. Allow me to orient you to our holograph model." The other officers moved out of the way so Victor could stand directly over the table. It was a holographic scaled-down model of the shipyard located near their warehouse base of operations. Victor could see thousands of shipping containers stacked in neat rows along the waterfront, where dozens of large ships were docked on their piers.

Major Silver used a pointer to identify the row of warehouses that they were now occupying. "We're located here. You will walk to the rendezvous point located here, at Pier 17. Once you are in position, you will send Omega a transmission notifying them of your position and wait till they arrive. From there, you will hand over the device to Omega and leave the shipyard. Our assault teams will be in position, here, here, and here." Major Silver pointed to several locations where groups of Soldiers were depicted on the holograph model. "Once you leave the kill box, the assault teams will open fire. It's air-tight. There's nowhere for Omega to escape."

Victor intently surveyed the holographic map in front of him. "What if they try to take me hostage?"

"Your sociograft will act as a homing device. The Quick Reaction Force (QRF) in this warehouse will be your extraction team if the mission goes belly up."

Victor wanted to poke more holes in the major's response, but there were more pressing questions. "What's to stop Omega from killing me right then and there and just taking the device?"

"We think that risk to be quite low, corporal. For all they know, you're on their side," said DeThroe with a wry smirk.

"I'll be armed though, won't I?"

"We don't think that's the best course of ac—" stammered Major Silver before she was interrupted by DeThroe.

"You will positively be armed, corporal. That's one area I may be able to lend some assistance to." DeThroe reached down at his side and unholstered his silver .45 caliber pistol. "When I asked what you would do if you saw that bottom-feeder father of yours and you had Selena in your hand, do you remember what you told me?"

"I said he deserves a traitor's death."

He flipped the revolver around so now the hand grip was within reach for Victor to grab. "This is his ticket, Corporal. You've got his number now. You do this, and you'll have set the universe right again. Not to mention, you'll have completely altered the course of your family's future."

Victor took the pistol in his hand and popped the cylinder open with a smooth flick of the wrist. The chambers were all empty. "Not sure how much good Selena will be if she's empty."

"Corporal, don't you remember her special trick?" DeThroe grabbed the revolver from Victor. He held the hand grip firmly in his right hand and did the same flicking motion that Victor did to open the cylinder. Except this time, when DeThroe opened it, the chambers all had .45 caliber rounds in them. "Like all refined women, she'll only reveal herself to those who know her best." DeThroe started to fiddle with his sociograft and then handed the revolver back to Victor. This time, when he grabbed it and opened the cylinder, it was still full of rounds. "I can only surmise that after they frisk you and find Selena's empty chalice, they'll probably think of you as a bit of an idiot." DeThroe chuckled.

Victor tucked the revolver into the inside of his waistband and smiled. "Well, that just means they'll be underestimating me."

"Too right, corporal! Now, I'll leave you with these parting words before I leave you in Dr. Desir's capable hands. The second most dangerous part of this mission will be when you turn on the device. Desir is going to show you how to turn it on and then turn it off. That is the extent of what you will do with the device, and that is only to prove to Omega that it is genuine. No funny business, you here?"

Victor nodded. "Got it, sir."

"And the most dangerous unknown factor of this mission isn't the device, corporal," said DeThroe, leaning in to whisper his next words.

"…it's you. If you see *him*, don't touch him. Don't so much as brush up against his hand. This is critical, do you understand?" After Victor nodded, DeThroe drew himself back up to his full height and proclaimed to the room, "Fireworks start at 0500, ladies and gents! Let's make sure we put on a good Fourth of July show for our friends in Omega."

As DeThroe, Silver, and their entourage turned to leave, a small metal crate suspended above the holograph table by ropes began lowering itself. When it reached a few inches above the table, the crate's metal flaps opened outward like flower petals to reveal the device. It was the same teardrop-shaped object that had appeared from DeThroe's desk during Victor's visit to The Fourth Branch. It ominously levitated under its own power a few inches above the holograph table.

Dr. Desir waited till the last officer had left the room before she started speaking to Victor. "How much do you know about the X500 device?"

"I didn't even know that's what it was called. So not too much."

"You need to know that it's the most…'"

"…dangerous device created by man. Yes, I knew that part."

Desir cleared her throat. "You also need to know that it emits enough theta waves to level a city."

Victor raised his eyebrows in astonishment. "*That* little thing could level a city?"

"That's not all it can do. Suffice it to say you need to exercise extreme caution when handling it. You need to sync with it to operate it. Take your sociograft hand and hold it out to the device."

Victor did as she said and raised his right hand toward it. After about thirty seconds of awkwardly standing there, he asked, "Is something supposed to be happening?"

"I've uh…never actually done it myself. Not anyone can actually calibrate it. It takes a…special individual to do it."

Victor tried to blink his frustration out of his next few words. "So you've never actually done this yourself? How sure are you that I won't level this whole building?"

"You won't…or it won't be our problem anymore," she said dryly.

That's reassuring.

Desir folded her hands behind her back. "Please try again."

Victor held his hand back out again. This time with an expression of terror mingled with absurdity. Fifteen seconds passed. Then thirty. Then sixty. It wasn't till a few minutes later that Victor thought he saw a purple sliver of light flash across the device's smooth silver surface. He was sure he imagined it until he saw another and another until there were thousands of flashes of light every second. With no warning, the device stopped flashing and floated silently until it spun pensively on its axis.

"Holy shit, I think you did it," said the flabbergasted doctor. Her obvious surprise was not lost on Victor and was the opposite of reassuring.

Victor put his hand down as they both marveled at the activated device. Its spin was erratic, more of a wobble, really. Victor cocked his head to the left to try to see it from another angle. The device moved its pointy top to the side. Out of sheer curiosity, Victor moved his head to the right. Once again, the device mimicked his movement. When Victor walked around it, its rotation transfixed itself on where he was walking.

"It's…it's following you," stammered Desir. "Okay, you should turn it off now." She was starting to sound scared.

"Just another minute," said Victor, entranced. The device was clearly connected to him in some way. Victor had spent enough time in Haiti with people who didn't speak English to recognize non-verbal queues. To the curious mind, mimicking was itself a form of communication to establish that you meant no immediate harm. And it was indeed curious how whenever Victor moved back and forth, and from side to side that the device wobbled like his reflection. Victor didn't know how or why, but he was sure that even though this device had no way of speaking to him, it had a lot to say.

"Turn it off now. That's an order!" Desir grabbed Victor by the collar and violently shook him.

The device began to sparkle with red and blue bursts of electricity.

"Don't you feel that?" she asked, shaking.

"Are you okay, doctor? You don't look so good." Victor was trying to maintain calm, but he could tell there was something very wrong with Desir. Her face had turned ashen white, as though she had just seen a ghost. The doctor's eyes became bloodshot, and she began foaming at the mouth. She lunged at Victor's neck, causing him to fall to the floor. She got on top of Victor and began choking him and screaming a primal yell. He tried to pull her off, but she was too strong.

"Help, help!" said Victor, gasping for air. No one could hear him through the thick concrete walls and blast door. She screamed in rage and in agony, her eyes bloodshot and bulging.

After what seemed like a lifetime, men in HAZMAT suits came rushing into the dome-shaped room from the blast door. A few of them ran toward Desir, pulled her off of him, and stuck her in the neck with a large syringe, causing her to pass out. Some were holding stretchers and medical equipment, while others had Geiger counter-looking contraptions that chirped loudly. A few of them escorted Victor into the decontamination cell.

Victor was thrown into the decontamination cell and the soldiers in HAZMAT suits began hosing him down. He saw others carry out Dr. Desir on a stretcher. Colonel DeThroe came strolling into the anti-chamber, as though he were taking a walk in the park. He didn't wear a HAZMAT suit over his battle fatigue uniform. He looked into the decontamination cell and grinned an unworldly grin.

231

17

Fireworks

"The show must go on, corporal," said Colonel DeThroe after Victor had finished changing into a new pair of clothes. "You're not thinking of chickening out, are you?" he asked as though Victor had just scraped his knee on the playground.

"What happened to her, sir?"

"Dr. Desir, you mean? Oh, she'll be just fine. You have to break a few eggs to make an omelet, right?" DeThroe pulled over a metal stool and sat on it, all while men in HAZMAT suits continued to go in and out of the room. "She's not like you and I, corporal. Not too many people are, and you've just proved that beyond any reasonable doubt here tonight."

"I don't understand, sir. How am I special?"

"Useful is a better definition of corporal. Sometimes, I choose the incorrect word. And in time, you will see how useful you really are." DeThroe pulled out the silver pocket watch from its chain in his breast pocket. "Do you remember my story on the train about our Haitian heroine Ms. Fatiman? Time to go roast some pigs." He oinked like a pig and laughed like a madman.

You could have heard a pin drop in the main part of the warehouse when Victor and DeThroe emerged from the dome-shaped room. The hustle and bustle from the once scurrying soldiers came to a complete standstill as the pair walked toward the main door that led to the outside.

DeThroe turned to Victor and patted him on the shoulder. "What you're about to do tonight will establish The Fourth Branch for the next hundred years, corporal, but…where's the device?" He looked around the warehouse at the still comatose-looking onlookers. "Will someone please get back to work and grab the device for the corporal? And for heaven's sake, make sure you grab Selena too!" He massaged his forehead with his thumb and fingers. "Sometimes, you really do just have to do everything yourself, corporal."

A soldier in a HAZMAT suit came sprinting over to Victor and handed him a backpack and the pistol. DeThroe beamed at him. "Make us proud, hero, and I'll see you at the festivities later this afternoon."

Victor tucked the pistol in the waistband of his jeans. As he slung the surprisingly light backpack over his shoulder, the floor beneath him began to rotate until he was outside of the warehouse. He shuffled down toward the shipyard, confident that even though he couldn't see the soldiers inside the warehouse anymore, they could still see him. If this was anything like a normal military operation, he knew for certain that there was aerial or satellite coverage of his every step and breath. Victor tried to pretend this was like a military operation to make him feel more at home, but the truth was that it was anything but. He was wearing a pair of borrowed jeans, a jacket, and a T-shirt and had a city-leveling device strapped to his back.

He walked into the deserted shipyard and passed row upon row of shipping containers, all stacked many dozens of feet above the ground. At the waterfront were dozens of piers and docks that stretched out into the river. At the water's edge were bright lights that dotted the shoreline for as far as he could see. Like a good soldier following Major Silver's last orders, he began setting up his sociograft to broadcast a message hailing Omega. "Here—end transmission."

Looking out past the piers to the east, he expected to see a sliver of pre-dawn light, but none was visible. The moonlight showed that it would be a cloudy day, and the smell of an impending morning shower lingered heavy in the air. Victor thought he must have been a weatherman in another life because he now felt a tiny raindrop land on his ear and drop down to his neck. He looked up toward the sky and felt more droplets fall onto his cheeks.

"Don't turn around," said a hoarse voice from behind. "Put the bag down and your hands out to the sides." Victor did as he was told. "Are you alone?"

"Yes."

The man began to frisk him starting from the shoulders on down. When he found Selena tucked in Victor's pants, he popped out the cylinder to check if it was loaded. Once he was satisfied that it was empty, he placed it back in Victor's waistband.

"Turn around," said the man gruffly. He completed his pat down while Victor stared straight ahead at the barrels of thirty rifles pointed right at his head. All of the men wore black and some sort of breathing apparatus with goggles that covered their faces from view. They were facing the lights from the docks, so even though Victor couldn't see their faces, he could clearly see the tactical gear they wore and the weapons they had pointed at him.

Once the man was done patting down Victor, he took a few steps back and lifted his own weapon toward Victor, who now knew the futility of having brought Selena with him. If DeThroe was watching on any satellite imagery, he must be getting a good chuckle.

"Empty the contents of your bag slowly and put them in front of you."

Victor took the device encased in its metal housing from his bag and placed it on the ground. When the men saw the device in its encasement, they all recoiled and trained their weapons on it.

The man motioned up and down with the muzzle of his rifle. "Take a step back, and don't move." Once Victor complied, another man came forward with the same Geiger counter-type instrument the soldiers had in the warehouse. The second he came forward and knelt down in front of the device, his instrument let out a high-pitched chirp and didn't stop till he backed up. He nodded to the man in front of Victor, who whistled a brief high and low tune.

This must have been a signal, thought Victor. Sure enough, he heard the thud of footsteps coming from behind the dense formation of men with guns. They made a space between their close ranks for the man to pass through. Raindrops fell hard on his dark leather trenchcoat and heavy-looking boots with metal buckles. He wasn't wearing the breathing device that the other men were, and when he walked right up to Victor, he swept his long gray hair with a frail-looking hand. He had deep wrinkles that criss-crossed his weathered face and sunken eyes were now plain to see against the pier lights. He wasn't the man Victor remembered, though it didn't take much time to recognize who this man was. It was *him*.

"Hello, Victor," he said quietly. "You've grown up since…"

"Don't," said Victor, holding up his hand in front of his waist. "We're not going to do this. You came for this. Now let's get this over with." Both men looked down at the encased device at their feet.

Mobius touched the case. Once he did, the encasement began to peel its metal pedals back, and the device floated eerily from it under its own power. It hovered about three feet off the ground, and Mobius' men took a few steps back, training their weapons on the device. Victor could almost hear them shaking in their boots.

Mobius looked up and into Victor's eyes. "I understand your anger,

Victor, but it is sorely misplaced. If you knew the truth, you never would have come here. In fact, if you did know, you never would have left home, joined their military, or fought in Haiti. The truth doesn't just hurt. . . sometimes it kills."

"How naive do you think I am? You are the biggest piece of shit in this country. Why would I listen to anything that a murderous terrorist has to say?"

"Because I care about you, Victor."

"Stop."

"And I care for your mother, too."

"Stop," he yelled before lowering his voice. "You…are not, my father. You're not my anything. You and your goons are Omega. You're terrorist scum whose killed tens of thousands of innocent people. And you have absolutely no right to talk about my mother. You left her…you left *us*!"

The rain was no longer a drizzle. It was now falling at a steady pace on this dawnless morning. Mobius looked down at the device and behind him at his men. He motioned for them to put their weapons down and swept his matted hair away from his eyes to investigate Victor's. "You're right about one thing there, kid, just one. I'm not your dad."

Victor winced. "What do you mean?"

"It means exactly what I just said. I'm not your father. I wish I could've been and that things didn't end up like they did. It just wasn't in the cards."

"But then…"

"You know more than you think you do. Trust me, kid. And I just don't have the time to explain everything." He looked down to check the time on an old-school wristwatch. "We need to move things along. I know your new friends will be here soon."

A chill ran down Victor's spine. *Somehow, Mobius knew that this was a set-up. If that was the case, then he also probably has a good idea of where an ambush would come from.* "I don't know what you're talking about."

"Your six o'clock on the boat, twelve o'clock, and nine o'clock in the shipping containers." Mobius was calling out the locations where DeThroe's ambush team was hidden. "I'm not stupid, kid."

"No, you're a murderer."

"I'm not evil, Victor, however detestable you think I am. I have good intentions, but that doesn't exactly make me a good person." He wiped trickling raindrops from his brow. "If it helps you sleep at night, I've never killed anyone that didn't ask for it. It's time to turn this sucker on, so I can make sure it's the real McCoy."

Victor didn't feel trapped before, but he started to now. If Mobius knew where the ambush was coming from, then he must have also employed a counter-attack team to destroy them first. And if that was the case, DeThroe's men didn't have much time and neither did Victor.

He needed time to think through the problem, so he did the only thing he could do, stall. "What are you going to do with it?"

"Get the revenge I've waited far too long for. We all have our interests. And I need to protect mine. I don't want to hurt you, but I'll do what needs to be done. Now activate it."

"Fuck you."

Mobius motioned with his head for one of his men to come forward. The same one who patted Victor down came home and struck Victor in the face with the butt of his rifle, knocking him to the ground.

"Let's not make this painful, kid. I have places to be," said Mobius as his man returned into the formation.

Blood dripped off Victor's lip. He looked up at the man he most despised in the world. Others may hate him for being a traitor and a terrorist. That is an impersonal hate, the kind that drives one to get into a cyberduel. No, this was not that kind of hate. It was a loathsomeness that can only be experienced by someone who should love you but instead betrays you.

"Is that why?" Victor asked, still on all fours as tears of physical pain and moral anguish welled up in his eyes. "Is that why you left us? Because I'm not really your son?"

Mobius looked back at his men and then stepped forward, leaning down to Victor. "I had to leave to protect you and your mother, Victor. You don't know what it was like in those days. If I had stayed, you both would be dead."

"She's in jail now because of you!"

"Not because of me, because of you. You have a choice that was never given to her or me. You can choose whether you want to be like *them* or tear it all down."

"What the hell are you talking about?"

"You've been given the gift Victor. Through the boy when you entered the E.C.H.O. Chamber with him. And now that you have it, they want you. They want you to be their tool. Lucier will do anything to get you to you. You're special, you and your friend. And you're connected in more ways than one." Mobius stood erect and spat off to the side, the rain washing it away immediately.

"The way I see it, kid, you got two choices. You could turn that damn thing on and come with me, or you could keep being their pawn."

Victor heard gunfire in the distance.

"You're out of time, kid. What's it gonna be?"

Victor knew he was out of time in more ways than one. Now, it was all or nothing. He raised his hand to the device and this time, it started sparking with its flashes of purple and red immediately. Mobius' men took cover behind some of the shipping containers, though Victor was still well within range of their rifles.

"Why are they afraid of it and you aren't?" asked Victor.

"Everyone is afraid of what they don't know," he said, staring at the device as though he were hypnotized. "Aren't you afraid of it?"

"No."

"You should be."

"It's just another weapon," said Victor as the sounds of gunfire drew closer.

"It's so much more than that, Victor. This is the sum of my life's work trying to create something pure and harmonious bastardized with an unbridled lust for power."

"So you aren't afraid of it?"

"I'm not. For the same reason a dog doesn't bite its master, it knows me. That doesn't mean I don't respect its limitless power. I don't have the full part of the code to control it, though. Only you do, thanks to Thomas Locke. It seems he still has some tricks up his sleeves."

"What has Thomas Locke got—ah, fuck!"

A stray bullet grazed Victor's leg. Mobius' men were now engaged in an intense firefight erupting behind them. Once the bullet struck Victor, his hold on the device started to wane, and it began to glow bright red. Sparks of red lightning began to strike all around them.

"Victor, turn it off now!" said Mobius.

"I can't. I can't control it!" The device shot up hundreds of feet into the air, and the falling raindrops around it looked blood-soaked.

The Earth began to shake under their feet. "You need to give me the code. I can shut it down!"

Victor still tried to maintain a grip on the device. "Fuck no!"

The quakes began to get so violent that the shipping containers began to vibrate, making screeching noises along the floor. "You have to. You have to let me touch you! I need your part of the code to shut it down. Victor, we're all going to die!" Mobius lunged toward Victor.

Using his other hand was not preoccupied with trying to regain control of the device, Victor pulled out DeThroe's pistol and shot Mobius square in the shoulder. Mobius reached for the pistol, and once he grabbed Victor's hand, a high-pitched ringing noise struck in his ears struck him like an oncoming freight train. By now, Victor was well acquainted with this sound. He was about to be transported elsewhere.

Sure enough, he wasn't at the shipyard anymore, and it wasn't raining, though it was nighttime. Victor sat by the door and played with his toy truck. It was his favorite thing to do right before his dad would come home from work. He'd walk in the door every day and scoop Victor up for cuddles and playtime. Today, though, there was nothing of the sort. His dad and mom got into a big fight when they got home from work that day.

It was so bad, and there was so much yelling. Dad started to walk out of the house, leaving mom at the door crying. Victor crawled out to the porch to follow his dad, who turned around and looked at him sitting on the porch in his onesie. His dad walked back to him, scooped him up off the porch, and hugged him really tight. *Finally, hugs.* Victor loved hugs, and this was the best one that Dad had ever given, but his dad looked so sad when he did it.

Victor's ears started to ring really bad again, and it felt like it was now raining outside and there were red flashes of light. The numbers 1-8-7 flashed red, quivered, and came crashing to the ground. Shipping containers were being tossed around like they were rag dolls in the wind. They collided mid-air, sending their contents scattered across the shipyard and falling on the shipyard inhabitants. Anyone still alive tried to make it to the water's edge and jump in to escape the shaking of the Earth, falling containers, and terrible red lightning flashing like fireworks from the flying device.

The last thing Victor saw before losing consciousness was Mobius making a series of rhythmic patterns with his hand up into the sky at the menacing device until the lightning stopped. He fell into the water and felt a strong pair of hands wrap around him.

18

America the Beautiful

Victor awoke with a cough and spat up water onto the beach, where he lay prostrate on the sand. His jeans and shirt were ripped to shreds. His chest pulsated in pain as though he had been hit by a semi-truck. A grazing bullet wound from his leg still oozed blood. He rolled over to face the sky and coaxed his eyes to open. By the look of the sun, it was sometime around mid-morning. He looked across the river to the far shore, where it looked like a bomb had just gone off. Small fires raged along the waterfront and piers, and somehow, a shipping container had blown through one end of a large anchored boat and was sticking out of the other side of it.

He massaged his head with both his bloodied hands. *What the hell happened?* He focused and tried to piece together the events in his mind. *The device, where is the device?* He sat up in a panic and looked around in vain for any possible clues. *Mobius must have taken it.*

Victor stood up and ran his fingers through his hair. Somehow, he ended up on the New Jersey side of the Delaware and had no idea where the most dangerous object in the world that *he* was supposed to look after had gone. And that's when he remembered; *1-8-7.* He

241

had seen it again, wreathed in a fiery red flame and shaking as though there was an earthquake. He had no way of knowing for sure, but he couldn't shake the feeling that people were in terrible and imminent danger.

A helicopter began approaching Victor from the mouth of the river. It soon landed next to him, and he saw Colonel DeThroe signaling for him to hop in. He limped over to it and was helped into a seat by some of the flight crew. DeThroe pointed near his ear at a pair of headphones for him to put on.

"You look like shit," said DeThroe as Victor adjusted the headphones and microphone.

"I feel like it, too," said Victor.

"You hurt?"

"Yeah, my leg."

DeThroe motioned for the flight medic to examine Victor. She took a pair of scissors and cut his pants off above the bullet wound. She applied some ointment and wrapped it tightly with a bandage. "Just a scratch."

"I've had worse," said Victor. He looked at DeThroe. "Did you recover the device?"

"No, but we'll track it down soon enough. Don't you worry about it, corporal. You've done enough for one day. You did good. Did you shoot that yellow-bellied bastard?"

"Got him in the shoulder," said Victor.

DeThroe slapped Victor on the knee. "That's my boy."

Victor took the pistol from his waistband and handed it to DeThroe, who tucked her away in his shoulder holster. "What about my mother? Where is she?" asked Victor.

"Still in a secure facility. You don't have a thing to worry about with her, corporal. She's in good hands. For now, look to the future. Speaking of that, it's time to make you look pretty for the cameras.

The grand architect will be arriving in Philly soon, and we can't have you standing next to him looking like such a ragamuffin."

The helicopter started to lose altitude and Victor began recognizing Fair Heights neighborhood landmarks. The park, Mr. Rizal's workshop with the big satellite dish on top, and James Wilson High School were now all visible. The helicopter began descending onto the Fair Heights Police Precinct landing pad. This was the precinct where Eli worked. *Maybe I'll see him here.*

As they disembarked, DeThroe shouted over the spin over the rotors to tell Victor. "The Fair Heights Police have lent their precinct to us. We'll be running operations out of it for the next twenty-four hours." Victor could barely hear him over the still spinning rotor blades as they approached the entrance to the police station's rooftop access. "The grand architect will be giving his speech and presenting you your award at the James Wilson High School," he said, still barely audible over the helicopter.

The soldier who handed Victor his uniform butted into the conversation. "Sir, I believe that when Lucier Corps purchased the high school, they changed the name to 'one-eighty-s...'"

"Thank you for that, Private, that will be all—ah, Chief Burgard! There you are!"

A portly police officer with a handlebar mustache greeted them once they entered the access stairwell. "Corporal, I'd like to introduce you to Chief Burgard."

"Good to meet you, sir," said Victor.

"The honor is all mine, son. We've got a hero's welcome for you down in the lobby." He eyed Victor from head to toe and back again. "You alright, son? You look like hell."

Victor hadn't looked in a mirror yet, but he was sure he was a site to behold. Half of his trousers on one leg had been cut off. And as far as he could see looking down at his arms and legs, he had bruises and dirt on nearly every inch of his body.

"It's been one of those mornings, sir," he said with a sideways smile.

"Must have been. You would've thought you just got off the plane from Haiti looking at you," he said with a chuckle. "We'll have a place for you to clean up while the colonel and I sort out some security arrangements with my team."

"Is Eli in the precinct, or is he on patrol?"

"Patrolman Abramson hasn't told you then. He's been placed on administrative leave as of this morning," said Burgard dismissively. He and DeThroe then began a very intense conversation in huddled whispers as they continued haphazardly down the stairwell.

Victor descended the stairs with them, but his mind had now gone to a completely different place. He had been with Eli just a few short hours ago, at the park, just after midnight. Eli didn't say anything about being put on leave then. *Something must have happened between that conversation and his reporting for work this morning, but what?*

The soldier who corrected the colonel handed Victor a black garment bag hanging from a coat hanger. When Victor gave him a funny look. "It's you're uniform, corporal. For the ceremony this afternoon."

"Oh, yeah. Thanks," said Victor as the group approached the access door leading to the ground-floor lobby. "Hey, you told the colonel that James Wilson High had changed its name. What did you say it was again?"

"I think it's now Private School (PS) one-eighty-seven."

All those visions of seeing the numbers 1-8-7 wreathed in quivering flames had come back to Victor in an instant. "Fuck me," he said out loud.

DeThroe and Burgard had just walked through the door leading to the lobby.

"You alright, corporal? You look…pale," said the private.

Victor tried to respond, but he was now being thrust in front of dozens of applauding and cheering police officers waiting in the lobby. Their mouths were all visibly open or closed if they were whistling, but Victor couldn't hear any of it. He felt as though he was watching the tellvision, and somebody had turned down the volume all the way. All he could hear now was a high-pitched ringing in his ears, and feel the hard slaps on his back as he walked through the gauntlet of jubilant policemen and women. He could see that their smiling faces were warm and welcoming, but Victor began to feel the room and all of its occupants closing in on him.

Chief Burgard got between Victor and his joyful officers and ushered him into a locker room off of the main hallway. Victor could see his lips moving as he motioned to the stalls of showers beyond a row of lockers.

Like a drone on an auto-pilot, Victor walked aimlessly with his garment bag over his shoulder to a row of sinks. He dropped the bag and hardly recognized himself when he looked at the face staring back at him in the mirror. He was dirty, gaunt, and haggard-looking. *Did you even sleep last night?* Victor couldn't actually remember the last time he had slept. He was having a really hard time remembering anything at the moment.

How did you get here? He started feeling lightheaded all of a sudden and opened the faucet to splash some cold water over his face. It helped a little, but not enough. He began getting dizzy, and that's when things started to go black.

He heard a voice whispering to him. "I'll be back for you, little guy. I love you." It was Mobius. He was holding a young Victor, who was barely bigger than an average-sized teddy bear.

The grown-up Victor was looking on as his dad said goodbye to him on the porch of their old house all those years ago. His mother stood with her hand over her mouth and eyes, crying. She picked up the toddler version of Victor and tried to soothe him as he also began to cry.

Victor felt a hand on his shoulder and turned around. It was Lewis. He and the other members of Tengo Squad (Chan, Sullivan, and Rojas) were all standing on the porch with him. "Can you hear me, man?" asked Lewis. "Did you go deaf or something?" Then he started to yell at him, "Corporal! Can you hear me!" Then he started to slap him in the face.

Victor became very confused and felt something cold splash on his face. He still heard someone yelling. "Corporal—can you hear me?" while slapping his face. But now he found himself lying on the locker room floor of the police station. His feet were propped up on a stool, and cold water was being poured on his face and neck. "Corporal, wake the fuck up," yelled a person with a very distinct Boston accent. *Anderson.*

"Alright, alright, I'm good, man, knock it off," said Victor, trying to smack Anderson's hand out of the way.

"You sure?" asked Anderson. "You know you look exactly like I feel most days?" he said sarcastically.

"One of those days," said Victor, rubbing his head.

"Here," said Anderson. "I never leave home with it." He tossed a couple Advil in his hand. Victor took a swig of water from the small bucket that Anderson had found to toss water to him. "You should probably get some sugar in you too. Here's some mints I nabbed from the office lady in the lobby."

Victor took them, scarfed them down, and looked into Anderson's scared face. "Was I there with you? On the beach that day in Haiti?"

"Yeah, you saved my ass," he said, helping Victor to his feet. "Along with dozens of other poor bastards. I...we all...owe you, big-time man."

Victor knew he would need some help for what would need to

happen next, and with Eli out of commission, Sergeant Abramson might be the next best thing. "Can I cash in on that offer right now?"

"You got it, corporal, anything."

"You still have your wheels?"

Anderson whipped his keys from his coat pocket. "Where to?"

Victor left the garment bag containing his dress uniform crumpled in a pile on the bathroom floor as both men walked out to the station parking lot.

Victor didn't have any time to waste. No one, including DeThroe or Burgard, would believe what he had seen in his *dreams* or *visions*. Victor had no interest in trying to prove that these hallucinations were genuine; he knew that they were, and that's all that mattered. Now, he needed cold, hard proof to convince others of the danger that Omega now posed. There was only one place he could get what he needed.

It was a very short drive to Mr. Rizal's parlor from the police station. Victor could have walked there, but his leg would slow him down, and time was of the essence.

Anderson pulled up right in front of the brick building, with a red, white, and blue sign over the door that read "E. Rizal Cyber Parlor." They found the inside empty. Victor knocked on the metal door using the rhythmic pattern of the theme song from the Rocky movies.

Deh...deh, deh, deh...deh, deh, deh...deh, deh, dehhhhhh.

"Is that Eye of the Tiger?" asked Anderson.

"Yeah...my friend, he's a big fan."

"Hey, who isn't?"

The narrow panel in the door slid to the left and revealed a thick set of eyeglasses. "Wow. It's you!" said Rocky.

"We need your help, man."

"Ah, man, I would. I mean, I want to, but my dad is inside the shop right now. He would freak out if I let somebody in. Plus, things are a little crazy in there right now."

"Rocky, you need to let me in. If you don't, there's going to be hundreds of people that die."

"Ay, Dios mio," said Rocky as he unlocked the door and swung it open. "Who's your friend?"

"This is Sergeant Anderson with The Fourth Branch. Anderson, this is Rocky." The two of them hurriedly shook hands, and Rocky ushered them through all of the security chambers leading to the parlor. Once inside, Victor now knew what Rocky meant when he said things were crazy inside. The first time Victor was in Mr. Rizal's parlor, it felt like he was inside of a freezer. All the cooling ducts pumped icy cold air to cool the farm of server stacks. Now, it only took a few seconds, and he had already broken out into a full sweat.

Victor made a beeline toward the center of the parlor. The teardrop-shaped E.C.H.O. Booster that used to glow purple now pulsated with a fiery red light. Mr. Rizal was sitting at a server workstation feverishly entering commands into the interface and wearing a tank top and shorts with a yellow sweatband on his forehead.

When he saw the boys, he barely even acknowledged them, except for a sideways glare at Rocky, and then he kept typing away. "Good to see you, Victor. How's your mother? Sorry if I don't get up, but you caught me at a bit of a bad time."

"Mr. Rizal, I know, er sorry for just barging in like this. I need the E.C.H.O. Booster's data report. It's really urgent."

Mr. Rizal now looked up at Victor and took off his glasses. "What… how do you know what this is called," he said with a frustrated glare at Rocky. He then pointed to Sergeant Anderson, all while glaring at Rocky. "And who on Earth is that?"

"I'm Sergeant Anderson, sir, I work for The Fourth Branch. And it's okay, I'm cleared access at Tier 2, so I'm permitted to be in any premises where there is an E.C.H.O. Booster." He held up his sociograft's credentials for Mr. Rizal to inspect. "I've already been to see most of the other ones around the world."

After Anderson held up his credentials, Victor did the same to show Mr. Rizal that he also had clearance to be there and hopefully lessen the backlash that was soon to befall Rocky. "It's crucial that I see a report of energy signals from the E.C.H.O. Booster," said Victor. "There are lives at stake."

Mr. Rizal put his glasses back on and entered commands in the user interface. "I've never seen the booster like this. Ever." He wiped the sweat away from his forehead. "There's such a build-up of negative theta wave energy. It's making the whole system overheat."

Victor remembered seeing the helix-shaped circuit cables glow fiery red just like the booster when he was in the power circuit tunnels last night. "What do you think could be causing it."

"I don't know, but it all started after the chant. And it's not just the one in Philly. Though ours seems to be the worst. All the other E.C.H.O. Booster maintainers around the country are having the same issues with theirs." He finished a line of code in the user interface and clicked the enter button. "Here, have a look."

Victor, Anderson, and Rocky all leaned into the screen in front of Mr. Rizal. The image showed tiny red dots that connected the E.C.H.O. Booster to all of the people with neurografts around the city. The energy signature that he was looking for wouldn't be tiny, like that of a neurograft. The theta wave energy being emitted from the X500 device must be enormous.

"There," said Anderson, pointing at the northeast quadrant of the map. Mr. Rizal zoomed in to expand the image.

"Wait, now there's *two* anomalies, look! Here and here. Right across the street from each other," said Rocky, pointing at two large orbs of energy on the screen. "This one looks like its at the high school, and the other one still at Madam Vixama's.

The school. The device is at the school.

"Wait…look. The bigger blob over Madam Vixama's is moving."

"What?" said Victor.

"Yeah, look. The bigger blob is moving closer to the other big blog," said Rocky.

Innocius.

"Innocius?" said Rocky with a turned up lip.

"We need to go now. Thanks, Mr. Rizal. See you, Rocky."

They made their way out of the parlor's security chambers and into the bright late-morning light of the Fourth of July. Parade-goers and protestors alike all began clogging the streets in every direction. "I don't think we're going to be able to take the car," said Victor.

"Nah. We're good," said Anderson. "It's too bad I left my snow plow at home," he said with a devious smirk. He unlocked the doors with the key fob. "Hop in."

They slowly made their way through the throngs of people, picketers, parade floats, and a mariachi band to get to the police station. The beeping from the SUV's horn helped, but what really parted the sea of pedestrians was Sergeant Anderson's incessant cursing and shit-talking.

"I can see why Omega would want to put the device near where the grand architect will be giving his speech. Those bastards," said Anderson between expletives. "And these protestors think I'm scary. Wait till they see that device," he said with a chuckle, adding, "It's a good thing it's summer break, and there won't be kids in the school, you know?"

That false hope hit Victor like a ton of bricks. "No. You're wrong. They will be in school!" said Victor in a panic. "Don't you remember? The mayor wanted kids to observe Independence Day 'from the safety of their classrooms.'"

"Fuck," said Anderson pressing on the gas and yelling even louder now.

Innocius' face was now burned into Victor's psyche, and the words 'protect the boy' now made more sense than ever.

As they neared the police station, the crowd had become too packed and dense even for Anderson to drive through. They hopped out and began elbowing and shoving their way through the sea of people. It got worse the closer they got to the police station.

When they finally arrived at the precinct, policemen were guarding the gate to the compound entrance. They asked Victor and Anderson for their IDs, and when they showed their Fourth Branch clearances, the guard laughed. "This isn't The Fourth Branch, you two. It's a police station. And in case you haven't noticed, we're having a little civil unrest on our hands."

"We need to see Colonel DeThroe and Chief Burgard immediately," said Victor.

"They're not here," said the guard. "They left a few minutes ago. It's not safe around here right now—you two should keep moving," he said as he waived off an unruly protestors picket sign out of his face.

Anderson began sending a message on his sociograft. "I'll message Colonel DeThroe that he needs to send a quick reaction squad to the school right away."

They turned to leave when Victor heard someone calling his name from inside the precinct compound. "Victor, wait up, you git!"

"Eli? What are you doing in there, Burgard told me you were put on leave."

"I was, I am. I went in to give him a piece of my mind. They're just fucking me about."

"But why?"

"Long story. Not really, actually. It's just more or less too stupid to comprehend. What are you doing here?"

"It's Innocius. He's at the school—he's in trouble. Come with us."

With Victor's leg still giving him problems, Anderson and Eli's anger issues were finally put to good use by parting the unruly crowd with leg sweeps and body checks. The crowd got even more violent and dense the closer they got to the school, and even Anderson and Eli had a hard time moving past them.

They rounded the corner where Madam Vixama's shop was, across the street from PS-187. She was outside of her shop trying to nail sheets of plywood onto the doors and windows, all while being jostled left and right by the throngs of people beginning to pour out from the school grounds.

"Ms. Rios, where is Innocius?"

"He's at school. I should have never let him go in that damn building, look at it. Look at all these hooligans running amuck around it and around my store. I sent Somera to go fetch him and bring him home. It's not safe for anyone here right now."

Victor's eyes were transfixed on the school. He couldn't separate the image of this school from the one in his Heads Up Display at the Battle of Les Rouge. To him, they were now one and the same. *I'm not going to let that happen.*

"You lot go on. I'm going to help Ms. Rios with these boards," said Eli.

Victor and Anderson continued pressing on through the crowd, who seemed to grow more agitated the closer they got to the school. In fact, once they got onto the school grounds, it seemed as though it were one big cyberduel. They were all acting rabid. As though they were under some evil wizard's spell. They looked as manic and deranged as Dr. Desir had looked when she was in the close presence of the X500 device. Victor was sure this was no coincidence. *We're close.*

Amidst the hair-pulling, wailing, and gnashing of teeth Victor heard "America the Beautiful" by Ray Charles being played on some large speakers that were set up next to a stage set up on the school grounds. "Ironic tune, eh?" said Anderson sarcastically.

Victor and Anderson ran up the stairs to the school's entrance and encountered a police officer guarding the door. "You can't come in here. Please step back away from the doors," he yelled. The school grounds started to rumble as though there was an earthquake, nearly knocking them off their feet.

"We don't have much time," said Victor desperately. If the device at the shipyard was any indicator of what was coming next, it was far worse than just a little rumble.

Anderson walked right up to him and clocked him right in the face. The officer slumped to the ground as the sergeant massaged his knuckles. "Come on," he said as he opened the door.

He and Victor rushed inside and barricaded the door to prevent any of the unruly protestors from coming in. Just as they did, they heard what sounded like a battering ram slamming against the doors. "Go!" yelled Anderson. "I'll hold the door."

Victor began running through his old school, the halls all eerily deserted. *The students and teachers must be held up in the auditorium.*

Based off of what he had seen from the X500 device, he knew where to go. The only place where it could possibly be deployed effectively was outside and somewhere high. *The roof.* He rounded the corner and was nearly knocked off his feet by Innocius being pushed in his wheelchair by Somera.

"Victor, what's happening out there? We saw it on the tellvision. It looks like a riot," said Innocius.

"I think it's a bit more than that now. You guys can't go that way. The door is—" Before Victor could finish his sentence, he heard what sounded like the horde of the underworld come barreling down the hallway. "We need to go now!"

Victor scooped Innocius off of his chair and began running up the stairs with him on his shoulder. Victor's leg was throbbing in pain with each step, but he couldn't give up now. He knew he was the only thing that stood between those mad people and this young boy and his sister. All that mattered now was keeping him safe and getting to that device before this city completely tore itself apart.

The three of them continued up the stairs until the only place left to go up was the rooftop access stairwell. When Victor pushed open the door, that's when he saw it and *him*.

Mobius' uninjured arm was outstretched toward the X500 device, which was so high up in the sky it looked like a little speck even from the rooftop. It was just now beginning to spark with fiery red flashes of light, while the rooftop began to quiver more violently by the second.

Mobius saw Victor out of the corner of his eye. "You can't be here, kid," he said, his voice strained. "You need to go before it's too late."

Victor laid Innocius down, and Somera sat behind him with her arms around him.

"You need to stop this," yelled Victor. "You're even more evil than I thought you were."

"You don't understand. I'm trying to stop it."

"Bullshit," said Victor, walking up to him and clocking him in the face. "I should have shot you in the head when I had the chance."

Mobius fell to the ground and got up to his knees, his arm still outstretched to the device.

"Either I'm telling the truth, or I'm here on a suicide mission. It can't be both." Mobius began panting loudly. "I saw your vision, Victor, when I touched your hand back at the docks. I saw you and I together when you were just a little boy. It was the toughest day of my life," he said with tears rolling down his cheeks. "And then I saw the numbers 1-8-7 and knew what kind of foulness you were up against. And..." his voice strained as though he were in a significant amount of pain, "whenever you decide to wake up and smell the roses, I could use a little help."

Victor considered the choice that this wretch of a man was offering. "So you didn't bomb all those people downtown? That wasn't you?"

"Jesus Christ, kid, what else do I have to do to get you to believe what I'm saying? Now, please give me a hand."

"Swear it to me. Did you have anything to do with that?"

"No, I swear it."

Victor stepped over to Mobius and helped him to his feet. He clasped their hands together and stretched them toward the device, trying to sync with it the same way he did when he was in the warehouse with Dr. Desir. Stopping the device now was a lot different than when he was back in the warehouse. When he shut it off then, it had only synced to one other person and he only heard her echo. Now, the device was connected to thousands of minds. And Victor's mind was filled with the echoes of their rage and spite. It was too much for him and Mobius to handle by themselves.

"We're not going to be able to do it," screamed Mobius, over the roar of the school's foundations beginning to buckle.

They needed someone else. *Innocius.*

Victor turned around to face the boy, who looked as though he were holding on to his sister for dear life. "Innocius, I know you're scared, but we need you." Victor's voice was muffled by the quaking of the building. This was the biggest Hail Mary Victor had ever thrown. Innocius had only ever shown an ability to change a radio station in the car.

That's it!

"Innocius, change the station! Change the station," he yelled again as loud as he could.

Cradled in his sister's arms, Innocius touched one hand to his neurograft and stretched the other toward the device. The effect was immediate. The quaking of the building began to still and, within a few seconds, came to a stop altogether. The device descended from its menacing heights and lowered itself harmlessly back into its metal case.

Victor ran to the edge of the roof and looked down toward the school grounds. If they weren't taking a seat in place, they were massaging their heads as though waking up from a deep, mysterious stupor. Victor threw his hands onto his head out of pure exhaustion. "It's over." Victor walked over to Innocius and Somera and bent down. "I don't remember summer school being this bad," he said with a smile.

Colonel DeThroe burst through the access door and walked without skipping a beat toward Mobius, striking him in the face with his cane. "You're time is up, Gates," said DeThroe, before whistling his dark eerie tune loudly.

Something came over Mobius. He began convulsing in horrific agony on the rooftop. He fell down and began flailing his arms and hands against his body as though swatting at some invisible flame that grew hotter with each change in inflection from DeThroe's whistling. "I learned a couple new tricks since the last time we met. This one's a real scorcher."

Mobius began rolling back and forth on the ground, all while screaming, "Make it stop, make it stop."

"Oh, I can oblige you there, old friend." DeThroe unholstered his pistol from under his jacket and aimed it point-blank at Mobius' forehead.

When DeThroe pulled his pistol out, Victor crouched low to shield Somera and Innocius from the line of fire. Victor looked on as Mobius continued to writhe and jolted in indescribable pain. *He was telling the truth. He was really here to try to deactivate the device. Not to harm anyone. If he deserved to die, it wasn't like this, thought Victor.* He ever so slightly raised his hand in the direction of DeThroe's pistol.

"Goodbye, Gates," said DeThroe while pulling the trigger.

There was no bang of gunpowder, just the click of an empty cylinder. He pressed it again, but still nothing. And again and again, until he had gotten through all six phantom chambers. "A misfire? Well, this is a first, Selena," he said, holstering his pistol with a fierce glare at Victor.

A dozen or more well-armed soldiers in body armor had stormed through the access door while DeThroe lowered his arm, relieving Mobius of his fiery hallucination. "Get this piece of shit out of my sight," said DeThroe. The soldiers put a nearly unconscious Mobius in handcuffs and dragged him down the rooftop stairs by his arms. "And for the love of God, would someone please remember to grab that damn device?"

DeThroe turned to Victor, still shielding Somera and Innocius behind him. "Corporal—you have a real knack for saving lives. I would be careful, though. You know what they say about too much of a good thing," he said while walking over to Victor. DeThroe bent down low so only Victor could hear his deadly serious tone. "And I would strongly advise you to *never* get between my prey and me ever again." He stood up, dusted himself off, and said in a much more congenial manner. "Now, does anybody need to see a medic? No? Very well, corporal, I sincerely wish we had the time to hose you down, but if you'd be so kind as to accompany me down to the stage. I believe you're almost late for your own award ceremony."

19

Major League Games

"Good afternoon, kind people of Philadelphia, and good afternoon, my fellow Americans. As Grand Architect of the United States, and on behalf of the entire United States government, I would like to wish you all a happy tri-centennial day. Three hundred years ago, we showed the world that free men and women could govern themselves independently of a monarch. Yet for nearly three hundred years, we were oppressed by other forms of tyranny. Not by one tyrant three thousand miles away, but by three thousand tyrants one mile away. We had to change, and so we did. As Americans, we led the world in ushering in the next great form of governance, the cyberocracy. A government where the will of the people can truly be realized, and freedom can ring true for all. The ever-vigilant and nigh omnipresent gaze of our cyberocracy, made possible by the most advanced quantum computing the world has ever known, ensures that the will of the people is never truly called into question.

But freedom is never free, and it never will be. There have been those throughout our history who have been traitors to freedom in the pursuit of selfish gains. I am pleased to report to the entire world that earlier this morning, one such traitor, Mobius Gates, has been apprehended and taken into custody."

The throng of people assembled around the stage and outside of the school erupted in cheers.

DeThroe continued.

"This man, who will now face trial for his litany of crimes against the state and to humanity, will finally have a date with lady justice. She won't need to lift her blindfold at all to see how wretched of a human being this man is and the damage he has caused this country. This country needs men and women of iron resolve to defend it from such enemies at every turn. And today, I am joined by one such young man. He has not only proven himself as a defender of freedom on the battlefield, but he has today proven himself once again as our nation's greatest hero, as the man who finally brought the rogue leader of Omega, Mobius Gates, to justice.

Ladies and gentlemen, it is my distinct honor and privilege to introduce Corporal Victor Gates, a national treasure, who will be presented with the Congressional Medal of Honor by the President of the United States and the Speaker of the House of Representatives. Madam President, Speaker Locke, and Corporal Gates, please come forward."

Victor, Speaker Locke, and the president rose to their feet and joined Valter Lucier at the pulpit. Lucier stepped aside for Locke, who pulled out a prepared script and began reading.

"Corporal Victor Gates, you are hereby awarded the Congressional Medal of Honor for conspicuous gallantry and intrepidity at the risk of life above and beyond the call of duty on December 24, 2075, at the Battle of Les Rouge. Corporal Gates himself destroyed an enemy stronghold that was intended to be taken by his entire task force. Upon discovering that the enemy had positioned deliberate ambush sites all along the coast, he began to systematically neutralize each one of their positions. At great risk to his own life, he fearlessly maneuvered his board and wingman within only a few yards of these enemy positions and assaulted their positions to allow his comrades time to move out of the kill zones. Corporal Gates exposed himself to hostile fire dozens of times by dismounting from his board through a shower of grenades and small arms fire to dress the injuries of the critically wounded under fire and evacuate them to safety. Through his outstanding bravery and unflinching determination in the face of desperately dangerous conditions, Corporal Gates saved the lives of many soldiers. This ends the citation."

After the president had placed the award around Victor's neck, the crowd assembled at PS-187 High School burst into uproarious applause. Lucier leaned into the microphone and said, "And for those wondering who wins the best-dressed award, that should also go to Corporal Gates as well. Speaker Locke, please see to that." Victor, who was still dressed in his torn jeans and T-shirt, must have looked like he had been working in a coal mine the whole day. He grinned embarrassingly and retreated with the president back to their seats behind the podium.

Thomas Locke remained at the lectern and pulled a piece of paper from his coat pocket. He cleared his throat loudly and said, "I wanted to take a few minutes to address the American public on the issue concerning the results of the investigation that inquired into yesterday's annual chant. We have conclu..."

Lucier interrupted Locke by placing his hand on the microphone and whispered a few short words in Locke's ear. Locke was clearly taken aback and placed his hand on Lucier's atop the microphone. After a brief tussle, Lucier took a step back and folded his hands against his belt.

"As I was saying, the House of Representatives has concluded its investigation into the anomaly detected during yesterday's annual chant. After an intensive review of the Sentient's code, we have determined that the anomaly had no bearing on the outcome of any of the chant votes cast. Due to the controversial nature of the final vote that approved a neurograft mandate, we reviewed those exhaustively. Still, there was nothing in the programming that indicated anything was out of the ordinary, and there is no evidence to substantiate any alternate theories of these conclusions."

A murmur spread throughout the crowd, and it looked as though Locke may lose control of them. Indeed, after this brief pause in Locke's impromptu remarks, it left Lucier a brief chance to lurch forward and seize back his podium.

Undeterred, Locke continued, "Unless you're a quantum computing expert, you may sometimes find yourself asking just how it all works. I think that lack of transparency is what caused people's tempers to flare the way that they do today. A wise man once said the doorstep to the temple of wisdom is a knowledge of our own ignorance. I'll conclude my remarks today with an offer," said Locke with what Victor knew was a quick glance in his direction. "An offer, with my personal assurance, to guide you to that doorstep and walk with you through it so you can be enlightened. Thank you." As he returned to his seat, Lucier practically leaped at the microphone to recover it.

"Thank you, Mr. Speaker, that was indeed enlightening. I also think that today's 'tempers' were caused by a 'lack of transparency.'" He said with a cough. "I think we've culminated here today. Perhaps not enough for the entire day, but certainly one early morning. God bless you, Philadelphia, and God bless The United States of America. Hopefully, I will see you all again later today at Lucier Corps Park, where none other than our very own local hero, Corporal Victor Gates, will be throwing the first pitch of the game. Hail The Fourth Branch!"

There was a smattering of applause that was drowned out by the playing of loud patriotic music as the crowd began to disperse. Those on the stage all wanted a chance to greet Victor, but Lucier beat them all to it. He walked over to him and adjusted the medal now hanging from his neck. "We're all proud of you. Damn, proud. This thing looks good on you. I know today must have been tough on you son, what with confronting *him*. I'm sure there's a part of you that still isn't quite sure what to make of it all. Just know that I'm here for you whenever you're ready to talk about it. No matter what, though, you just remember that you did the right thing. Somehow, Victor Gates always comes out on top. And this business with your mother, don't you worry about a thing. I think it's just a big misunderstanding. We'll have her home in no time. How are you and Ms. Earhart getting along?"

Victor could feel himself getting a bit red in the face, thinking back to their time together in the power circuit tunnels. "Er, pretty well. Why do you ask?"

"Cause she's right behind you waiting for me to stop boring you," he said with a laugh.

Victor turned around and right into Abiana's hands, grabbing him by the cheeks and pressing her lips against his. When she was finished, she gave him a hard push. "Way to leave me down there all by myself!"

"I thought *you* left *me* down there."

"No, there's a back way that I didn't show you," she whispered.

"Richard, you old devil! I knew you couldn't be too far behind this lovely, feisty young woman," exclaimed Lucier as he shook Richard's hand.

Richard gave Victor a hearty pat on the back. "I would never pass up a chance to see America's greatest hero, Valter. Especially one that my daughter has taken such a liking to. And you know Valter, I've never had to wait so long for someone to accept a job offer from me before. It seems Mr. Gates is trying to play hardball," he said with a wink.

Lucier's eyes lit up. "Now you know that I can't be involved with Lucier Corps' day-to-day business anymore Victor, but in this case, I'll just dip my toes in a bit. Richard will offer anything you want. You just name your price. We need good people over there, and that is where you will be able to make a *real* difference. That is unless you had other plans."

Victor started to shake his head no but couldn't get a word out before Abiana cut in. "Do you two ever stop conniving? The answer is yes, and yes. Of course, he'll take the job, and he *absolutely* has better plans than hanging out with a couple of old dudes the rest of the day."

"We'll talk more at the ball game, my boy!" shouted Richard as his daughter yanked Victor's arm and forcibly removed him from the stage.

"They never would have left you alone," said Abiana, locking her arm with Victor's. "They mean well, but I don't think they ever stop thinking about global domination."

"Well, they are two very powerful men. What do powerful men always want more of? More power," said Victor.

"Careful. If you tell them that, they'll jump your bones faster than I did."

"Ew." Victor laughed. "You have a really dirty mind, you know that, right?"

"You know you like it," she said with a mischievous smirk.

Victor realized they were just following their feet with no real destination in mind. "Where are we going to anyway?"

"Back to your place, you big goof. We have to get you cleaned up. Look at all these people," said Abiana as they waded through the dissipating crowd toward Madam Vixama's store. Many either pumped their fists up in the air when they saw Victor or gave him a pat on the back if he was close enough. "Just a few minutes ago, they were like rabid dogs, at each other's throats, trying to tear each other apart. What in the hell happened?"

"You didn't see it?" asked Victor.

"Saw what?" said Abiana.

"The device," whispered Victor. "It was above the school. That's what caused everyone to go nuts."

"You sure it wasn't just those anti-neurograft drones just causing shit? That's a much more plausible story, Victor." She put a hand on Victor's chest and let out a short shriek. "Innocius!"

She ran up to give Innocius a big hug as he, Somera, and Vixama were all in the process of struggling to remove the sheets of plywood from her storefront windows. Victor grabbed an extra hammer in a toolbox lying on the sidewalk and got right to work helping them.

"Thank God you two showed up. I don't know where Eli went after all of the protesting ended. He hammered these boards onto the windows so deeply, they are so hard to get off," said Vixama.

Victor yanked out the first sheet with ease. "It's no problem. We were on the way back to my house to get ready for the big game." He handed some of the nails he pulled out to Innocius and asked, "You're coming, right?"

"We don't have tickets," said Innocius.

"Psh, don't you worry about that. My dad has the VIP box. You guys have to come and do the Fourth of July right."

"Mom, can we?" asked Somera.

"Of course, you can," said Vixama giving up on using a hammer, and grabbed a crowbar instead. "Victor, I didn't see your mother with you on the stage. Is she alright?"

"Oh, yeah, I think so. She had an appointment she had to go to." Victor wasn't sure why he lied, and now that he thought of it, he wasn't sure that Vixama and his mother had even met. In fact, he couldn't be positive that he had ever mentioned her to Vixama, even in passing. Regardless, he assumed she was just being polite out of gratitude for Victor's and Abiana's help with the store.

"Good," said Vixama, now giving up on the crowbar and wiping sweat from her forehead. "I will go inside and make sure that there was no vandalism on the inside." They all laughed when she went inside after taking several overly dramatic deep breaths. *Obviously, there would be no vandalism inside. How could anybody get into the store when all the windows and doors were boarded up?*

Victor had already taken his half of the store's boards down and moved to Vixama's side. "Hey..." he looked up and down the street to make sure nobody was coming before asking Innocius and Somera. "Are you guys okay after...you know?"

Somera's face contorted into a look of puzzled astonishment mingled with fear. "I've just, I've just never seen anything like that. That thing..." She let her hammer fall to her side and turned to face Victor. "You, and that man, and Innocius...I don't understand. What was it, and how did you stop it?"

Innocius through a fist full of nails into a bucket on the sidewalk. "It's like I could feel it. All those people who were down there protesting and fighting. I could feel their..."

"Misery and despair," said Victor.

"Yes. That's exactly what it was. All those people that were yelling and shouting were so numb to one another. All they could feel, all I could feel, was..."

"Icy cruelty and red-hot malice?" said Victor.

"Yes. Just like that," said Innocius. "I wonder if that other man could feel it too."

"He could," said Victor. He couldn't know for certain, but Mobius' complete look of exhaustion told him all he needed to know about what demons he was grappling with.

"Christ, that sounds awful," said Abiana in disbelief. "What kind of sociopath would make such a thing?"

"Mobius told me that it was his life's work gone wrong," said Victor, throwing the hammer in the toolbox and stacking the last sheet of plywood against the brick wall.

"Big surprise there," said Abiana, laying on thick notes of sarcasm.

Somera made a small pocket of her dress by tucking it up a bit, dropping in fallen nails wherever she found them on the ground. "And that man, the man with the cane, it looked like he was torturing the other man. Like he was lighting him on fire or something like that?"

"Can we change the subject, please?" said Innocius quietly.

"Our mother would say that he was like a Petro Loa or a voodoo fire spirit. I can't believe that is the same man that comes into the store sometimes, right Innocius?"

"Somera!" yelled Innocius, clearly becoming upset.

Somera bent down to give Innocius a hug, spilling the nails she had tucked in her dress. "Sorry, little bro. You know I didn't mean to upset you."

"I don't think it was voodoo, but it was definitely strange," said Victor. "But Innocius is right. What we *really* should be talking about is how many hot dogs we'll be stuffing our faces with soon." He cracked a smile in Innocius' direction, hoping it would catch on.

"Yeah…hot dogs," said Innocius with a vacant expression on his face. "I think I'll go in now."

Abiana walked over to the door so he could go inside. "I'll send a car

for you and your sister and your mom, too, if she wants to come, okay?"
Then she bent down and gave him a kiss on the cheek and whispered
loudly, "I bet that Jacky would be super impressed by everything you
did up there kiddo. I know you have the hots for her—you want me
to put in a good word for you?" That got Innocius to smile wider than
Victor had ever seen before. Then Abiana whispered something that
neither Somera nor Victor could hear, but they both looked at Victor
and burst out laughing.

"What are you two scheming about," said Victor, folding his arms.

"Just between me and the power circuit champ over here," said
Abiana with a wink at Innocius as he went into the store.

Once the door closed from behind him, Somera went up to Victor
and Abiana and said, "He's always been very sensitive. More so than
the other kids at school."

"I get it. That was some pretty traumatic stuff up there. Not many
people will ever see the stuff that guys got to see on that rooftop.
Abiana and I are here for both of you, okay?"

Somera nodded appreciatively.

Abiana checked her sociograft for the time. "Shit, we need to get a
move on Vicky. I wouldn't let you into a fishing shanty looking the
way you do right now, let alone a VIP box at Lucier Corps Park. We'll
see you there, Somera, I have to take this guy and hose him down."
Victor reached in to try to kiss her, and she contorted herself so he
didn't make even the slightest physical contact. This put Somera into
a fit of giggles as she waved goodbye to Victor and Abiana, who were
rounding the corner.

They had only gone a few steps when Victor stopped and smacked
his palm to his forehead. "Dammit!"

"What?" said Abiana.

"Ah, I forgot my damn uniform back in the station."

"No one's going to take it. Just leave it there. You can come back tomorrow and get it," said Abiana with a heavy eye roll.

Victor had been conditioned by the military to never leave your issued gear unattended. The mere thought of leaving his dress uniform still on the floor of that station locker room was unthinkable, even downright criminal. "Yeah, but we're right here already. I'll just run back in real quick and grab it. You just want to stick around here and keep the Rios' company?"

"Fine," said Abiana, exhaling dramatically. "I'll go get my palms read or something. Don't you keep me waiting, Victor Gates!"

That was a direct order coming from a superior officer if Victor had ever heard one before. He took those words to heart and broke out into a light jog down the street where the police station was on the opposite side of the school from Madam Vixama's. It was about an eighth of a mile away tops, thought Victor. He'd have been gone for five minutes at the very most. General Abiana must not be displeased, and Victor wouldn't dream of it.

He raced up the row of stairs leading to the police lobby, grabbed the door, and swung it open wide. He completely ignored the woman at the desk in the lobby, who only got out a few words before she recognized him and figured he knew what he was doing. Victor checked his sociograft before kicking the door to the locker room with his foot. "Got here in two minutes, right on time..." He looked down on the cold tile floor and stopped dead in his tracks.

It was Eli. He was lying face down and prostrate on the ground. "Eli," he yelled, lunging onto the floor next to his friend. Victor turned him over to find a syringe stuck deep into his forearm. Victor immediately checked for his vitals, and there was a pulse. "Help, help, help me. Somebody help!"

The woman from the lobby came in, let out a shriek. "Oh, my God." She ran out to call for a paramedic. One was quickly found in the station, and she immediately administered a vial of purple liquid into his system.

Eli's head was resting on Victor's lap when his eyes began to flutter and let out a raspy murmur. Victor let out a sigh of relief and began to rub Eli's head gently. "I thought I lost you, buddy," he said tearfully.

"We'll need to get him to the hospital," said the paramedic inspecting the syringe in Eli's forearm. "This definitely looks like neuro-drip."

Eli continued to murmur as the medical team came in with a stretcher, and Victor helped load him into the ambulance in front of the station. Before the paramedic shut the door, he asked, "Want to ride along?"

Victor didn't hesitate. He leaped into the back of the ambulance and held his friend's hand as he lay helpless on the gurney. He couldn't stop asking the medical team, "Is he going to be alright," all the way to the hospital.

Once they got there, Eli was rushed into the emergency room, and Victor was forced to stay in the waiting area. He began pacing back and forth between rows of stiff-backed chairs, sending sociograft transmissions to Abiana and getting a flood of them in return.

"At the hospital."

"Oh my God, what happened? Are you okay? I was waiting for you? The car picked us up, and we're going to the game right now."

"It's not me, it's Eli. He's hurt pretty bad."

"Poor bastard. Is he gonna make it?"

"I hope so. Can you tell your dad and Lucier that I won't be at the game? I'm going to wait with him here. I don't know if I'll be there in time for the first pitch. I'll try, but I don't know right now."

"Okay, no problem xoxo."

Victor paced and sat down and then paced again. He fidgeted with his hands and picked at his nails nervously. He began getting a headache and tried to sprawl out on the sparsely cushioned chairs. All along, he kept wondering the same thing. "How could Eli do this to himself?"

It seemed like forever before a doctor finally came through the Emergency Room's double doors into the waiting area. Victor sat up in the chair when he saw that the doctor was walking in his direction. "Did you come in with Eli Abramson?" he asked.

"Yes."

The doctor looked at Victor's still unkempt appearance from head to toe. "Were you, uh, with him when he did it?"

Victor knew the doctor must think he was either a dealer or one of Eli's seedy drug den friends. "No…well, yes, but I just found him. What I meant to say was, he was unconscious when I found him."

"Okay. He's stable now and awake. You can go and see him if you'd like, but only for a few minutes."

The doctor led Victor back to the emergency room area and pulled one of the many curtains back to reveal Eli lying on a hospital bed, looking both gaunt and delirious. "Oi, I knew Philly's hero would save the day." Eli pointed with his eyes at Victor's Medal of Honor, still hanging from his neck.

Victor took the medal off and tucked it in his pants pocket.

"Eli, what did you do?" he asked as the doctor closed the curtain around them. Victor walked over to Eli and gave him a hug across the chest. "I thought I lost you, man."

"Me too," said Eli groggily. "Those bastards put me on leave, Vic. Somebody framed me. They stashed drugs in my locker, and then there just so happened to be a surprise inspection where they searched the row of lockers that mine was on."

Victor screeched a wooden chair closer to the bed and slumped down in it. "Why would anyone, especially your co-workers, want to do that?"

Eli looked down at the thick hospital blanket now covering him. "I have no idea, mate, I really don't."

Victor tried not to sound too judgmental. "But you *are* using again. I met Lou in the slammer, remember?"

"I'm not stupid enough to bring it to work and hide it in my locker. I can be thick sometimes, but damn Victor, have a little more faith in me. Listen, I just do it at home sometimes. When Jacky isn't there and when I don't have to go in to work the next day. I would never do it on the job, mate. You have to believe me."

"I do, Eli, but then how did you end up half-dead on the bathroom floor?"

Eli looked embarrassed. "Yeah, I know it was stupid. I wanted to show those bastards what they did to me." He started to choke up a lot and struggled to get his next few words out. "I...I couldn't bear the thought of having...Jacky was taken away from me...even more. I barely get to see her as is."

Victor grabbed some hand towels from the sink nearby and handed them to Eli who blew his nose loudly in them. "Jacky doesn't want you to take yourself away from her, Eli. You can't be there for her if you're..." Victor couldn't bring himself to say it.

"I know, Vic," he said with another big blow. "I just know that the ex is going to try to use this whole locker business against me, and...it's really hard for me to bear that. I'll lose my house...So I did the only thing I could do..."

Victor took Eli by the hand and said, "There's always another way out, man. You're like a brother to me, okay? I'm not going to let anything bad happen to you or Jacky. You guys are family."

Eli fought back tears by tightly closing his eyes. "Thanks, mate. I should have talked to you."

If Victor was being honest with himself, he hadn't been completely candid with Eli either since he got back. Instead of telling him about how he had mistakenly targeted the school in Les Rouge he had chosen to tuck it away, hoping it would go away and no one would ever bring it up. It's exactly the same line of short-term thinking that landed Eli in a hospital bed. If Eli had the wherewithal to talk about what was hurting on the inside, he never would have wound up here. What's worse, Victor constantly lashed out at Eli whenever he called him a hero. Eli didn't know what happened down there, and Victor never manned up and told him about it. He could change that now.

"I need to tell you something, Eli." He took a deep breath. "I haven't been straight with you. At Les Rouge, I destroyed the wrong target. It was a school. That's what they told me afterward. I'm sorry for jumping down your throat whenever you'd call me hero. I should've told you about it. It's probably why I sleep like shit and get headaches all the time."

"You're still a hero, mate. Even they wouldn't have given that medal to you if you weren't. You *saved* a lot of lives down there. And you may have even saved one or two up here, too."

They didn't speak anymore after that, not until a nurse opened the curtain and asked Victor to leave. "I'll come back in a bit, alright."

Eli nodded with a slight wave as Victor walked through the curtain and started to pull it behind him. "Mate," said Eli.

Victor held the curtain open. "Yeah?"

"You look like shit," he said with a smirk.

"That makes two of us," said Victor.

* * *

Due to several unfortunate twists of fate, Victor was somehow able to make it in time for the National Anthem and throw out the first pitch into the catcher's mitt. Evidently, there was a 'threat' on the grand architect's life that turned out to be nothing more than some kids playing with firecrackers next to his motorcade. That, and the ensuing traffic jam that it caused, allowed the start of the game to be pushed back by a full hour and a half.

After he threw a lackluster pitch, the tellvision crews swarmed him and couldn't stop badgering him as to why he was dressed so shabbily.

To top it all off, Richard Earhart and Valter Lucier would not stop cornering him about accepting the "job of a lifetime." Abiana didn't help matters by drinking too much and loudly proclaiming that he should take the job and that they should "get a place together." Somehow, by the top of the fourth inning, he had agreed to both. Then there were the endless photo ops in the VIP box and the people he had no clue who was badgering him about how many people he killed. All of this right off the heels of having just come from Eli's bedside.

Innocius and Somera seemed to be enjoying themselves in the VIP box. It was more than most Fair Heights kids got out of a baseball game. They would have counted themselves lucky to have been in the nosebleeds for a game on the Fourth of July. They were the one bright spot in all this. And Victor was glad they could have a good time. He decided just before the ninth inning started that he was going to sneak down to one of the open-air bars. He grabbed a seat at the nearly empty bar and kept the drinks coming, watching the game on the big screens and throwing nuts at them whenever the Phillies slacked off.

The teams were tied at the end of the ninth inning, and when the announcer said there would be an extra inning, everyone at the bar downed their drinks as fast as they could and raced back out to their seats. All except Victor, he didn't have a seat and there was no way he was going back up to the box. He flipped his sociograft off and tried to focus on anything but his mother or Eli.

"You alright, kid?" asked the bartender.

"Yeah, I'm fine. Just wondering how things end up so shitty sometimes."

The bartender picked up a glass and started cleaning it. "Ain't that the truth? After three marriages, you think I would've learned my lesson." He finished cleaning the glass and asked, "You're him, aren't ya? The hero."

Victor took a long swig of his brew and ended it with, "Yip."

He handed him another gold-colored ale. "On the house, kid."

"Thanks."

"Hey, you gonna be here a while still?"

"Yeah, I guess so."

The bartender scratched his armpit and spat on the floor. "You mind watching the register for me for a minute. I gotta go take a dump."

"Sure thing," said Victor, followed by another long swig. He could hear deafening cheers coming from the field, but when he looked up and down the breezeway, it was deserted. Until it wasn't.

"Congressman Locke," said Victor, nearly spilling his beer all over his shirt. "Jesus, you snuck up on me."

"Don't tell me the great Victor Gates gets a little jumpy by an old man in a tweed overcoat," said the congressman with a friendly smile. "You are *the* Victor Gates, are you not?"

"I don't think there's another one," said Victor, taking a long swig from his mug.

Locke looked up and down the bar. "Where's the bartender?"

Victor shrugged.

Locke did a quick back-and-forth scan before reaching over the bar, grabbing a glass, and filling it to the brim with the tap. Victor snorted out his beer and lifted his glass to Locke's.

"What are we drinking to?" asked Locke, already drinking deeply from the glass.

"The Fourth Branch?" asked Victor jokingly.

"Ha!" said Locke. Victor knew he heard Locke murmur "fat chance," under his breath after taking another long drink. "How about we drink to Mobius." Victor's smile faded. "Or maybe your mother, or perhaps Mr. Abramson?"

Victor pushed the stool out from underneath him and stood within a few inches of Locke. "What, in the fuck, did you mean by that?"

"Are you angry, Victor?"

"*What* did you mean by that?"

"Because if you are, you're not nearly angry enough."

The bartender came back from his trip to the necessities and began cleaning glasses absent-mindedly. He glanced over at Victor, who stood with muscles flexed and a narrowed brow, and a congressman who sat totally unperturbed. "Hey, can I get you something?" asked the bartender.

Locke raised his glass and smiled at the befuddled bartender. "Oh no, I'm fine. Thank you, though." Locke looked at Victor and said calmly, "You should sit down, Victor. You're angry at the wrong people for all the wrong reasons."

"Are you fucking with me?" asked Victor, pulling the stool back and sitting back down but with shoulders still squared against Locke.

Locke stared in the direction of one of the tellvisions behind the bar. "No. I most certainly am not fucking with you." When he made eye contact with Victor, he lowered his voice to a murmur. "Don't you find it odd that you met a young boy at the E.C.H.O. Chamber and then just started having scarily accurate hallucinations whenever you touch someone? Do you think that meeting that boy was a strange coincidence? And is it just happenstance that he can control that device far better than you or Mobius could? No, I'm not fucking with you, Victor, though I can't even count how many people are trying to use you."

Locke took another deep drink from his mug. "It seems even the Sentients themselves have taken an interest in you. And your friend."

Victor started to get a few words out before Locke interrupted, "We don't have much time, Victor." Locke kept his eyes on the tellvision behind the bar. "Phillies are about to throw the game," he said, stuffing a handful of peanuts into his mouth. "You've hardly scraped the surface of who you are and what kind of game you're playing."

Victor emptied his glass and slid it across the bar, stuck a finger in Locke's chest, and slurred his words. "You know you sound exactly like that twisted old kook, Mobius." Victor's voice began to get drowned out by the deafening screams of the crowd and he had to yell. "He was talking the same mumbo-jumbo bullshit when we were at the shipyard."

Locke leaned into Victor and said as loudly as he could without talking over the roar of the crowd, "That twisted old kook and your mother saved your ass more than once. You should be grateful. But now they've thrown themselves into the fryer, and they're not here to help you anymore, Victor. You're not where they wanted you to be, and you're not where you *need* to be."

"How would you know where I need to be? I'm perfectly fine where..."

"Son of a bitch!" The bartender swore up and down and grabbed the hand he had just burned, tossing some French fries into the sizzling oil. The crowd began pouring out from the field into the breezeway, raising all kinds of hell about the Phillies throwing the game. And before Victor had a chance to turn to Locke and say something, he had already vanished.

"Damn Phillies. Way to ruin the Fourth of July." The bartender stumbled over and placed Victor's empty glass in the sink. "You want another one, killer? On the house."

"I'll take two."

Victor Gates will return in
The Fourth Branch: Sentients

Victor Gates will return in
The Fourth Branch: Sentients

About the Author

T.B. Kramer is an American author and former US Army Officer. He got the idea for The Fourth Branch series by thinking of what it would be like if a supreme AI ran the government and what the implications would be for a society that never seems to run short on anger. When he's not writing, he can be found in central Pennsylvania spending time with his wife and two children.

To stay on top of all his latest projects, subscribe to his FREE newsletter!

Navigate to the URL below to join.

You can connect with me on:

🌐 https://www.kramersremarks.com

Also by T.B. Kramer

Did you enjoy The Fourth Branch: 2076?
Leave a review!

Just scan the QR code with your device, or navigate to the Amazon page HERE

The Fourth Branch: Sentients
Continue this epic journey with Victor Gates and pre-order the series' second book today!

Just scan the QR code with your device, or navigate to the pre-order page HERE